Actual Love

A Novel Inspired by True Events

Kevin Logan

ISBN: 978-1-4834-5415-3 (sc)
ISBN: 978-1-4834-5414-6 (e)

Library of Congress Control Number: 2016910099

Lulu Publishing Services rev. date: 7/8/2016

Conditions of Sale

Your kind
of novel?

- An exciting romance / thriller.
- A weave of historical and modern tragic love.
- Three story-strands entwined into one.
- A trio of fascinating finales.
- The answer to 'What is Love?'
- Divine honesty and realism in love and sex.
- For all who love to learn while being entertained.
- Themes and ideas to lift your own romance.
- Inspired by the Greatest Love Story ever told.

*

Modern novels tend to reflect life without
reference to life's Author.
This saga celebrates that there is more to our
human story than our five senses can communicate.

Dedication

To my wife, Ann, and my supportive family.

Contents

Acknowledgments

My name is on this book, but 101 others could
also be mentioned. They include friendly critics and
proofreaders, a patient and extensive prayer team, and
my supportive family and friends. The editors, advisors
and staff of Lulu Publications have been wonderful.

Without all of those mentioned above,
this novel would not exist.

CHAPTER 1

Nightmare

"Kill her!"

Sleep-sodden passengers stirred in the dimmed cabin of the overnight sleeper Flight TA 437 out of Tel Aviv, Israel.

"I'll kill the ... the ..." The voice trailed off, seemingly reluctant to curse.

Some now lifted eyeshades, wondering if they really had heard the shouted words or whether they were eruptions from their own restive dreams. One or two stretched to switch on their overhead lights. One woman, halfway down the EasyFlight cabin in the row that overlooked the yellow-painted port-side wing, burst into sobbing gasps.

"I knew it!" The words were a strangled wheeze. "What did I tell yah, Hal?" Each phrase she spoke was squeezed

1

from tubes hoarsened by asthma and now rising hysteria. "Should never ... gotten on board."

"Now, now, Mavis." The man next to her patted her buxom left arm, squeezing an inhaler into her flapping palms. His soft, Southern states, maple-syrup drawl coated his wife's nerves to no avail. "Now then, old girl," he said, chuckling, "only some guy having a nightmare. Easy does it, dearie; no danger, darlin'—"

"He shouted, '*Kill her,*' Hal." The rasping was punctuated by comforting sucks on the inhaler. "Twice he shouted it, Hal. I heard it plain as—"

"Sure you did, honey," soothed Hal. "Just a little ole bad dream, that's all. Nothing more. Nobody's going to be hurt."

An English flight attendant, her chest labeled Monica, arrived at their row. "Is everything okay, madam?"

"No problems, miss. Surely no need to wake the flight marshal." Hal guffawed. "Just a bad dream a couple of rows—"

"Flight marshal!" echoed a startled woman with an English accent across the aisle. "You've got a—"

"No, no, no, madam." Monica waved a calming right hand while the left jabbed an overhead attendant button three times in quick succession. "We don't have such things on EasyFlight, and"—she swiveled to bestow her brightest enamel confidence on all around—"nor do we need them. We just have one single harmless passenger having a bad dream."

"Kill her!"

2

The words this time were just as terrifying, despite the fact that the Brooklyn brogue sounded drowsier.

"*There!*" Mavis was panting while rising. "He said it again." She collapsed with a gasping whine, saying, "Hal, honey, who's he going to kill? Remember that Boston Marathon bomber ... and that Sikh temple shooting?"

"Easy, Mavis. that's enough." Hal's tone, still patient, was stern, suspecting that 9/11 might join his wife's list of terrorist activity.

"Please, madam," Monica said, smiling confidently, "just relax, and be sure we can handle this from here." Already two other flight attendants were approaching with unhurried efficiency, one from either end of the single central aisle. More overhead lights now flickered on, and questioning murmurs rippled along the stirring cabin.

"Excuse me, sir!" Monica had moved up two rows to look down on a large man with a comb-over attempting to self-consciously hide the shine of his well-tanned scalp. Getting no response, she leaned down toward his arm, which was resting on an open laptop.

"Sir?" She gently nudged the slumbering figure, overriding EasyFlight's no-touch rule.

"Hmm ... oh!" the man jolted forward, almost losing the laptop down his slanting legs, and releasing what looked like a parchment scroll stuffed beneath. He grabbed at everything, catching all at shin level.

"Sorry ... sorry." He laughed pleasantly, looking up. "Who, er, what were you saying, honey?"

"You okay, Monica?" The forward flight-deck attendant came alongside.

"Fine, Trevor. I was just about to ask this gentleman to give us a moment at the rear of the plane." Flashing a professional smile at the passenger, she said, "Would that be all right, sir? We just need your help with a few things, if you don't mind."

"Sure." His voice was still slightly slurred, but then he briskly collected himself and rose to his full height. "Yes. Yes, of course, if I can help. I'm only too happy to oblige."

That was definitely a first for Monica, not one included in her flight-attendant training manual. Usually, she got a drunken curse, an argument, or a less than enthusiastic agreement, never smiling cooperation. Also, the view looking up at the man was far more appealing than her earlier overhead viewpoint. A strong but unshaven jaw on his bright, thirty-something, sun-bronzed face held no hint of covert terrorism. In fact, at face-to-chest level, with his neck slightly bent to allow for the luggage locker, she thought he was rather cute.

"Thank you, sir. Follow me, if you will." Monica turned and bumped into the flight attendant who was just arriving from the rear section.

"We can all settle back down now." She sweetly smiled with a full 360-degree pirouette, which owed much to Miss Mountjoy's Saturday morning ballet lessons back home in Surrey, England. Monica was amazed and a little relieved to see some nearby passengers still soundly asleep. "Everything is now well in hand, and before you know it, we'll be making preparations for a peaceful descent into Luton."

"Thank you, miss," drawled Hal with a thumbs-up. "You handled that real nice." He then glared up stonily at the towering passenger who was following, clasping laptop and scroll to his chest. It looked as though they were the only treasures he would save in any emergency.

CHAPTER 2

Scrolled Treasure

"Is it a sick passenger or something else, miss?" the stooping passenger asked Monica as they reached the rear galley.

"I beg your pardon?" Monica's cut-crystal Home Counties sounds contrasted sharply with his easy Brooklyn burr.

"Well I, erm, thought you wanted my help."

"Why should we want that, sir?" Monica was flummoxed for a moment.

The passenger shrugged and smiled. "Well, I mean, how do you want me to help? Isn't that what you wanted?"

"Are you a doctor?"

"Of course not." The man grinned, yet perplexity furrowed his brow, almost a mirror of Monica's frown. "I'm a minister. It's on my ticket—the Reverend David Jackson. I thought you'd seen it and maybe somebody was panicking and needed a bit of good old-fashioned pastoral care."

"Excuse me, Reverend—"

"Dave." The passenger nodded. "Just Dave; still not used to the 'Rev' bit, even after all these years."

"I'm afraid you don't quite understand, Reverend." She icily ignored the suggestion. "You are the one who has been causing the panic. You may have only been having a bad dream, but you shouted out loudly twice, and some of the words weren't very reverent."

"Well, honey, I, erm—"

"Sir." Monica stuck out a hostile jaw, trying to wipe a widening grin off Reverend Jackson's face. "You need to take this seriously. Causing panic in midair is a grave offense that carries—"

"Forgive me." The face became serious, and the furrows deepened. "I don't quite get the panic bit."

"You screamed out, 'Kill her,'" hissed Monica as she leaned toward him. "Twice! Now, I don't want to know the ins and outs of your private business, sir, but whatever you were dreaming about has caused us and not a few passengers a bit of, well, shall we say, anxiety. Never a good thing at thirty-five thousand feet, I'm sure you'd agree."

"I really had no idea." Dave looked disappointed. Monica was not sure whether his apology was for causing near panic, for using irreverent words, or because his pastoral help was now no longer required.

"Take a seat." Monica pulled down a basic crew bench hinged to the galley wall, adding with equal crispness, "I need passport and boarding card, sir." She found civility difficult, and briskly added, "You'll stay with us down here while we check your flight details with our Luton HQ."

"Well, yes, if you're sure that's necessary, honey." He reached into his inside jacket pocket for the requested items.

"It is, er," she said, speed-reading the documents, "Reverend Jackson." She snapped the passport closed. "This is the Tel Aviv flight. I'm sure you understand that we do have special precautions in place because of, ah, well, because of security issues." Monica made a mental note to drop the nervous-sounding hesitations in future incidents. She rushed on. "In any case, a quiet time down here will do no harm and give other passengers time to settle."

Rev. David Jackson squirmed on the letdown seat, more from discomfort than embarrassment. He immediately understood that the seat was designed to inform cabin crew that EasyFlight was not meant to apply to them. It gave zero encouragement to sit down on company time.

He quietly gave thanks for years of laid-back training in his own job. Now it was second nature for him to receive surprise news without reaction. As a reverend, he had heard everything and was prepared for anything. For example, a parishioner back at Boston General had once asked the reverend if he would give his left leg "a good Christian burial." It had appeared that the gangrenous limb was destined for the hospital incinerator. On another occasion, only days before Reverend Jackson's Israeli trip, a tearful cleaner at the Oxford, England, college where the reverend now worked had collapsed sobbing into his arms as he turned to descend some stairs. Her dead divorced husband's spirit, she claimed, had returned to kill her new boyfriend on the eve of their wedding. Her ex had often threatened to kill any other man she dated on many occasions before he died from a broken neck after falling down his staircase. Only that morning, the cleaner's new fiancé had tragically died, again in a stair fall. Dave had then spent an hour musing on life's coincidences and giving pastoral care. He finally gave the cleaner a comforting hug, lost his balance, and somersaulted headfirst down a flight of uncarpeted steps.

"Oh my God!" the distraught cleaner had screamed. "Now he's killed the reverend!"

Dave had slowly levered himself onto an elbow and managed, "Nope! Missed me altogether!" He thought it unhelpful to mention the throbbing kneecaps and two swelling, probably broken, wrists that had taken the full impact.

Dave was certainly not going to be phased by a mere nightmare in the presence of a flight of sleepy night riders and a business-brisk EasyFlight attendant. He was tempted to pass off the dream as the result of a tummy upset due to a suspect cheese bagel at Tel Aviv airport, but clerical honesty forbade him from doing so. He knew precisely from where the "kill her" shout had originated. He knew at whom it was aimed. And he also knew, at the moment of wakening, that something deep down within him had actually meant it.

CHAPTER 3

Mary's Story

Remanded in polite custody for causing midair panic, the reluctant prisoner perched on his torture seat.

Dave Jackson concluded that work was his best diversion, while his warders checked on suspected darker deeds via contacts in Tel Aviv and Luton. He had assured Monica and Trevor that being an Episcopal Anglican minister and Oxford lecturer did not sit well with murder or blowing up a plane full of people.

"And in any case," he'd smilingly assured both of them, "the treasure I've found in Israel leaves no room for such activities."

Trevor had peered over his bifocals with an uncertain, wry twist to his mouth, and Monica had offered nothing but a blank stare. As they resumed their inquiries, Dave sighed in submission and adjusted his laptop on upwardly sloping thighs, the seat being rather on the low side. He logged on to behold the most precious file he had ever dared entrust to a computer.

"That thing in flight mode?" Monica snapped over her shoulder as she stowed away bin liners bulging with in-flight snack leftovers.

"Trust me on this one."

Dave received a vexed "Hmm!" in response.

He fondly gazed at a file's icon placed in splendid isolation to the right of his desktop page. So valuable to him was it that he had instructed the cloud to back up changes every ten minutes whenever he was online. At the close of every session during the last precious weeks of translation, he had also diligently backed up his work on two separate hard drives. His pedantic push toward perfection ensured that there were always improvements to be saved. His overkill on saving was verging on OCD, yet there was no way he would lose this gem of a find to stupidity or the devilish gremlins of technology.

Thirteen weeks ago, he had been wretched. His life was smothered in ruins: there was no sign of the son he yearned for, his job was under threat for lack of students, and his marriage was gasping its last. Hope was in short supply, when a single message pinged on to his mobile and blessed revival dawned with the news of a new Dead Sea scroll find. His life was transformed in an instant.

11

Lovingly, he now opened the file, simply titled "Scroll," and gazed at it with an expression verging on adoration. Eleven of the weeks had been devoted to deciphering the precious document that even now continued to demand expert unraveling, stretching his rusty Hebrew.

He began to read, stopping for occasional corrections or pausing to savor a more dynamic translation. Monica, the flight, and even the pain of his rump on the unpadded ledge seat faded as Mary's story once more commanded his whole attention.

His mind was yet again lost in 74 AD and the siege of Masada. First, he reexamined the crude map of the Masada fortress that Mary had laboriously scratched onto her parchment scroll. He smiled, glad that he'd had an Israeli artist tidy it up and label it. Only then did he begin to reread and add polish and prose to her incredible diary. It began, oddly, with an entry that was seven days late.

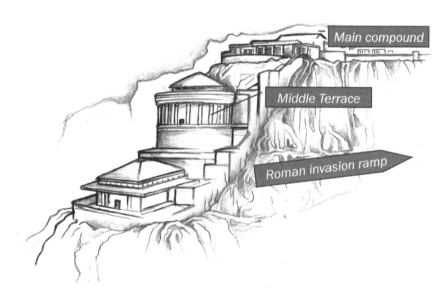

Illustrating three levels of Masada's fortress.

CHAPTER 4

Masada

Day 7

Can I find courage to kill my five precious children?

The world has gone mad down there. When it reaches us high in the sky, we must die. This is the lesser of evils, so we were told at our first planning meeting last night.

We will each kill our children first, and then all the adults will die. This ice-cold resolve is set. Not even the searing heat that hammers down on us on our high haven of Masada can melt it.

And yet still an inner whisper momentarily mocks, "Kill your babies? Snuff out the lives you have lovingly nurtured?" Immediately the meeting ended, I spent some thinking time at the edge of Masada. I gazed down, with the help of a full moon, on the sluggish turquoise jewel that is the Dead Sea of Israel. Never had its name been less comforting.

My chronicle begins with this tragic end, and yet my people have a long history of miracles. Who knows?

I am Mary, a leader in the uprising against an empire that believes its might carries the right to rule all. Rome rules, and all must obey. We Jews choose to disagree—forcefully!

Diaries should begin on Day 1, yet quill and papyrus need peace and quiet. Days of flight filled with fear have not provided these. So much had to be done, with the enemy often strides behind our sandals. Defenses had to be strengthened, children organized, siege stocks counted. There was not a sane moment to think, let alone scribe.

Last night allowed time for debate and our eventual decision to be our own executioners. This bloody resolve may appall those not of our world. If this scroll is found, I ask only that readers defer judgment.

"Slavery is living death," had cried Eleazar ben Jair, our "Moses" in the terrifying exodus from nearby Jerusalem. To me he is Uncle El, which is all I could manage as a babe. "El is a God name," he had said, smiling. Fine by me: Uncle God seemed perfect.

Six hundred listeners last night squashed each other on the cramped middle terrace of our stronghold. The rest—children and minders—were distracted high on the plateau by a torchlight hunt for planted treasure.

"Freedom!" we had hissed as Eleazar discussed the cruelty of Roman slavery. The word should have resounded, accompanied by ram's-horn shofars and crashing cymbals, enough to ripple the sluggish waters below and maybe even strike terror in the enemy camped on its shores. Yet we whispered lest our treasures—hunting treasure—became infected by the terrors that gnaw adult minds. Pitiful to the ear, maybe, but not to the eye! Body stances and faces, yellowed in flickering torchlight, told of a never-surrender resolve. "Freedom in death!" we growled as short sica daggers flashed from the folds of many robes.

"Friends." Eleazar had risked a loud single voice. "We arrive at this death pact fearing the dreaded alternatives. Absence of freedom forced us into war. To surrender our babies and our own lives for Roman use and abuse would be high wickedness, and how then should we stand before our Maker or even each other?"

"Unthinkable!" cried Rueben, a gray-haired elder. Supporting whispers swelled to produce a clamor that Eleazar hastily waved down.

"Nor must we take our own lives," Uncle El said, resuming. "Life is a gift; not ours to steal." Silence underlined this as his steady eyes swept all. "The elders propose death by a loving hand. We can do nothing more."

Day 8

My beloved and much-missed Joseph gave me my three beautiful daughters, followed by two handsome sons.

He was felled by arrows in Jerusalem, and yet still he was forced to work on clearing stone after stone from our charred temple. The last time I saw him, as I took water to our workers, I swore through hot tears to keep our children free from Roman harm.

We both knew even then that death might be the only way. The course we have now chosen is embraced with deepest love. Each parent will act swiftly and at the same prearranged time to ensure the least fear for the little ones.

When I am away from the crowd, that mocking whisper haunts, even now as I scribe. In such lonely moments, I scream without sound as my insides wrench skin and bone. Logic nods at necessity, but the maternal revolts. Knowing what our foe does with captured children sustains me. One more thing: we Jews have had divine support for centuries. "God help," the human prayer as old as Eden, is our daily breath.

This morning a leaders' meeting settled the details. I am to help oversee the adult deaths; my writing and administrative skills will assist the ten executioners. When our duty is done, my assassin will be the elder I most admire, my husband's closest friend, Isaac ben Judah.

He is skillful and strong, and I know he loves me as his best friend's wife. Strange to scribe, but when free from that haunting whisper, I feel safe in his hands. The remaining ten will draw lots to decide who will be the final executioner. Only he will commit suicide, falling on his sword of love.

Day 10

One argument raged at the end of our leaders' meeting: how much longer will we live?

"Maybe a whole year," old Rueben had stubbornly declared. Usually, this gnarled elder makes sense, but not this time, according to my Isaac ben Judah. "Three months at the most!" he had claimed with noisy support from the skeptical Sicarii.

"Maybe not even so long," one had said, sneering.

The Sicarii are always angry, forever pessimistic. They are the hottest of hot-blooded Jews. We minority

Zealots have our eruptions, but the Sicarii are us at our fiercest. They are named after their solution for everything—their sica daggers. We Zealots prefer sharp words. Uncle El's fury at the "weak feebleness" on our side of the family is well-known.

"Zealot softness let the enemy trample us into servitude," was the oft-chanted mantra of the Sicarii.

"Reckless Sicarii assassins caused our last-stand mess," was always the Zealot counter. Our words cooled eventually around one uncertainty: none of us truly knows how much older we will get.

What is known is sobering: nine thousand enemies are in five encampments. They have begun piling rubble on a rising spur on Masada's northern flank. Some of it looks like the square white stones from our sacred temple. Centurions, served by as many slaves, scurry like ants below us.

Pessimists claim the spur gives the Romans a massive start. Rueben and his optimists claim the spur will crumble. The pious, mainly the tiny band of holy Essenes, remain silent and consign our future to supernatural hands.

The truth is frightening. Ignorance runs as deep as Masada is high. Few understand what earthwork is needed to take thousands of marching feet, plus a ramming tower with hinged walkways, to bridge Masada's massive fortress walls. As the debate ended, most favored half a year or less.

Unanimity without argument reigned on the last point: we must be cheerful for the children and each other. Camp rotas and sentry duties would help.

Isaac announced that the men will build a second wall. The enemy will batter through the existing ramparts with their tower ram, while archers above will protect haulers and pushers. Our planned inner wall will be layered with stone, then wood, and then more stone to absorb the ram's impact and give us extra days. The women will have the children and the cooking, and I will have extra administration duties.

And yet I yearn to do more, especially when my little ones sleep, the quiet time when the fears of what I must do will be most persistent. I therefore have decided on a special writing project.

Day 12

Sanity reigned over Masada yesterday. All slowed in the dry heat of the plateau for our second Sabbath, a small victory over the scurry far below.

I resisted starting my new project because of the guilt of our scramble for survival on our last Sabbath. Then, settling into our Masada retreat, we had so feared the enemy would pounce before we could repel them. Yesterday, we gave our Creator his day, and each other permission to recover. All strolled with weary smiles, shadowed only by the knowledge that the lightest of all evils looms in the distance.

Discord jarred midmorning for the leaders. One of our older boys scaled the northern wall and saw everything. He was excitedly telling of soldiers and a giant tower before he and his friends were herded to the middle terrace, where we confidently, if vaguely, spoke of escape plans. There were hints of rich rewards for the silent and of dire punishment for chatterers. A deal of silence was sealed.

Later, my own family declared war. Eldest Joseph, named after his father, had a poison of the throat. In the poor light of flickering tinder at sunset, I could only guess at a dark rawness at the back of his tongue.

"Stop being a baby," Gad had delightedly taunted his brother, two years older than his mature six. "Be a man like me." The girls, all older than the boys—twins Rebecca and Rachel and my firstborn little dove, Jemima—had giggled and goaded, multiplying the power of the original taunt.

Day 13
My brood have roosted early, especially a still-drowsy Joseph. I have had time to extend this diary scroll for my special project.

My passion is to pass on the family saga that kept me sane in that sad world below. We all love a story, and perhaps a love story best of all. I claim no originality, for I am merely the storyteller. This is a handed-down account, warmed by campfires and under cozy rugs of generations long gone, of the great romance at the heart of our universe as lived out by one of our heroes of old.

The inspired saga of Hosea has kept our people grateful, amazed, and amused for nine centuries. The original is now hidden in the caves below our high plateau, together with other sacred writings.

Only the Dead Sea saw the Essenes hide them, and it has no way of telling its secrets. One day, no doubt, they will be found and unfurled before brighter and more receptive eyes. When Jews followed these scrolls, we prospered; when we ignored them, we descended into war and famine. I am not alone in my amazement of how we stubbornly failed to see cause and effect.

In ages long gone, Israel had once again lost touch with its roots and books. Then, a great-great-great- (I lose count) grandmother began to retell Hosea's love story through the supposed eyes of his sister.

"A woman's words should be heard," she had told her bedtime children. "Better still is a mother's point of view. All the tomorrows to come must hear the solutions often ignored by our stubborn menfolk."

And so the story came down to us. It was not divine, and not sacred scripture like the hidden scrolls; it was just gloriously human tales, cruel, sometimes savage, yet filled with the bittersweet emotions sifting for sense in the ever-shifting sands of our sun-soaked centuries.

Am I too fanciful to hope that a mere love story will save a fractured, hate-filled world? Of one thing I am certain: none can let evil go by without challenge. If we let evil thrive, then we ourselves become evil. If only one of tomorrow's mothers is saved from the horror that I and my family now face on Masada, then this scroll will be blessed.

My scratchings are better than no words, and so I now pledge the rest of this scroll to the handed-down love story of a prophet's sister.

One final thought: It takes but a brief gossip to stroll around Masada. Hundreds of families now live in space that once would have supported just one family. For a people used to rolling tribal lands, these confined months will be an ordeal like no other.

From time to time, I will interrupt my love story to report on notable events.

CHAPTER 5

"Come ASAP"

A gentle two-tone alert, plus Monica's service trolley brushing his knee, recalled the Reverend Dave Jackson. His mind scrambled back from a first-century Masada prison to his own incarceration in the galley of Flight TA 437.

"If you have empty cups or cartons," cabin steward Trevor droned into his handset, "my colleagues are now passing among you with refuse bags."

The two tones echoed Dave's mobile signal and conjured a smile. He immediately recalled the life-changing message of thirteen crazy weeks before. It had initiated a surprise start to a writing sabbatical from his day-to-day task of imprinting Old Testament skills onto the green, embryonic ministers in his charge.

His leave had been booked for the following summer's break, but the startling text from Israel prompted a rethink. Delighted college authorities granted him immediate leave plus an all-expenses-paid trip. "As much for our reputation as yours, Dave," the dean of studies had said, beaming, upon hearing that his struggling Oxford college might enhance the glitter of its literati.

A last-minute online EasyFlight open return to Tel Aviv secured, Dave had stuffed two holdalls with essentials, slung his bagged laptop over a shoulder, and walked out on his wife with only the briefest of notes propped against their forty-two-inch flat-screen. *More consideration than she gave me when I caught her with the ethics lecturer on the kitchen table!* he thought.

The bitterness was ever present, whether he was asleep or awake. His eyes moistened and then squeezed tight, vainly trying to stifle a vivid and unwanted vision. Feeling his stomach muscles tighten and his diaphragm rise, he snapped open his eyes, thumping his tanned skull against the bright white bulkhead of his hinged galley seat.

"Something wrong, sir?" Monica swung around. Dave shook his head, forced a smile, and willed his thoughts back to the surprise message.

"Come ASAP," the first text from his department's Dead Sea dig chief had read. "A find u won't believe!!!" A smiley face plus a face with spiraling eyes and a wide-open mouth accompanied the exclamation marks.

"Spill," Dave had immediately texted back. His mobile trumpeted Handel's "Hallelujah Chorus" after a few moments.

"It's Stan." The thick Lancashire flatness of his third-year-student dig leader was unmistakable. "Dave, grab a flight. Honest, mate, yer just gotta see this for yourself."

"Stop shouting." Dave laughed into the Samsung, a little from his ear. "Quickly, run down the what, when, and how." Dave hadn't believed they would find anything in the remote caves below Masada. It was no more than a fun fieldwork trip to the Holy Land for his near-reverend charges. Had not the caves already been plundered, rifled, and searched by two generations of archaeological sleuths?

"S'not from a recognized cave." Stanley Ramsbottom had sounded either short of oxygen or hyperventilating too much. The rapid gasps burst forth as he said, "'Ardly a cave at all. More a hollow on a ledge almost filled with dry sand ... a giant scroll ... eye-witness stuff ... torn in two. ... Looks like the tear edges match ... nothing like t' others. ... Not scriptures. Yeah—disappointing, I know, but good all the same. Disintegrating at t' edges, but—"

"Whoa! Stan. Who, erm—" Dave stuttered.

"What? You mean who wrote 'em, who found 'em, who has 'em, what?" Both were laughing in confusion.

"All those," Dave excitedly shouted. "Sorry, Stan. Shell shock. Never expected this in a million digs; brain's overdriving at Mach 1. Look, hang up and then e-mail me a meaty report. I'll check flights while I wait."

He had then sat, mobile clasped in fist, beaming at nothing in particular, surrounded by dark oak-clad walls in his study. He had just hit the biblical equivalent of gold and was savoring the incredible moment.

"Thank you!" He had chortled. "Thank you, thank you, thank you!" he shouted past a ceiling chandelier, but he giggled at doing precisely what he had told his students not to do. "Why look up?" he'd chided them. "You know he's not the bearded old man in the sky! He's all around, omnipresent!"

"Excuse me, sir." Monica's voice was less icy. "We're starting our descent into Luton, and we need you back in your seat."

"Fine, miss. No need for handcuffs, then?" He raised an eyebrow and smiled while automatically adjusting his comb-over.

"Think yourself extremely lucky, sir, that..." Monica suddenly lowered her thunderous eyebrows, and a half smile caught the corners of her mouth. The news from London had backed up the reverend's story. He was "a university professional, an EasyFlight regular," and what's more, his comical macho bigness perched on his pop-down seat twinned with almost naïve shyness showed he had not the slightest inkling of how attractive he was to the opposite sex. Monica's maternal and not-so-maternal instincts ignited, and she suddenly wanted to protect this giant at large in an alien world.

"Sir." The professional resurfaced. "Try not to doze off again. Please! Do you think you could manage that small matter for us?" Her lips finished in a slight kiss-pout below innocently elevated eyebrows.

Dave rose quickly, letting the bench seat slap loudly against the bulkhead. His treasures clasped to his stomach, he strode into the now-sloping aisle with an over-the-shoulder quip: "Impeccable service, Monica."

"Hal." A whispered whine drifted up as Dave neared his row. "That Yankee killer's back again."

"Hush now, honey, sweetie pie." Hal patted her belted tummy. "Everything is just dandy."

"Sorry for the commotion." Dave's apology to them was sincere, "Just a nightmare—probably a dodgy Tel Aviv bagel," he white-lied. Mavis shrank away from her midair psycho.

"Would all passengers please return to their seats and ensure electrical items are switched off?" Dave stowed his laptop overhead to Monica's well-practiced landing monologue, and then belted up before unfurling his small scroll.

"Little beauty!" He smiled even though it was merely a photographic image of the real thing.

The original, giant scroll was hermetically sealed in a dark Tel Aviv vault, now a protected and preserved part of modern Israel's archaeological trove. Stan's well-schooled team had created a comprehensive photographic record before their tutor had reached the airport on his outward flight. Dave had had it copied on parchment paper and set in a velvet-lined box, ready to present to the dean of studies and his department's rich sponsors in the city of London.

Once again, he fingered the hastily scribbled Hebrew stories. He smiled and again frowned at the odd crossings-out and corrections. As a norm, such scrolls were precise, crafted by professional classes of old.

Some of Masada Mary's scribbled characters had caused him grinding, nightlong headaches. Some, at the scroll's edges, required educated guesses. Other words had no exact equal in English, so he had been forced to choose what he believed to be living equivalents in today's English. There was still a mass of work ahead, but he now had a readable, if unrefined, version of Mary's beautiful love saga.

A deep irony tickled his brain, not for the first time: how weird that a disaster in the affairs of the heart must now relay a love story to a world as lost to love as he.

Of course, he could do nothing else. Was he not honor-bound to pass on Masada Mary's work? He smiled shamefacedly and mouthed, "At least such was my first intention."

Translating his mixed motives was harder than decoding ancient scripts. He had long ago established the first principle of deciphering conflicting desires: a human's first gut instinct is surely the purist. To be honest, less-worthy motives had rapidly crowded in. He wanted his name on another book. Why not? Had not every soul a book lurking within? The Everest of unwritten novels challenged the mountain range of all other human resolutions.

Sure, he wanted to impress his friends, and yes, oddly enough, even Colette, the wife he loved and hated in equal measures.

Of course, a popular paperback edition would be the first stage. Once the duty of passing on the message was accomplished, scholarship would follow. Precisely what had his team found? Was it merely the fanciful tales of ancients? Could anything be verified? Could it add meaningful information to the library of knowledge that was already shelved on the infamous Masada siege and, perhaps, even on the Old Testament itself?

Could it enhance his reputation? Ah, here was the rub: was this not the real motive? The original sin of pride was certainly chief contender to his original altruism. Dave Jackson had reveled in the fame of his one and only volume so far. Part of him desired more of the same.

And while on the subject of honesty, the candid part of his mind thought, flitting into an area he fought to keep battened down, *what of Colette and this ethics lecturer—or lecher?* Dave sometimes preferred to refer to the man with whom his wife had committed adultery as the latter.

Again, the kitchen table scene swam into his mind just as clearly as it had in his earlier embarrassing nightmare. He dug his nails hard into his palms. When this did not distract his thoughts, he banged his head to the beat of a catchy chorus coming from the speakers set into his headrest, anything to fuzz his focus. He quickly scanned the distant lights now coming into view and tried to fathom the flight path. The plane obligingly banked, and city lights replaced the dark swath of the Home Counties. The two-tone alert sounded.

"Ladies and gentlemen," Monica said, sounding sad, "Luton has set us in an unavoidable holding pattern. Please keep seat belts fastened for what we hope will be only a short delay."

Dave grimaced. Desperate for distraction and unable to use his computer, he unraveled the small scroll to reexamine the original Hebrew of Mary's love story.

Fast as light, he was yet again outside the sky-blue chapel in a hillside cemetery in Safed, northern Israel, as he reread the hasty scribble of Masada Mary about a prophet's sister.

CHAPTER 6

The Sister's Story

I paused for breath, having caught up with the carriers who were stumbling beneath my brother's embalmed and tightly bound form. My ears pounded from haste under a climbing sun, but I could still hear the crunching slap of the carriers' sandals on the downward-sloping cemetery path.

I cooled beneath a gnarled olive tree and inhaled air that was too warm and arid-dry. I gulped to deliver my message, but a male growl of a question left me open-mouthed.

"How did he survive so long?" the lead carrier asked, flinging the words over his plainly aching shoulders. I held back, grateful for another breath on the errand for my mournful family, still straggling a long slingshot back up the hill.

The last of the six bearers missed his footing, maybe surprised that another voice had punctured his own thoughts. It was a well-asked question at my brother's funeral. I winced at the blood oozing from the dislodged nail of a big toe belonging to the last bearer, staining his hide sandal while he battled to gag his curse in a sacred place.

"His wife had murder in mind in the early days," the injured carrier said as he gasped out of a mouth devoid of teeth. "Poison, they say."

"Royal assassins were the biggest threat," a middle bearer cawed through his gaps. It looked as though the town's tooth pullers might retire off the earnings from this decaying party. This last nibble provoked more vicious pecks.

"Those Assyrians put a huge price on his head!"

"The stoning mobs of unholy priests had—"

"Stop it!" I shouted.

The procession shuffled in the embarrassment of a family member catching them up, catching them out! My message that they slow down forgotten, my eyes blazed while theirs examined the dirt path. My beloved Hosea, strides away from his final resting place, deserved more than a shredded character. Their gossiping beaks might gorge back up the hill in Safed, but not in our family procession, not while bearing the only human who loved me, my protector, my image of what our God must be like.

My glare pinioned each bearer as I picked my way past them. Stepping around the squatting lead man, I suspected my outburst had a cause unrelated to the callous carriers. Guilt, maybe: Had I not also questioned my beloved Hosi being gifted to me for so many years? Fifty-five!

Hosea had been my shield from scorpions, bears, and mountain lions. He was an ever-hovering hand as I toddled. He was my sage, my teacher, my comforter during my growing pains. He was a brother who was a mother after ours had died giving me life. He was my ever-bright, sometimes irritating sun that rarely dimmed, illuminating the scary recesses along my scrambling path to maturity.

He did all this while loving kings and priests who wanted him dead. He would have even smiled at the insensitive body bearers. Hosi was hesed in living flesh, hesed indicating a special love, a tough, unbending, ever-forgiving, never-condemning acceptance that embraced all. Hesed, Hosi had often told me, was a divine kind of loving. I had never seen a human-expressed love to match it, save, perhaps, in my brother.

Maybe, just possibly, Hosi really was the prophet he claimed to be. It was so difficult to be sure, to believe that my own flesh and blood could be so extraordinary, despite all the astounding events I had witnessed.

Perhaps, after all, he did have the ear of the Great One. Often he had claimed guidance from the One who saw all possibilities and predators, the Unseen One whom we know simply as Yahweh, "the One who is."

Maybe this was the One who really had directed and ordered my brother's brave and foolhardy tongue. It would make sense of his life lived crazily without heed to his personal safety. He should never have reached twenty-five years, let alone fifty-five.

My glaring silence prompted nervous mumblings from the fallen burial party.

"Sorry!"

"Yes, should have known better."

"Unforgivable in the circumstances."

I made myself smile, as Hosi would have. He too had marveled over what kept him going. In a climate that tended to age men rapidly, maybe a divine youth-giver had nurtured his assets to ensure clarity and delivery of a divine message.

I raised a flat palm to hush the carriers. "Please wait a while." The bearers straightened with renewed reverence, holding my brother at waist height and fashioning their faces as paid mourners.

Fond memories kept flooding back in waiting moments. I now remembered sitting on the teaching stone where I had entered the world twelve summers before. Hosi, my font of knowledge with a three-year head start on me, gushed forth on the subject of caterpillars, moths, birds and bees, and birth.

The flat oval stone, an upthrust of gray limestone thrice my length, tilted slightly toward our whitewashed eight-roomed house, double the size of normal village homes. It angled away from a separate bakery, out of which our father had just shooed us, dramatically ending our bread-making shift.

My tears were drying. I was not going to die after all, it seemed. Before the boulder Hosi stood, hands on hips with feet splayed in his teacher-storyteller stance, wisps of chin fluff waving in a warm breeze.

"You screamed and bellowed like a baby bear deprived of mother's milk," my Hosi said while laughing, "and you flailed and wailed under a full moon, demanding we all forget our sleep and devote the midnight hour to you and you alone."

I giggled, lying back with my bare, blood-smeared legs kicking in the air, shaking out the stiffness from treading the day's dough. My fears of moments before were quietening, and I delighted once more in tales of my entry into the world at immense discomfort to my parents and brother. Hosi had this extraordinary art of centering the world round me, remolding life each time it cracked under my fresh fears of growing up.

Only an hour before, death seemed moments away as the dough beneath both of us streaked scarlet. Cramping pains had clutched at my middle, causing my scream of terror.

"Now you're a woman!" Hosi had cried triumphantly, eliciting in me a fresh yowl of despair. "I told you it would happen. Remember?"

He had grasped both my shoulders and knelt down in the ruined dough to gaze into my appalled face. He soothed me, quietly telling me of the changes needed for a time when, like my long-gone mother, I would be able to make babies. Hope was in his words, yet my innards needed more.

"Look!" Hosi clasped a handful of red-streaked dough. "You're changing just as this!" I had pouted at the comparison with a shapeless lump.

"No." Hosi had laughed. "The leaven! The starter lump! Changing water and flour into bread?" I nodded. "Well, your girl's body is—"

"Out!" Father had screamed as he discovered the day's dough and tomorrow's village order ruined. "And how many times have I told you not to use your feet?" Father hated change. "Heel of hand, not unwashed foot!"

Hosi had swept me up over his shoulder, carried me out to the flat rock to wash me down, and added graduation touches to my womanly education. "Be excited, little sister! Are you not the delicate grain bursting into barley, a freckled egg cracking open to reveal the graceful, gold-winged bee-eater?"

"No, I am not." I puckered my lips as he sat me down. I peered down my nose haughtily, recovering my little-sister sulk. "You silly boys know nothing of our mysterious feminine secrets."

"Aha!" He greeted the return of his normal nag of a sister. "Then you are a giant green-mottled egg, cracking open into a fearsome, scaly she-dragon with brown runny warts all over your fire-breathing nose!"

"Nooo." I perched, royally aloof, on my stone throne. "I am a pale, dainty blue-white creature of beauty, springing and fluttering from her chrysalis as queen of all butterflies."

"You." Hosi smiled with arms opening wide. "You are a soft auburn foal growing into a graceful gazelle."

"Of course," I said, accepting the declaration with princessy primness before falling with gales of laughter into his strong arms.

"Useless!" Father's angry bark crushed our merriment as he strode from the bakery. "All totally ruined!" He looked like the prophet of doom he had once been in his younger days.

"Sorry, Daddy Beeri." I offered a smile spiced with finger-twining archness. "You see, now that I am a woman—"

"Enough!" he growled, determined not to be wound around the finger of the villain who had just canceled his afternoon nap. "You'll be a woman when you learn to behave like one. If your mother could see you now ..." Daddy Beeri trailed off, as he always did with this oft-repeated regret.

I miss my mother even though I saw her but once. Hosi said it was his earliest memory. She was lying on our best bear rug, which was flung over the rock table. My birth night was oppressive, even though Safed perches high in our Galilean hills. Outdoors was a healthier, brighter childbearing arena, illuminated by a massive Levant moon and blazing tar torches. In flickering orange-yellows, Mother gazed down at moments-old me with strength only to offer a little finger for me to grasp and suckle.

"I felt so sad," Hosi told me when I finally extracted words from him. "I looked up beside the rock and Mother smiled down, first at me, and then at you lying beside her on the rug. Then, she just seemed to go out." Sadness stung my eyes. I stared through the watery glow, wanting more. Hosi turned

39

as if to close the subject, but powerful curiosity made me jab him so vigorously that he gave a strange sob and glared back at me.

"One moment, Mother was bright in moonlight." Hosi had little trust in his voice. "Tears leaked onto her cheeks, and her eyes widened and twinkled with tar light. Then color, reflections; everything, faded, and she ... she just went somewhere else."

The day Hosi told me all this was the first time I wondered about God and me.

Now, let me get this part right. This was not me and some great power out there. It was not cold logic as when Hosi gave me God lessons. This was not the Almighty of Abraham, Isaac, and Jacob, all rules, rites and rituals, and distant religion. No. This was personal. For the first time I sensed God might be real and, strangely enough, not very nice.

Any God who loved and controlled everything was not so great if he gave babies but stole mothers. The day I became a woman was another God-and-me moment. He gave nice things like babies, yet at the cost of painful installments paid every month. Not a good God impression.

I tell of my deep moments so you may fully understand what I am to reveal about my Hosi. He was big on God moments, even getting messages from above, or so subsequent events seemed to prove. It began with one more God-and-me time when I shouted for him and he definitely growled back at me.

I had wandered aimlessly away from home, walking down a hill of yellowing grass strewn with white-gray rocks. I found myself beyond Safed and among the hillside shrines of Baal. Father was appalled at such "wicked places" where one god even demanded sacrificial babies, but on this day I was tired of being his good little girl. Maybe Hosi had been especially bossy about counting loaves or discussing why clouds could spit rain and fire bolts. Too much can hurt little brains.

"Later, you need to know about some of the five hundred birds that pass through Safed each spring," my know-it-all brother had shouted at me the last time our paths had crossed.

Maybe he would miss me and have to come looking for me. Or perhaps I just wanted freedom, like those birds he wanted to teach me about. This day, I was migrating along my own path. This was to be about me and nobody else. This was not to be about gods who ate babies, or stubborn family males who consumed my patience. I was one of Hosea's songbirds flying off to exotic parts.

"Oh, you sweet thing," I cried out as I rounded one of the shrines. "Where's your mummy gone?"

There on an overgrown path was a mewling ball of fur. Big eyes pleaded for a cuddle. As I reached down, falling pebbles made me look up to an avalanche of fur and claws. I ran, bursting into gulping tears, quickly hiding behind a Baal shrine. "No see, no eat," I reckoned, not knowing then that bears detect the world through wet noses.

Hot breath and a furious roar came around the shrine, and for first time in my life I had a serious conversation with the One who had made me as well as the bear, praying that he would be more on my side than on the mother bear's.

My shallow faith in this Maker was demonstrated with a swift circling of the shrine so that the roar and the hot breath stayed at least one corner away from me. Then I stumbled. Roar and breath and bear all bore down.

"No!"

That was the word I was about to scream, yet, oddly, it came from another. Roar, breath, and steaming body all hesitated. The "No!" had come from another shrine, and the mother sensed new danger for her cub.

"No!" I heard once again.

Such certainty: I could not put the right word to it then, but I know now that it was authority. It commanded beyond argument, and it belonged to my brother. The bear could obviously see him. The giantess swayed above me, keeping one eye on Hosi and one on her baby bear.

42

"No!" Hosea said again, only this time his voice was nearer. The bear was bigger than Daddy Beeri. It was broader than two fathers, with paws the size of my head. Hosi stood no chance.

"God, help us!" I screamed, immediately clamping both hands across my stupid little mouth as the she-bear bellowed and crashed down on all fours, aiming her quivering snout at me.

"No!" came once more. Impatiently, the mother bear reared up and turned toward the voice of my foolhardy savior. Nailed paws again slapped down, this time pointing away from me. I sobbed with relief as the bear's haunches rippled away. I was on my feet, climbing the shrine until I could see over it, until I could see my beloved brother standing in the path of an enraged mother.

"Hosea!" I screamed as the bear sprang.

"No!" shouted my brother, turning to one side and thrusting the long handle of a baker's oven scoop into the bear's throat. The wooden shaft shattered as Hosea's end met the ground, deflecting the bear's attack and sending her skidding in the direction of her mewling cub.

The mother turned to attack but then halted as Hosi breathed hard and quietly sang, "Nooo." He stood square in front of her, his eyes ablaze and steady. Staring! I gasped when he took one tiny but deliberate step toward the mother.

"Nooo!"

This was quieter. The bear now sensed that the word no was an indication of pain. Hosi's eyes still drilled into the mother's, and then he advanced one more step. To me, it meant nothing but stupidity! Why didn't he climb a shrine? To the mother bear, the small step seemed to be everything.

She flinched, blinked, and then snorted. She took a step back, swinging her massive head to look for her nearby cub. She faced an authority to match hers. There was her aching throat. She rose to her full height, and roared enough to shake my shrine before cuffing her careless cub into line behind her retreating buttocks.

"You can close your mouth now." Hosi smiled as he lifted me off the shrine.

"She b-b-backed off," I stammered.

"She decided she had won." Hosi shrugged.

"No!" I yelled back. "You won!"

"Should we call her back and discuss it?"

"You told her no."

"Maybe." Hosi grinned. "Or maybe you got a prayer answered." I knew my mouth was gaping again. "You screamed out for God's help?"

It was not to be the last time my brother deflected danger. Greater powers than bears would back down in the face of this strange power my brother possessed. Perhaps here was the secret of his many years.

It certainly made me glimpse his God as my God. It dawned on me that this Almighty was rather more complex. Yes, he took babies' mothers away, and certainly he was a pain to women's insides, but he also heard and answered a little girl's terrified screams.

Possibly!

Enough of my childish tales! Now I must tell you of the woman who should have proved the early death of my brother. Woman, did I say? Actually, Gomer was not much older than I.

CHAPTER 7

Princess and Prostitute

"Ladies and gentlemen, we again apologize for the delay in landing." Dave Jackson detected tiredness creeping into Monica's cut-glass English vowels. He blinked to lubricate his drying eyes, determined to remain alert and to leave the now sleeping Mavis and her inhaler in peace.

"We now understand that the technical issues at Luton will take several hours more to resolve. Therefore, we have no alternative but to redirect to Heathrow. We are sorry for this unavoidable inconvenience."

A sleepy groan rose in the dimmed cabin. Dave sighed and once again reached for his scroll. He smiled with pleasant anticipation at reaching what he considered to be the real beginning of the sister's saga. He settled contentedly as he felt the plane bank away from its Luton holding pattern.

He was grateful for the change of pace in the main story. Freed from the sometimes staccato diary entries, Masada Mary seemed to relax into the color, character, and words of the storytelling sister.

∗   ∗   ∗

"Hello, Gomer."

Outwardly, it was a pleasant enough salutation whenever we passed on pathways or in town. Within, uglier feelings seethed. For a start, mere words of greeting were clearly inadequate. A bob of the knee or a reverential nod seemed to be expected. She got neither, much to the irritation of the old woman who invariably accompanied her.

"You!" was what Gomer haughtily aimed at me and others on the rare occasions she required attention.

"No better than us!" we village girls would mumble, though not loud enough for her ears, and certainly not for those of her rich daddy. Even if Her Highness had heard, she would probably have stifled a yawn at such trivialities.

She was two seasons older than I and far prettier. She had more shape, which was emphasized by her robes being darted in hidden ways. Men and boys who walked by me with no more than a friendly nod would slow to a drooling shuffle when Gomer glided by.

She sashayed from the other side of Safed, the pagan priest district of massive mansions with Baal shrines at most pathway junctions. Not that she and her family were pure Baal believers. These days, most bowed to Jewish priests on Sabbaths and to Baal statues every other day of the week. Seeking spiritual insurance, bulls or birds were offered to two or even more gods. Who could be sure where to aim the sacrifice?

Gomer's family played the religious game well. They were good Jews up front, but they entertained Baal in their back-garden shrines. Toward the bottom of their terraced lands, extending beyond the green Galilean hills and out to the faraway shores of Lake Kinneret, was the White Temple of Fertility. Daily, it praised or pleaded with the weather god Hadad—Baal to commoners like us, for only "holy ones" decreed themselves worthy to utter his sacred name.

"Baal rhymes with gale," Hosi had once growled in distaste during a grudging afternoon lesson on other religions. "Easy to remember, because they think he rules the wind that brings the rain."

Baal's fertility temple was a mystery to us young ones, even those who had reached womanhood. We were far more interested in the produce of Gomer's land surrounding it, boasting orchards of the finest figs, dates, and grapes, and a dozen other fruits. The lands of Diblaim were one of the wonders of the sun-blessed Levant, which extended from the Philistine shores of the Great Sea across to the River Jordan, and which descended as far south as Egypt and climbed beyond us and northward to the heights of Syria.

"Our family might have enough to weather the odd crop failure," Hosi once taught me, "but the fields of Gomer's father are dotted with crop silos sufficient to outlast the most crippling droughts. Diblaim has vast influence in our tents of power."

"But we have plenty," I had argued.

"But of course." My brother-teacher had smiled at my family pride. "But Diblaim could keep half the tribes of Israel from starvation until normal fertility returned."

Clothing was another area where the Diblaim dynasty reigned. My workday wear was a brown tunic over rough wool robes with thong-tied sandals of hard hide, tiny miniatures of the Phoenician-coast barges trading at our market ports. Not Gomer. She wore silks in the purples of princesses, the color being so precious because it needed a colony of mollusks to color just one bolt of fabric. Peeping from her fine hems were delicate slippers carried to her by exotic Eastern caravans via the great trade routes threading their precious and precarious ways through our mountain passes.

For years now, business had boomed. We were the only land bridge across the center of the world, and all travelers coming from Africa or the intriguing East, or from the Roman West or the savage North, had to come through our hills. Impatient traders, those who liked a gamble, sometimes chanced their fortunes on the quicker sea routes, but even hugging coastlines held risks.

"Far safer through our back garden," we would often chide travelers who complained of highway taxes and road robbers.

Our main wealth poured from the heavens. For years now, the rains had arrived at intervals best for wells, watercourses, and crops, and our lush abundance well qualified us as the western tip of the great Fertile Crescent arching round the heart of the Levant.

Hosi and Father Beeri had taught me well about such things, especially because my family role, even at my tender age, was to care for the shekels of the caravan swarms. I did what Mother would have done, while Father and Hosi, so they insisted, dealt with high affairs of business that only males could comprehend.

"Always know you trade with thieves," Father Beeri stressed with a wagging finger, "vagabonds, and murderers who must be whipped or won over with the sharpest of wits."

I kept my wits well honed, and even delighted in improving them by extracting extra tuition from well-traveled rogues. My wits were especially helpful if a good deal depended on impressing the young bookkeeper of Beeri. The travelers ranged from the newcomer customers of Greece, lightly bronzed with heart-fluttering beauty, to the dark traders of Egypt, Ethiopia, and below. There were even bizarre and exotic customs and goods from travelers with eyes shaped like our almonds.

One evening, after discussions with traders of various faiths, I teased my teacher-brother, saying that he was too narrow in his thinking and beliefs.

"Baal is a mighty god of many names." I laughed at Hosi. "The Greeks in Phoenicia call him Zeus. The Romans call him Mars, whereas the Egyptians insist that Baal is really called Set. Does not this great god of many names control the whole world's weather?"

Hosi ignored the teasing with a strange sadness. My mockery demanded an argument, but he seemed to be lost in himself.

"When a hot summer trespasses into winter," Hosi had said, eventually leaning toward me as if trading in great secrets, "then business will be brisk for the temple ladies."

"Who?" Even as I mirrored my brother's conspiratorial lean, I knew my mouth stayed in the *oo* position. Suddenly, my interest in my own argument faded and I was hooked like a golden sandal fish on a Galilean line.

"The ladies who pleasure men," Hosi said without hesitation, though his forehead creased and his eyes flitted nervously for fear that Father had overheard. "It's time you knew. Father will never tell, and there's no mother's knee for you."

"Ooh," I said while smirking, confidently tossing my long black hair back across my shoulders, "you mean the *zonah*."

I laughed out loud in Hosi's face. "You are funny, dear brother. We all know about them in the bazaar booths. They sell themselves on street corners to men who have no woman of their own, and even to some of my friends' daddies ..." I trailed off as Hosi slowly shook his head. I leaned in further, and my lips formed the *oo* again.

"The *kedeshah*," he whispered.

"The what?" My nose wrinkled, showing the disdain of the young for older ones who made no sense.

Hosi patiently repeated the word with a slow nod and an expression I had never before seen on his handsome face—a wistful sadness as though he were longing for something lost; something that should not have been.

"The kedeshah are mostly chosen from young girls who have never been with a man." Hosi had raised both eyebrows, and I nodded to show I knew his meaning. "Well, they are usually from the best families, and they have great beauty and comeliness. They are not like the unfortunate zonah, selling themselves just to eat or because their debt owners force them into it."

"So, should I join the kedeshah?" I giggled archly.

"They are set apart for what Baal believers see as a sacred duty of encouraging new life," my brother said, as if he hadn't heard me. His sadness seemed to grow heavier as he continued. "When fields remain barren or crops are browning, weather-worriers form long queues at the temple, especially the farmers."

"Why?" I had often pumped Hosi mad with this word, but now I wanted real answers.

"A temple prostitute a day keeps the drought at bay." Hosi looked at me seriously. "Ever heard that?"

"'Course not!"

"We call it sympathetic magic," said Hosi, using his stick to draw a Baal figure in the dirt—a bulbous bountiful tummy below a long neck ending in a tiny round head. "Rain-thirsty crops or even a family's barrenness can create queues of worried males. They come to make babies in Baal's maidens while praying that the god will sympathetically bestow similar bounteous blessings of fertility and life onto barren lands and wives."

"Tough work for you poor men." I risked a cheeky smirk.

"Oh, the wives are just as bad," Hosi replied.

"That I do not believe!"

"It's true! In bad times, they really do make sure their men turn up for services in the White Temple."

After a moment's thought, I added, "I suppose when things are going well, like now, with good rains and plenty of passing trade from luxurious caravans"—I paused, still working it out—"business at the White Fertility Temple might not be all that brisk."

"Right!" exclaimed Hosi, breaking into one of his smug teacher smiles, as though he alone had produced my reasoning. "Well done."

"So, what happens when business is bad?"

"The Baal priests offer men something they can't refuse."

"What?" I barked. "Who?"

"Gomer!"

This, I was not expecting. Nor did I anticipate the strange look that made my brother's face sag. For a moment, he seemed lost, almost—strangely—at the point of bursting into tears.

I was missing something important; a feeling intolerable to little sisters who needed to feel in control of their menfolk. Intuition whispered that this had more to do with Her Highness than with his sadness about false gods.

CHAPTER 8

Nightmare on Masada

Another airport, another holding circle, this time stacked at five thousand feet above west London. Heathrow always had enough to handle without having to cope with a competing airport's cast-offs.

Worse, Dave Jackson was revisiting yet another turbulent snag in his precious treasure. Three months it had now nagged him: one scroll, two stories, different time periods separated by eight centuries, two narrators—Masada Mary and Hosea's supposed sister.

What to do for the best? To research both women in scholarly depth was to invite burnout. Perhaps he should just do one tale for his Masters and then, later, do the second for a doctorate. In that case, should Masada be first, or should the biggie take preference, with its fascinating dictators and despots of eighth-century Israel?

The conundrum hit at this moment because, once again, Masada Mary's diary was claiming his attention with an update.

"Maybe I should do three books," he said, frowning.

Book One could glue them together for a paperback. After all, each tale was strong, both had great plots and endings, and popular readers would enjoy a two-for-one bargain. The reader also got the added bonus of variety.

Then, once the paperback had whetted appetites, the detailed scholarly dissections of each tale would be produced for Books Two and Three.

Dave glanced out as the plane banked lazily over a halo of lights around a junction of the M25. All was circles: the roundabout, the M25 looping the capital, the plane's holding pattern, and especially the literary ideas that orbited his inner space.

Enough! was his inner exclamation. There was still plenty of time to decide, what with his marriage in tatters, no chance of offspring to cosset and guide, plus long, lonely hours to fill. He should be glad. He shrugged, wondering why he didn't feel it.

He turned toward Masada for distraction.

* * *

Day 30

Planning for failure even when all is fertile is, to us Jews, like breathing.

Our history has taught us well, and this is why we captured Masada five summers ago. Even then we knew rebellion might need a last stand.

"Wheat, pulses, oil, dates, and wine are holding up," the man who will kill me reported at our leaders' meeting this morning.

"At least we will die in good health," Isaac ben Judah added dryly.

I should shiver in my executioner's presence, yet such is not the case. Indeed, I smile whenever I see him. He has become good for me, especially for my children, who are missing a father. They often cling to Uncle Isaac, something that I, of course, could never do.

In honesty, this diary should report a strange recurring nightmare. I awake in terror with my husband slamming his bloody sword broad side down onto our eating table while shouting, "Stop behaving like a whore in front of my children."

The first night it happened, I scrambled from bed to cringe in a corner, sobbing, "Nothing's going on, Joseph! You know I love you." I crumpled into silent tears that I could not, and did not, want to control. As the light of a new day filtered through the gaps around the wall-opening covers, the tears dried, leaving an emotional residue I feared to name. It nagged and unsettled me.

Our water reserves are also good. They will also outlast us, thanks to old King Herod's insecurities. When his rule was imposed upon us by Rome four generations ago, he had Masada fortified to protect himself and his family as his final redoubt. He had planned well with a network of channels all leading to large storage chambers deep in the rock.

I hope the sister's part of this scroll is good for you. I try to fix each episode in my mind before my late-evening scribing, yet time tempts me to rush. Forgive the many corrections. The educated Essenes would be horrified with my blottings on their plentiful parchment.

Hosea is a great inspiration. I too marvel at how he escaped for fifty-five years. My constant prayer is that his God will also turn up for us. I still shiver at our fate and blank out thoughts of how I will kill my five precious ones. I should make plans, but it is too horrible to dwell on. I still entertain wildly unrealistic hopes of another ending.

Day 31

Today, we had sight of our chief adversary, halfway up the enemy ramp. Roman Governor Lucius Flavius Silva straddled his white mare, unfortunately well beyond the range of our archers.

We are cheered that the ramp is only progressing slowly. Flavius Silva's siege army remains about the same number, but they have established three more camps. We face their impressive Legio X Frentensis, according to fluttering standards. Four auxiliary cohorts look after equipment and also guard the thousands of Jewish prisoners working on the ramp. We must not blame those captured. Down there in the madness, they do or they die. And Silva is clever. All major works are in the hands of his trusted legionnaires, giving no chances for any fellow Jews who might wish to delay Rome's upward advance.

There are two wings of cavalry, one stabled on the coastal plains, its riders bathing daily in the waters of the Dead Sea or wrestling in mud baths. The second wing camps directly in Masada's shadow to provide horsepower on the ramp. Cunningly, Silva is building his ramp on our main exit and entrance. There is an alternative on the eastern side—the Way of the Serpent—narrow and steep, infested with deadly snakes. Also, it twists and turns as a viper in death throes. It ends its thirty stages, or slopes, where the first cavalry section camps.

We sent a small scouting party down in the early days, and only one man returned. His tales were so horrendous that we never tried again. Sending raiders down to hinder the ramp work was also outvoted. Even the Sicarii have little appetite to kill our own people.

The good news is that the children continue to be happy. They are unaware of their future, and we count this a blessing.

I am enjoying my storytelling. It is a blessing that I know the story so well, for it has been a favorite since childhood. It recalls happier times and enshrines our identity as Jews.

Time and ramps and enemies are impatient things. I must press on.

CHAPTER 9

The Day They Met

"The Marriott serves breakfast in your room at whatever time is convenient to you, Reverend Jackson." Neither the night maître d'hôtel's bright artificial smile nor his immaculate, waistcoat-neat welcome betrayed the predawn hour.

"We're quite used to comings and goings round the clock." He gave a generous shrug and held out his arms. "So, please, please, please, never think you're at all putting us out, one little trifle."

A travel-weary Dave Jackson bathed in the bright-eyed beam, booking a continental breakfast for eleven before tipping the maître d' less than the gushing smile asked for, although more than his tutor stipend could afford.

"A pleasant flight, I trust, sir?" The bellboy, obviously unaware of the delay and rerouting, ushered Dave to a wall of elevators and bubbled with mock enthusiasm, determined to improve on the receptionist's reward.

"Hmm," Dave discouragingly mumbled, and then he carried on, savoring yet fearing the idea of seeing his wife later that evening. He had booked a table for two online at their favorite bistro pub, one of Oxford's finest. He'd texted an invitation and added that he would ring her as soon as he awoke.

His stomach muscles lurched not so much in response to the fast lift but to a sudden inner laugh as he twinned his present pleasant anticipation with the earlier "Kill her" nightmare. Hate and love, next-door neighbors along the inner corridors of lovers, were forever arguing these days. Sweet mingled with sour in a marriage made in either heaven or another place. These days, Dave could never quite decide.

The bellboy came a poor second to the receptionist. An absentminded Dave showed him nothing but the door. He then collapsed across a king-size bed, fatigued as much by the incessant circling above airports as his contradictory emotions.

Dave disappointedly fisted the hotel's iron mattress. "Doomed to a pea-on-a-plate catnap," he muttered, and then he comfortingly allowed his thoughts to wallow a few more moments on the downy softness of his Colette. He recalled the first time of feeling her smoothness, the incredible delicacy of her fair skin and the sweet tingle of it touching his.

"Hi." He'd held out a large right hand, while the other made sure his supersideburn was properly draped over his baldness. "I'm Dave, one of your new appointments from the other side of the pond."

"Delighted." She'd bobbed, giggled, and held his eyes, dusting her fingers across his offered palm, seemingly confident in the impression she gave.

"Just arrived in town yesterday," he mumbled, mesmerized by the waves of titian tresses that flamed about her delicious face and crowned a petite figure that was much too curvaceous for a theological college senior's common room. The emerald-green cocktail dress gloriously set off the orange-brown hair, and the Irish lilt of her first and only word was enchanting. Her face was wide, open, and trusting as she gazed up at him, with a hovering smile that hinted at much mischief.

"You're the brainy book boy, the one Dad's not stopped talking about for a whole week? He's the dean, don't you know?" She tilted her head to the left, allowing Dave to recognize the inherited features of the large round man who had interviewed him in early spring. "He thinks you're going to make our college sponsors jump for joy. Are you?"

"Yeah!" Dave, still wide-eyed and captivated, used the affirmative more as acceptance of the exquisite vision before him.

"Not strong on humility then, are we?"

"Well, erm ..." Dave had flustered trying to recall the question he had distractedly answered, but he then relaxed, hovering above her approving grin.

"And you, big man, sure you'll not be having too much trouble reaching our college basketball nets now, will you?"

"You always this cheeky, miss, erm ...?" he'd quickly bounced back.

"Depends," she replied, her red lips pursed and her eyebrows raised in mock affront, giving no response whatsoever to his fishing "erm." Her eyes had then flicked above his gaze, and the glint of mischief ignited. "Sure, you ought to be going the whole hog with that wispy top tail of yours. Would you not be best just donating the poor thing to the cushion industry?"

"Asperger's, is it?"

He was pleased that her eyebrows took off in astonishment. "No." He lifted a staying hand before her pout, pausing to savor the upper-hand moment. "Let me have another shot ... er, yes, ma'am, I have it. Tourette's syndrome! You just can't help rudely spraying out any antisocial thought that lollops through that pretty little space behind those twinkling eyes."

"You could be fun!" She prodded his chest, bubbling out a rich chuckle.

"So," Dave said, still feeling in charge, "tell me, impolite offspring of the Reverend Dr. Michael O'Hara"—here he mimicked her Irish lilt—"would I be right in assuming I could call you something shorter?"

"Ah well, now, I only give that information out to friends, don't you know?" The prim expression looked odd when it winked at him. "Now, Mr. America, would you be moving along and stop blocking the poor door with all your great galumphing bigness?"

She ended her dismissal by waving cheerfully through the door to attract another of her father's guests. Dave had no alternative but to step into the crowded senior common room.

"Ah, Dave, so good to have you with us." Her father, a few strides away, waved at him. "And I see you've already got yourself acquainted with my Colette's delightful banter. To be sure, she'll need a strong hand one of these days, you mark my words. Between you and me, those poor darlings she teaches at that infant school of hers daren't so much as put a foot out of line."

Dean O'Hara had then smoothly placed a guiding hand in the small of Dave's back, adding, "I have a few folks who are absolutely intrigued to test your interesting theories." He'd waved a book toward a distant group, the cover of which looked surprisingly like Dave's own *Wellhausen Unwell*.

Dave's popular demolition of a once widely acclaimed theory on who wrote the Old Testament had turned him into a minor campus celebrity. His blunt, yet learned, dissection of two centuries of inaccurate biblical criticism had annihilated an authorship theory once held universally by generations of Bible scholars.

As a result of the work Dave had done for his masters, hardly one modern academic now supported the documentary hypothesis of Julius Wellhausen. Most had accepted that this German theologian's theory was based more on untried and untestable speculation and dubious presuppositions than on sound science and literary criticism.

Dave had shown the theory to be wholly inadequate and unsafe in accounting for how the old scriptures had come to be written. They had also hopelessly contradicted what Jesus had claimed for the Old Testament, throwing up far more problems than the theory claimed to solve. Dave had concluded that Wellhausen's ideas and others' variations of it were faulty, and therefore unreliable.

"Loved this in your summary," one college sponsor gushed, hardly before the introductions were completed. With a mini tablet in his palm, he read, "So-called solid theories claiming the Bible to be a collection of legends have now themselves been shown to be sickly myths. Wellhausen may not be dead just yet, but he is certainly far from well."

Even as the backslapping continued, Dave reconnected with his petite hostess across a chattering coffee crowd. When their eyes had hungrily met once again, there was a wink from him and a wicked glint from her. By the end of the third week of college, nothing separated them as they shared a double bed in a small hotel located in a picturesque Oxford village on the River Thames.

CHAPTER 10

Miscarriage and Marriage

Within a month of coming together at Saviour College, Dave and Colette were beginning to receive invitations as a recognized couple. In less than a year, they were sending out a special invitation of their own.

On the named day, each separately had wondered, between waking and walking down the short college chapel aisle, if they were not about to make the biggest of all domestic blunders.

There had been a delightful bout of mutual proposing three months into their great passion, but the cause of this had subsequently dissolved in a tearful miscarriage.

Relief colored by an odd, ill-understood sort of grief produced embarrassed hugs and cheek kisses. They had simultaneously whispered to each other, "I'd still have wanted to marry," before erupting into self-conscious laughter, Dave chortling and saying, "Great minds think alike," while Colette refused to echo with, "And fools seldom differ."

Dave remembered this well. What he was never privy to was what his fiancée actually thought about that event.

"I mean," she had said, splaying her hands before her best friend, Bridie, in a premiscarriage teary angst, "what is love, anyway? What does it do or say? How're we to recognize it at, er, what is it?" She had sniffled and glanced at her wrist. "Four thirty on a Friday afternoon in real life, in real-time Oxford?

"And another thing," she'd continued almost without taking a breath, "I'm twenty-two, for heaven's sake, still in my probationary teaching year, and am I really ready for a full-time screaming, pooing, spewing miniature of me with a giant of a boy who still acts like he's at school and thinks with the wrong part of his body?"

In another heart-to-heart, this time post-miscarriage, Bridie had hesitated when invited to be maid of honor at her friend's surprise nuptials. She had casually wondered out loud, behind a cocked skeptical eyebrow, how real life in real-time Oxford had abruptly produced a miraculous number of answers to Colette's questions on love, and in such a tiny number of days?

How, Bridie casually wondered, had her best friend now arrived at "'til death do us part" love and wedding bells from her recent gloomy starting position? "Has there been a miraculous change in your heart as well as the one in your womb?" she bluntly queried.

"Maid of honor, is it?" Colette had glared back, holding her open left hand palm upward. Then up came the right hand to make balancing scales. "Or are you after playing devil's advocate?" She seesawed both in a balancing motion. "You choose!"

Bridie had nodded to Colette's "maid of honor" hand, vaguely feeling guilty for not carrying out her full brief as friendly advocate, devilish or not.

The newlyweds were halfway through a Lakes-of-Killarney honeymoon, sharing a disappointing three-quarter-sized bed with a dip in the middle, before each separately concluded that they had little in common but sex. By the sixth night, even that was suspect, with each privately wishing that the valley in their mattress could have been inverted into the Rockies or the Mountains of Mourne.

"Mars Bars all over again," Dave had glumly, if oddly, concluded quietly to himself. He was remembering vomiting halfway through his sixth bar on the day he had discovered the pleasing confection at a lower Brooklyn stall under the archway of an overhead rail track. He'd wedged his seven-year-old frame against a stone support plinth as trains screeched and grated overhead, while a not dissimilar action and soundtrack was repeated deep in his innards.

Colette had been his first and only lover, what with him being previously of the virtuous theological-college opinion that students should not hop into and out of bed without the combined blessings of God, the church, and the law. This relationship had been the one-off exception to an otherwise celibate norm, and he'd done the man thing and gorged himself on the physical side of the relationship. In one of his guilt fests, he had, in a rare personal talk with his bedfellow, stressed that she had been his first and only one.

"Same here," Colette had hastily assured him, "absolute one-off—hardly ever been kissed. I don't want you thinking I do this with all of Daddy's new tutors. This is totally unique, David Jackson, definitely, absolutely!" Dave, rather unchivalrously, began to wonder whom she was trying to convince.

Beyond this, they had discussed little else about the actual act. Wasn't it enough that they were doing it illicitly? Did they have to turn it into a human biology sex-degree course? Never once had they deliberated how many times they might indulge. No intimate chats accompanied by giggles or tender looks regarding their likes and dislikes had occurred, not even the setting up of no-go areas or must-go areas.

Whereas Colette didn't want to sound too educated in such delicate subjects, Dave preferred actions rather than words. He was too busy assuming it was free every night and especially in the morning—and why ever not? The bride was tolerant in the hope that experience might miraculously teach him a better way.

"He's not a total caveman," she had confided to Bridie shortly after arriving home from Ireland. "He only knocks me out with occasional compliments and flowers, not so much as a club or a grunt within sight or earshot."

71

Then she had confided her greatest fear, something that was only then dawning. Her involvement in lovemaking, she revealed, appeared to be the means to provide the necessary friction for Dave to satisfy himself. Blessed relief for her came only when he turned over and fell asleep.

"For heaven's sake, Bridie, didn't God gift him with a brain as big as Einstein's?" she'd shouted one day. "Does he not have half of Oxford in thrall to his divine and godly intellect, and wouldn't you think he'd take a tiny break from God to Google what makes a woman happy? He might even take a peek in his precious Bible and read the Song of Songs for some useful tips. Fine thing, isn't it, when the Good Book's a better lover on paper than your hubby is in the flesh?"

Bridie had smiled sadly and nodded wisely, and was about to add deep words from her own experience, when she was inundated with yet another tsunami of anguish.

"And where's all this submitting to each other, and loving communication? Oh, and Bridie," Colette said, lifting her hands in helplessness, "this God thing of his is something else. He spends so many hours lost in divinity and theology that I'm turning into a God widow, for heaven's sake! I'm jealous of the big man in the sky, would you believe it?" At this point she was shouting.

"Every time he goes into his study, it feels like he's off to see his other bit on the side. I ask you: is that healthy? God's keeping my husband from me. Is that weird, or is that weird?

"Tell me, Bridie." Colette's persistence gave her once maid of honor no time to respond. "Wouldn't you think, now, that the great buffoon would find time to come and ask me what makes me happy? Wouldn't that be what love would do? Am I missing something here? A bit of loving listening and talking, isn't that what we all want now? And, Bridie, what's wrong with just cuddling and a little kissing on its own? Does it always have to end up with the full-blown thing? I'm getting to the point of being scared to even touch him in case he springs on me and pins me to the floor."

"Well, Col, you know what I think now, don't you?" Bridie had paused with the surprise of being allowed a contribution. "What you need, my girl, is a—"

"Sure, he's a child himself! What would I be wanting one of my own for?"

"To love and be loved, wouldn't you think?" Bridie had quickly retorted. "Or maybe compensation for the one you lost when you were courting. Oh, I don't know, maybe a child who'll need you—"

"Haven't I got twenty-five needy ones five days a week as it is?"

"That's different, and you know it," Bridie had said, huffing. "Teaching's teaching. What you need is a lesson in love and to be loved."

Two years and two miscarriages later, there was still little improvement on the Dave front.

With the elastic patience of her maid of honor at the breaking point, Colette had begun to find substitute comfort most evenings in a glass or more of Irish gold. At least it brought blessed sleep and escape. The whiskey, its odor heavily camouflaged when necessary with sugar-free mints, brought one more amazing plus—a glowing inner confidence to surpass the fake confidence she wore on the outside.

She had begun to use this newly acquired assurance to sledgehammer the castle-wall thickness of Dave's defenses. One criticism was lobbed after another. A grappling-hook barb would be slung over the top of his battlements as she tried to scale his thick exterior, trying to break into the inner keep of his soul.

"Tell me what you want me to do." He had eventually surrendered to her frequent evening alcohol-fueled sieges.

"You shouldn't need telling," had been her quick, if slurred, counter. "If you loved me, you'd know what to do. And you'd do it without me having to tell you." Most of the confrontations began this way and didn't progress much further.

"What's the point of me telling you how to do what you promised to do at the altar?"

"Right." Dave had interrupted Colette one night as she sipped her golden nightcap. He was thankful that she only began drinking as she prepared dinner, once the school day was tucked up for the night. "Right," he continued, for the first "right" had been used up as he bolstered his own flagging confidence. "Right, here's a notebook and a pen."

"And what on earth would I want with those at this time of the night, you great big lummox of a numbskull?"

"Well now, you don't have to tell me what to do." Dave had grinned. "Just write it down. Just set down a list, and just you see, Col, if I don't get on with it first thing tomorrow morning."

He'd tossed the items into her lap, grinning widely at his clever academic solution to all their problems. He had then ducked nippily to the floor before his wife's flying glass of liquid gold put him there. Colette had then stormed out.

Dave flinched at the memory as he fidgeted to find comfort on a hotel mattress that insisted on ignoring the contours and needs of his stretched-out mass.

As sleep finally stole him away from the Marriott multichannel TV and gaming console, the ethics tutor and his Colette took leading roles in a drama conjured out of his own subconscious self. The nap he took before heading home turned into a fitful nightmare of tossing and turning and grinding teeth.

Replayed in the full rainbow of colors was the night when Ethics Man had first come to visit. The fool had tried to preach heaven but ended up taking them to the pits of hell.

At this, Dave shot bolt upright on the hard mattress, and then just as quickly slumped back, desperate for good-quality horizontal sleep. Normally, he fuzzed this sort of thing out of his mind or busied himself with other matters.

Now, desperation brought him back to the upright sitting position. He plumped his hard pillow into a passable backrest. Once again, he unraveled the presentation scroll and forced his mind back to a more ancient, and therefore safer, past.

CHAPTER 11

Betrayal and Betrothal

"You mean... she is a..."

I gestured toward Hosi with my hands splayed before me, unwilling to use either the common or sacred description of Gomer's prostitution. Neither "street-corner zonah" nor "sacred kedeshah" sat comfortably on my lips. I might not like her, but girls in Safed village did not brand each other so easily.

"She began preparing a year ago," my brother spoke flatly, "and five months ago she was initiated into the kedeshah." Not one inflection suggested his opinion, but I did sense a vague sadness. "She is now coming toward the end of her temple duty."

I stayed silent. I feared the words that would pour out if I lost control. How dare she laud it over us? What cheek! Hypocrisy was the word my Greek traders had for it. They used it to describe the swapping of handheld masks to play different roles in their torch-lit plays once their traveling souks had stopped trading.

This two-faced madam had paraded daily with both noses stuck in the air. How could she let men do to her whatever it was they did? Hosi had given me the basics during our butterfly talks, but I was still hazy on precise details. It must be more than money, I thought. She could buy Safed with her clothing allowance. The buzz of questions began to focus on my brother's sadness. I could usually read Hosi long before he himself unraveled his own mind, but not now. This time the text and meaning were cloaked.

"What do you think about this?" I stressed the "you," and Hosi's eyes melted. I was shocked to see a single tear brimming as he shuffled in his misery. "Tell me, Hosi. Let me help."

"I love her."

"You love her?" I echoed unhelpfully, and then I stood stupidly, my arms hanging loose and

77

awkward, as I tried to order the myriad reasons for why he should come to his senses as soon as possible.

"We are betrothed. We have been as good as married for five years."

Had I wildly guessed this answer, I would never have expected it to be announced in the lifeless flatness of his previous statements. For the first time in my brother's company, I had no words. Even questions fled. Betrayal flooded my whole being.

Betrothal was one of the big matters of childhood. It was discussed in families, over cooking, and during laundry time at the Safed springs. I had often wondered why nothing was ever said of Hosea's future. On occasions I had asked him outright, only for him or our father to deflect me toward a more enticing subject or a make a half promise to answer at some unspecified future time. For betrothal to have taken place secretly in a family did not make sense.

How could he teach me and even laugh with me all these years and still keep this terrible secret? How could he absorb my endless criticisms of the one he was promised to and still remain silent? Nothing made sense. I was lost for something sensible to say. In a moment I would burst into tears.

I turned and fled.

* * *

Running away was not possible weeks later when Daddy Beeri received Gomer's daddy, Diblaim, and his ornate entourage.

I had been bluntly warned to do and say absolutely nothing that would disgrace the family. Me! How could I possibly shame the family more than my big brother had?

When Gomer's father arrived, there was no sight of Her Highness, and for that I was grateful. Our best pots were spread over my teaching rock, displaying our finest breads. Daddy Beeri understood that the pleasure of entertaining an intended bride and family was also good for business. Was this not his air and his lifeblood? Our famous breads would be consumed, yet always with the hope of attracting future orders. Hospitality also demanded the best vintage of our renowned brew of lemon sweetened with spices and herbs. For this day, Father gave pride of place to our fig and date bread, highly appropriate for entertaining the Levant's first monarch of figs.

Father fussed with customary pleasantries, and his eccentric compliments were richer and more exotic than usual.

"To Diblaim, noble and high prince of the people!" My father was creative with the high-flown compliments in his welcoming toast. So, in turn, was his honored guest.

"In tribute to the bounteous Beeri, the overflowing breadbasket of our beloved Galilean Hills," was the gushing response. And with each successive wave of praise, accompanied by bows and smiles, both men appeared to be on the verge of joyous laughter, as if neither could wait for the finale of his performance. Eventually, a moment's quiet descended as if to allow the men to savor the lushness of salutations, who knew the greetings to be but the subtle overture.

"We meet for the security of our two excellent families, yes, my friend?" Diblaim beamed at Father, who readily reflected back the warmth. Both immediately switched on serious and sincere expressions, each squatting cross-legged on the rugs in the hospitality arbor of rose trees between bakery and teaching stone.

"Your presence, Diblaim, most assuredly enhances the excellence of my humble family."

"Ah! Exactly! Quite right, my esteemed friend." Diblaim's business allowed no false modesty.

"And it is certainly in our hands to ensure our future and mutual prosperity. That, I most happily drink to." Father Beeri delicately waved in goatskins of his finest wines. The business about to be conducted demanded more than spiced lemon.

"We have some success with figs…" Diblaim waved a dismissive multi-ringed hand, accompanied by a modest smile and a careless shrug that acknowledged his understatement... "while you, my dear and good friend, have your own outstanding accomplishments with your superb ovens."

"Most kind of you." Father humbly inclined his bearded head.

"Alone, we manage ..." the chief guest said, trailing off, his eyebrows rising over a confident arch smile.

It was always frustratingly so, I mused, watching from between two bushes of red roses. This was the way with men at bargain. Nothing was said, as little as possible was risked, and yet so much was understood. Put two women in the same conversation and all would be stated, and then repeated to ensure that the meaning was absolutely established and fully understood. I knew where things were going, yet no vital questions were being asked, and no definite statements agreed. Of course, I did not interrupt. I kept my sullen promise to behave. This was "maledom." Between two patriarchs no woman should venture, and certainly not an inexperienced maiden.

With the mere wave of a hand, the trailing off of words with barely half sentences uttered, and finally a suggestive tilt of a drinking vessel, a whole conversation was proposed without the risk of common words for fear of a snub or worse.

Even with the scarcity of words, I understood that it was time for the betrothal of my brother and Gomer to move on to the next stage, marriage. I could not help but glance to see how Hosi was taking it. His face was quite readable. It sagged. It was sad.

There was just a moment's pause before Father Beeri waved his goblet and produced a matching smile of agreement. "But together," he said, raising the vessel, "working in partnership, eh?!" It was not so much a question as an exclamation of mutual agreement.

"It is enough," said Diblaim, laughing and waving a drinking salute to Father, and then to each person in the circled entourage. I was astonished. Daddy Diblaim did not even acknowledge the subject of the agreement reached. Hosi stood next to me, mute and rooted without expression. Hosi, a man with authority to take on bears, was accorded not the slightest significance in this arena.

"How dare you!" I wanted to scream in defense of my champion, my feelings of betrayal set aside for the moment. "How could you, Father?" I wanted to add, knowing my brother to be worth a dozen Gomers, despite all her finery and flounce. "How could you have promised my beloved brother to a woman who loves only herself, who makes love to other men?" So much remained unspoken.

As was our custom, no date was set for the consummation, or the marriage banquet that would soon follow; there was merely the understanding that now was the time to prepare. Once the wedding arrangements and feast were ready, then wedding heralds would be dispatched to all those invited.

This day remains my greatest moment of regret.

I should have shrieked my protest. My mind often replays all the things I should have done, the many questions I shouldn't have left unasked. Where was Gomer? Why were no women involved? Why did my brother stay silent?

This was the day our lives changed forever, the day I truly learned the real pains of becoming a woman. Our true troubles did not come once each month. They were felt every time our menfolk behaved as though we did not exist.

* * *

"You are not going to marry her!" I cried the moment Hosea and I were alone together.

"You sound very certain."

"Oh, I am, Ho-sea, sim-ple son of Beer-i." My chin thrust out with every staccato syllable. I must have looked like one of my manic hens pecking her chicks into line, but somebody had to mother a family whose menfolk had fawned away their senses. As is the way of mountain womenfolk, learned at the

Safed laundry lagoon, this was no time for brotherly pet names. Only stern full titles might underline the stupidity of what was proposed.

"Have you grown so old, little sister, that you think you are my mother?" My infuriating brother grinned, rising for the first time from his worrying flatness. "I'm the big man, remember? You are—"

"And why all the rush?" I stuck a thumb into his face in the way other village matrons nagged. "And why no questions, like where, when, and how, and what does Gomer think of her absence from the matchmaking?" By now all five fingers were splayed in front of my idiot brother's face. "She is spoiled, is full of herself, is always demanding her own way, treats people like they are dirt on her fancy Eastern slippers. ... Hard as rock on the outside, cold and ugly within. And why would anybody—just tell me this, dear Brother—why would any sane man marry a pagan Baal witch who sold herself to sad old men?"

"Because I believe that—"

"No!" I yelled, now holding both hands splayed rudely in his face. "Do not dare!"

"What?" A wide-eyed brother peeped around my hands.

"None of your God stuff," I pecked. "For once, I am not your pupil. I am not some poor little sister who has to be schooled and tutored in all those big words to do with God's will and all that mystical,

84

spiritual stuff. Why do you always have to bring God into the argument? Can we not just leave him to one side for a moment? Just give me a straight answer that I can understand. Why are you so determined to throw your life away on a whore?"

"What?" Hosi looked as shocked as I felt. It was the first time I had ever spoken back with such boiling anger, and especially without a care for the words uttered.

"Answer me!" I yelled after a brief pause, striving to ensure he did not deflect my attack.

"Go and marry a prostitute." Hosi smiled sadly. I gaped.

"Is that it?" My chin thrust forward. "Do you actually think you have given me an answer? Tell me, dearest Brother, who has lost his wits and forgotten the basic rules of making good sense— answer me this: who told you to go and marry a prostitute?"

"That I cannot tell you." Hosi shrugged.

"Cannot? Will not? Who?"

"You told me not to bring him into it."

"See!" I fumed, and beat him on the chest with small clenched fists. "There you go again with God. Well, let me put you straight, dear brother tutor, dear know-it-all son of a prophet, you are listening to the wrong one. The real God does not tell us to go and marry prostitutes, especially not those who

85

worship Baal. This is not right, Hosi. This is exactly opposite to all you have ever taught me. This, my dear, mad brother, is not using your mind and heart in prayer. This is using another part of your body to do your thinking."

I was now shouting into his face, yet no anger came back. Flatness and a sense of grief descended, and he was as he had been before.

Had I gone too far? It was like watching a sunset, and not a pretty one. His earlier, bright face was eclipsed by violent and violet clouds. He had returned to the dark place that made me afraid for him, that made me fear for myself.

He quietly turned and walked away. I wanted to rush and jump on his back and become his carefree little sister again. Stubbornness refused me permission to move, as did something else—a whispered intuition that such innocence was now gone, lost forever.

If my brother would not listen, then Daddy Beeri would have to. And anyway, what was one of our old prophets like Daddy Beeri doing backing his son? Why was he giving his blessing to marry a prostitute who worshipped another god?

Something was wrong, and I was determined to know what it was.

CHAPTER 12

Cave of Hope

Day 42

"We will fight you if try to stop us," Magdalen snarled at me through her toothless mouth this morning.

I am not surprised, even though it was totally outside my friend's normal character.

It has now been a whole week since she hinted at escape with a band of other widows and their children. I had reacted without wisdom. I had immediately warned her that I would have to pass this on to the Masada council. She had promptly turned on her heels and raged away with speed and energy that belied her advancing years.

Even before her scurrying figure was out of sight,
I had calmed enough to know I would take it no
further. Extreme Sicarii elders and even some Zealots
might feel duty-bound to make examples of lone
dissenters. Most of the leadership are surprised that
an anxious six weeks has not proven to be fertile
soil for dissent. In our hearts we suspected that
our original commitment would not always go
unquestioned.

"Magdalen," I said, smiling at her during
our meeting today, "I am sorry. I have no right to
demand that you join in the lesser of evils."

"Forgive me, too." Magdalen looked shamefaced.
"My words poured out before I could stop them. I
would find it hard to hurt a cockroach, never
mind a friend who has become most dear." She half
smiled, and I felt the usual warmth that made this
woman so special.

"We have a good plan," she whispered, with an
expression on her face that pleaded a hearing. This
time I stayed quiet. We had been through much. I
owed her a brief listening ear.

"We have found a small hollow on a goat path
just below the south lip of Masada's plateau, directly
opposite to where the invasion will come." She briskly
tilted her ancient head to indicate the direction.

She and her energy made me smile. I often felt
drained looking after five children on my own in a

place that was not home. She had made my burden lighter, taking the children for walks or games. The twin girls and Jemima had delightedly adopted her as their honorary grandma.

"Joshua, one of Abigail's boys, found the cave while trying to catch a runaway kid," Magdalen bubbled. "The scared creature had dived into this niche off the path as Joshua threw his rope. The kid just vanished. He went closer and saw a small jagged hole. With his crook, he began to poke and dig. Before long, he had opened up a long and low cavern.

"Mary, come with us when the soldiers invade." She reached out to touch my shoulder. "We can easily make room for all of you. We already have some food stored, and once the Romans have conquered and gone, we can crawl out and be on our way to safety down the Snake Path, or even," she said, chuckling, "down their own ramp."

"Magdalen, please think this through."

"We have!" Her cracked and tanned face hardened. "It will work. There is no way we can afford to let it fail. We have thought of nothing else for days. Mary, it makes good sense. When the Romans find dead bodies and none to fight or sell into slavery, they will plunder what remains and leave for someplace more civilized.

"Mary, we can save ourselves and your precious children!" she exclaimed with a brighter face. "My children!" she added with a nervous laugh. "Oh, Mary, the twins and laughing Jemima and those grand strong boys of yours, they are so special." Emotion caught and she gasped. "It would be terrible to end so much joyful life."

I considered hitting back, telling her she was being too optimistic, that cunning Zealot or Sicarii minds had already imagined all possible escapes before settling on the lesser of evils. This all faded as my friend buckled inwardly in soundless sobbing. I took her in my arms and joined her. A good cry is such a rarity up here, especially for me as a leader. Suddenly, it had become too tempting.

"But you cannot tell any of the other leaders." She pulled away with a force her slight frame belied. "Please!" Her hands came up to mine. I remained quiet but relaxed, and she took this as encouragement.

"We women without husbands must stick together, Mary. We must look after ourselves and our children." Her tone was quickening and rising all the time. "This plan to kill our precious ones is too cruel."

Magdalen stopped again, on the verge of tears. She battled for control but finally dissolved into rasping sobs, gasping while saying, "That's it ...

nothing… nothing more…" She allowed me to keep hold of her this time. I stroked her dark hair down the center of her back. Her sobs lessened. I felt her back muscles harden as she eased away.

"Magdalen," I coaxed gently, "you were not around a few summers back, were you? We have seen what the enemy does to the conquered and caught." Her back was now to me. She did not respond.

"Listen to her!"

Both Magdalen and I swung around to face Isaac ben Judah.

"I thought he was away visiting the lower terraces," I shouted apologetically, whirling back to Magdalen. She looked as though she could have cheerfully saved my friend the trouble of executing me. Isaac beckoned for me to continue, but Magdalen's last look sucked my remaining energy and I slumped to a stool.

"Masada was not ours on those days," Isaac spoke gently. I was instantly grateful for his lead. "It was a Roman garrison that dominated the Judean desert and all its routes around the Dead Sea, and the plains and hills running up to Jericho and Jerusalem. They ruled just as cruelly as Herod had two generations before." Magdalen made as if to go; I think she feared what Isaac might do.

"Worry not," he said, touching her shoulder. "If Mary is keeping this to herself then so will I."

Magdalen at least turned back. Isaac added, "However, we would not be your friends if we did not tell you what you desperately need to know." She nodded.

"He who has Masada has power, Magdalen. Herod knew that when he developed this high garrison. The Romans saw its value and took it for their own. After our war with the Romans began, the Sicarii tricked them and managed to capture it. Once you have the high place, you do not easily let go. Once the centurions scramble up here, they will be masters of all below. They will not leave. Magdalen, you and all who hide will have to surrender or face the even crueler death of slow starvation."

"I cannot be part of killing babies," wailed Magdalen, her shoulders drooping so that I wanted to wrap my arms about her again.

"Please sit, Magdalen." He said it with warmth. My youngest had once called him Daddy Isaac because of this tenderness. "You and your group will be free to do as you wish when the time comes, and that is still some weeks from now. The ramp is proving more difficult for the Romans. We all have more days, more time, to think."

Magdalen nodded. She gasped inwardly a few times, making her shoulders jump.

"The second point you need to think about is what will happen to your group, and especially the children, when you come out of hiding. I think we can forget the option of staying put and starving to death. That is not going to happen with children, is it? So, the soldiers find everybody dead except a handful of women and your children. These are not kindly, caring men, Magdalen. Understand what I am saying?"

"We're not stupid," sniffed Magdalen. Isaac was just about to continue, but then she shouted, "But if we can stay hidden, we can wait for a good moon, make our way round to the Snake, and descend without them ever knowing we were here."

There was silence, a standoff. Isaac was at rest, giving time for thought. Magdalen was trying to look hard but was not entirely succeeding. Stifled sobs kept catching her breath. I felt the guilt of my helpless silence.

"The Snake will be guarded top and bottom and will be patrolled day and night, Magdalen," Isaac spoke quietly, shaking his head. "I didn't finish; I was about to explain what happens to those who are captured. I was hoping not to put it into words, yet I do not want you to have false hopes. First the soldiers will use you as they wish. Oh, they will not be too rough. Those fit and well fetch good returns at the Judean auctions, especially your children. You must understand that men want boys and girls for their own amusement."

Magdalen shuddered, shaking her head as though trying not to listen.

"I am truly sorry to be so blunt." Isaac took her right hand in his. "It is your decision. Discuss it. You owe it to the other women to share this with them, and I know you are a woman who will do the right thing. Think hard, and may our God go with you."

Magdalen wrenched back her hand and looked to be at the point of fleeing. I reached out to embrace her, but she pushed me aside and walked quickly away. Isaac caught me as I was falling off balance. He and I ended up embracing for mutual support.

It was so natural. Our community strongly discourages men and women from mixing in public, let alone touching, but norms seem to have subtly changed at this high altitude and anxiety.

Traditions, as with our lives, seem in suspension. Life is lived increasingly in the present, for we have no future. As for the past, it forever made us who we now are, the centuries and stories cascading from Abraham over the Sinai Mountain of Moses and the Ten Commandments and onward in a millennium walk with our Maker. All of it described us. All prescribed our ways, yet the embrace of Isaac was too warm, too comforting, to move away from quickly.

To be wholly comforted in another's arms, to be possessed and consumed by a lover, was strong and overwhelming. His smell was pleasant, his body strong and hard against mine. I relaxed to enjoy what had been denied to me for too long, ever since Jerusalem and Joseph.

Isaac gently grasped my upper arms and pried himself apart from me. He smiled and nodded. I could see he felt exactly as I did. I was on the point of melting back into his arms when he let go of me and stood to one side.

The disappointment was so acute that I turned away quickly, lest he see it in my face.

I heard his steps take him away from me, and I turned, my mind in a muddle. The feelings tumbled within: I was sad that he was honorable and strong, glad he was strong enough not to use me, and mad that he remained only a friend.

The bitter-sweetness of it all made me want him more.

CHAPTER 13

The scroll slipped from Dave Jackson's hands, rolling off the bed to bounce on the plush tufts of the Marriott carpet.

Sleep came, but not peace.

His large frame jerked occasionally and his breathing became erratic as the past seeped yet again into the unprotected present. The Welshman and his own Irish colleen had unrestricted passage into his evolving nightmare.

* * *

Caractacus Llewellyn, known across the Oxford campus affectionately and otherwise as Carac the Moustache, fell in love with the art of ethics upon learning as a six-year-old the origin of his name.

Dave was treated to this unwanted information on only their second meeting in their senior common room. Llewellyn seemed so full of himself that Dave disliked him intensely, long before finding him and Colette embracing on Dave's own kitchen table.

Grandpapa Llewellyn had taken the youngest of his clan to knee in the front garden of Delfryn, a solid pebble-dashed four-bedroom detached house with pretty views on an equally picturesque hill of Higher Gwespyr. He pointed hundreds of feet down and a mile out to the Bay of Talacre, sweeping a dozen miles from the winding wheels of the old Point of Ayr Colliery to the beginnings of Prestatyn sands.

"All this great stretch and a thousand more of seashore, scenic lakes, black mountains, and green valleys was all that was left for the original Britons," boomed Llewellyn the Elder, "and Caractacus led them into this Welsh retreat. There, he defied the world champions of his day—the centurions of Rome."

"Did they kill him, Gramper?"

"They did not, my little one." His fulsome cheek-to-cheek moustache, one just like Caractacus himself had sported, twitched with pride.

"Why didn't they kill him, Gramper?"

"He shamed the Romans into letting him live."

"How, Gramper? How did he do that?" pleaded little Caractacus, slipping off his grandfather's knee to jump up and down.

"He looked the enemy right in the eye and challenged their pride and their greatness with a killer question."

"What, Gramper?"

"And can you then, who have such possessions and so many of them, covet our poor tents?"

"Was that clever, Gramper?" Carac had wriggled back onto the knee, excited by Gramper's rising Welsh baritone. "Is that what you want me to do when I grow up?"

"It is, lad." Gramper nodded gravely. "Caractacus told the Romans they had no right to steal his life, nor his land, nor his freedom. He stood out against the evil that had captured his wife and children, and he fought to be free, to be or not to be without hindrance."

His bristled grandfather peered over half-moon spectacles. The lilt of his story voice hardened. "Caractacus, my boy?"

"Yes, Gramper?"

"You have a hero's name to grow into and to fill. Our valleys cry out for a modern-day Caractacus, and you must take up the challenge. Will you do this for me now, boy-o?"

From that day forward, little Carac told all and sundry who cared to listen, and especially each new student intake who had no option but to listen, that he immediately jumped from his gramper's knee and devoted himself to the rights and wrongs of human behavior. Now, just into his fifth decade, with "the little wife" back home in Aberystwyth and his brood of four having flown the nest, Caractacus was in his prime, a handsome ethics man graying at the temples, yet as heroic in his own view as his original namesake.

He sported his own flaming-red moustache in memory of his hero and Gramper. Actually, it was now more ginger with gray flecks, but he considered that only a minor ethical point.

*   *   *

Dave Jackson struggled to escape back into consciousness, to find he was no longer propped up on pillows but spread-eagled over a disheveled bedspread. He swung his aching limbs off his pea-on-a-plate bed and perched on the edge, wondering if Caractacus also considered Colette to be one of his minor ethical hiccups.

How could a committed Christian and theological lecturer steal another man's wife? What warped mind could major in right and wrong and then choose such an evil path? Even as his anger wallowed in this injustice, the scholarly side of Dave's brain remembered Israel's King David taking a soldier's wife before arranging for him to be killed in battle.

Dave snorted away the comparison and bustled about his bedroom, quickly scooping traveling paraphernalia into a holdall. He scanned the airport compensation deal he'd been given. It included a hired car, which he would later drop off when he collected his own car at Luton. Soon he had checked out and was chugging along on the inside lane of the M25, wondering why his unfaithful wife was still not answering her mobile.

"Dave, you've got to come and listen to the new man." He now grimaced, remembering how Colette had first thrilled over the Welshman. He never imagined then that the invitation would lead to his dreaming of murder at thirty-five thousand feet somewhere over Europe.

"Come on, Dave," Colette had urged when he did not immediately respond, "Daddy's got him for a couple of terms on loan from Aberystwyth University. He's like a breath of fresh air in this stuffy old college."

"I've already met the Reverend Caractacus Llewellyn at a staff meeting earlier this week," Dave had replied, trying for a neutrality that would not spoil his wife's enthusiasm. "Seems a pleasant enough chap." But then he couldn't stop himself from adding, "Though perhaps he's a bit full of himself, hogging conversations at our coffee breaks."

"He says he'll see us both if we give him—"

"Pardon?"

"Well, erm." Colette had immediately suspected that this abrupt blurt might not have been her wisest. "Dave, Caractacus has been talking to the campus wives, and it seems he's hot on counseling. He's written books on marriage, with some chapters devoted to marital problems, and one of them deals with miscarriages and their effects on couples. When he heard of our baby troubles, he went out of his way to come over to me. It was as though he could see and read the hell churning inside my head and even—"

"Could we not have talked about this first, Col?" Dave had wanted to reach out and agree, but instead he felt cold. He had no interest whatsoever in sharing his grief with anybody, and certainly not with a silver-tongued, ginger-headed lecturer who styled himself on a gift-of- gab historical character skilled in charming his way out of sticky situations.

"Please!" Dave had still felt cold. "Pretty, pretty pleeeease?" That was unfair. Colette knew he was a sucker for her pretty-pleading. If he didn't say something definite soon, she would just go on adding "pretty" after "pretty" until he eventually caved in.

"I've a class waiting." The coldness sounded in his voice.

"Later, then?"

"Col, it's a choc-a-bloc week."

"Oh, well go to heaven then," she cried, meaning the precise opposite. It was her shorthand for the times when he put "the whole divine shooting match" before her and her needs. She swiveled and stormed off.

"Great, Dave!" He had sighed at the time, knowing it might have been more peaceful to play along until she had gotten it out of her system, even if it meant agreeing to a quick coffee with moustache-face.

Thus it transpired a week later. Dave had finally been coerced into counseling in an alcove of the senior common room with a Celt who loved the lilt of his own Welshness far more than the wide twang of Brooklyn.

When Colette spoke, Caractacus listened to her colleen brogue as though savoring the sonnets of a great eisteddfod bard. When Colette wept, he cradled her forlorn hands between his and stroked the silken backs with soft, gentle thumbs. Occasionally, a comforting arm would slide across her shoulder, all kindly acceptable in public, but far too much for Dave. And, in any case, weren't counselors supposed to have a no-touch protocol?

On the occasions Dave spoke, there always seemed to be a speedy Welsh interruption, a qualification, a question, or a view that rolled onward like the forever foothills of Snowdonia. When his Celtic tormentor reached the peak of one sentence, it was certain that yet another would have to be endured.

When Dave offered an opinion, there was an immediate, though well-disguised, bristle, almost as though Dave were an invading Roman centurion about to plunder and pillage the precious possessions of Prestatyn.

Occasionally, Dave's ego reared as a rampant red dragon on a Welsh flag, but always his lively defense would be followed by a reproachful look from Colette, marking him indelibly as the guilty party.

"It's his fault," Dave had wanted to scream in a schoolboy cry for justice. *Why should he get away with an ethical monologue? This is grown-up conversation in which all have the democratic right to an opinion.* This had roared through his mind as Caractacus launched what Dave suddenly felt to be an all-out attack.

"If you got knocked down by a double-decker Oxford bus on your way home tonight, Dave, would you end up in heaven?"

"I beg your pardon?" Dave was incredulous. Had Llewellyn flipped into another universe? Had Alzheimer's suddenly plundered the Welshman's middle-aged wits? Had this Caractacus chap forgotten he was addressing a leading lecturer on Old Testament studies, an acclaimed author, an ordained, fully revved-up, dog-collared theologian?

"Will you end up safe in God's arms?" The ginger moustache twitched to one side over a crooked charming smile. An eyebrow arched innocently to highlight the inquiry.

"What sort of fool question is that?" Dave blustered. "Counseling? Remember, that's what we're doing. Marriage guidance! Coping with miscarriages! Relational issues! All that sort of thing!" The exclamations were bullet-pointed and forceful. "And now you suddenly turn into a Billy Graham Bible thumper?"

"Dave, he's only asking." Colette's wide-open eyes seemed to implore him. "For God's sake, for our sakes, Dave, we need solutions, not punctured professional pride."

"Sorry, Dave." Caractacus smiled, cradling a mug of tepid coffee in his cupped hands. "Humor me. I like to cut to the heart of problems via the scenic spiritual route, if you see what I mean?"

The reproachful Colette still glared. Dave offered a grudging "Of course!"

"Of course what?" Again the annoying raised quizzical eyebrow.

"Of course we can hope to be with him when we die."

"Why?"

Dave placed his hands on the edge of his chair.

"How do you know you'll be with him when you die?"

Should he push up? If he did rise, should he push off, or stay and push this pompous Welsh twit over the back of his own chair?

CHAPTER 14

On a Brooklyn Hydrant

Dave sat out the rising fight-or-flight panic. If he exploded, his wife's look might deteriorate into something far worse. He dreaded any repeat of the emotional horrors in the wake of their miscarriages, the second one especially. It had almost finished them. Perhaps tolerating Welsh smugness was his less evil choice.

He smiled when recalling how one group of his students had dealt with a pompous, hairy-faced know-it-all. Maybe he too could later nail Llewellyn to the college lawn with croquet hoops and then shave off half his facial hair. That ginger moustache needed putting out of its misery almost as much as Caractacus did.

Dave continued to smile over his cooling coffee, and then he slowly sipped as the pause stretched toward embarrassment. "What's New, Pussycat?" thankfully intervened. Llewellyn apologetically wrestled open his mobile to kill Tom Jones midsong, which allowed Dave's mind to flick away frantically and back through his past.

He was desperately hunting for a put-down answer to his obnoxious colleague. His mind, trained to order complex ideas, began to bullet-point memorable God-colored scenes from his past, such as the following:

❖ He had stood blindfolded on a water hydrant opposite Captain America Church on 125th Street in lower Brooklyn, with hordes of kids screaming, *"Fall back, Dave!* We'll catch you." The last Sunday school lesson about trusting God had turned into a game of Dare. Young Dave, having no faith in the kids and little in God, ripped off the blindfold, jumped from the hydrant, and ran.

❖ He had sat on the same hydrant six months before. His seven years of life had taught him to stay put. His drug-addicted ma would soon return. Hadn't she always turned up, usually later rather than sooner, with tears of guilt and treats of remorse? Three hungry days and sleepless nights later, his trust was ebbing.

❖ Rescued on Day 4 by the Captain America pastor who fed, watered, and then housed him. Captain America, it turned out, was a character in the wonderfully mad lessons of the church's Sunday school, together with

Superman, Yogi Bear, and Batman and Robin. It was a crazy circus of athletics, games, dramas, stories, and—best of all—iced donuts and cupcakes to die for. It turned out that the church's pastor had also been abandoned on the streets of New York when he was around the same age as Dave. If God could save his pastor, why not him?

❖ Then, months later, he bounded forward with a hundred other elementary kids to give his life to a Jesus, who, so he was assured, had saved him from his sins and hell. He didn't quite understand how a man dying on a cross centuries before could do this, but he did have a strong faith in the savior who'd fed and loved him—the kindly pastor.

Maybe I could tell Caractacus this and shut him up, Dave had mused as the Welshman's mobile conversation rudely continued. Colette had offered Dave an encouraging smile. In return, he had grimaced and then promptly escaped back to his time traveling. There had to be something stronger to strangle the Welshman with. For God's sake, didn't he have a dog collar for his final passport?

Back at the water hydrant, this time selling crack cocaine as a ten-year-old, black-bandanna-wearing pusher for the Brooklyn Brothers—the token white in a gang of many colors—Dave was accepted because, even then, he towered above those of his age group. Dave's trust now centered on a homemade pipe gun stuffed in his waistband ("just in case") and on his cool gang of brothers who saluted with straight arms ending in clenched fists.

"Sorry about that." Llewellyn had now dropped his phone into his shirt pocket. "Take your time, Dave." A patient smile accompanied the raised eyebrows of Ethics Man.

"I sure will," Dave had drawled within but smiled outwardly. He then took childish delight in excusing himself "for a quick visit." He knew he was stretching his wife's patience as he departed for the john, not particularly needing it as much as buying more time to stroll down memory lane.

- ❖ This time, he had been alone in a cage for three days in a Brooklyn precinct. Now he was a twelve-year-old loner minus his pipe gun and any drugs to push, deserted equally by black and not-so-black brothers. *"Trust!"* Dave had screamed into the frightening blackness. "Jesus, help!" he then whispered in exclamation, testing if this cross-dying character might be more of a savior in reality than his Captain America pastor was. He was also responding to something deep within, a childish feeling that, despite all, somebody was there for him.
- ❖ "Jackson, we're giving you a second chance," the lady judge had said upon releasing him the following morning to the custody of his pastor. "Prayer works," a quiet voice inside his head had whispered. "Coincidence," his academic mind replied.
- ❖ Slurping from the court's water fountain while waiting for his new guardian, he had wondered if he could

really trust something that no one could see or touch. Why couldn't life be simpler, maybe such as bending to a fountain to drink in happiness? Wiping the back of his hand across his mouth, he had decided it was time to find answers to life.

On his way back to Caractacus and counseling, Dave's steps slowed to a crawl while his mind raced over more God-wrestling moments, still trying for that killer quotation to quiet his Welsh tormentor.

❖ Middle school, he mused, had seen him dump a Creator in exchange for a big bang. No divine hand guided, he was assured, just ancient eons haphazardly fashioning lighter, and then heavier, elements—and then planets. Life bubbled out of a chance dance of chemicals with electricity or deep-sea vents, or maybe unidentified flying objects wafting life seeds from outer space. Yet wasn't all this merely another set of beliefs, religion minus God? He still had to take a massive number of things on faith. And how on earth did such beautiful complexity and seeming design come from a big bang, when every other explosion he'd ever witnessed produced utter chaos? Science was good but surely not that good. Well, not on its own and unguided!

❖ And what of his math lessons and also music and astronomy, all obeying perfectly designed laws? How did a chaotic blast produce such order? Was all this precision just a massive fluke, or was there really a Designer, like his pastor preached? Didn't a universe that looked designed demand a designer?

❖ Biology was his biggest puzzle. How could things that weren't alive invent things that were obviously alive? How could dead clays, crystals, or chemicals produce life that could then reproduce more life? How could nonlife produce a self-replicating cell complete with its own power station, exhaust system, and vital protein-making machines all folded with deckchair precision, plus a hundred other components needed for life to start and go on? For unguided chance to hit on just one self-replicating cell seemed about as far-fetched as scooping Mega Millions and the world's other lotteries all in the same week.

❖ And what about having a brain that could think such things? Was it really intelligent to think that his intelligence merely bubbled out of a non-intelligent stagnant pond or fell from the tail of a passing mindless comet? Dave's intelligence cried out to be fathered by, at the very least, an intelligence bigger than his own.

As he neared the door of the senior common room, Dave found that all he could say with a fair degree of certainty was that the mindless big bang of his high school lessons didn't sit well in his mind without at least some external mighty assistance. Neither his faith nor his reason was happy with unproved maybes and possibilities of billions of years, not without some Superguide.

What he had seen in his three decades needed a producer. It needed a beautiful mind to invent the fine-looking laws and forces on which a whole universe was hung. Such a one, in his opinion, deserved at the very least to be called God.

But—and here was the "but" that Llewellyn was getting at—was this Governor of the Universe the personal God and Father of Dave? That's what the Welshman was after. Dave had long ago concluded that he rather liked being his own god, thank you very much.

True, he loved the old Bible stories, and was quite fond of some of the New Testament as well. And yes, he did make his living on his ability to think new things about sacred literature. But did that really mean he had to submit his whole life, his future, and even his purse and credit cards to this God?

This brought Dave back to Caractacus's big question: did he know for certain that this all-powerful being liked him enough to swing wide the heavenly gates to welcome him after he departed his present earthly address?

Could anybody know such a thing?

Would it not be rather presumptuous to declare that this God of the Universe had a special heavenly slot already reserved for him—merely one of many billions of souls to have paced this planet?

If you were a near-orphaned kid who couldn't trust his own mom to provide a home and love, how could you believe that an unseen heavenly Father would?

On top of everything else, why should he deserve such a heavenly reservation? Had he gotten enough credit? Did he deserve it? Most days he doubted it. God was supposed to be good, but Dave Jackson certainly knew he was not. How could holy absorb unholy and still stay good?

"Sorry, folks." Caractacus Llewellyn was once again tucking his mobile back into his shirt pocket as Dave returned. "It seems like we're destined not to chat tonight. Bit of an emergency over some exam results. Can we take a rain check, as you Yanks say? Seven tomorrow evening, same place?"

There was a disappointed nod from Colette, which Llewellyn took as settling the matter. He glanced briefly at Dave, flashed a genial smile, turned on his heels, and hurried off.

Dave's rumination on his extended trip to the water closet must have worked at a subconscious level. He was suddenly relieved to see large white W.C. letters on a looming blue M25 service-station sign.

On his way back to the car, he was tempted into Starbucks and was soon seated with a double-caramel black coffee propping up his precious scroll.

He needed a diversion. Checking the next stage of the sister's tale became suddenly attractive.

CHAPTER 15

"They Want to Kill Our Babies"

"Hosea!" I screamed as I ran up the lane.

I dropped my hoisted skirt and frantically reached out to unloop the front gate's rope, tripping full-length in my hurry. I scrambled up to catch sight of my brother and Daddy Beeri in deep discussion down in the rose garden.

"They want to kill our babies!"

"Stop blaring like a ram's horn," Father snapped.

I gathered my skirt once again and marched forward. No matter their topic or their irritation, they urgently needed to know what I had just discovered. They must also understand precisely how all their senseless marriage talk was endangering me, them, and our village children.

"Slowly." Hosi smiled, sensing that my trumpeting was about to rise an octave. "Breathe slowly, and then tell—"

"Two priests are down from Dan," I said, cutting short his condescension. "They are prophesying the good times and saying that the rains will soon end. Droughts will be as bad as in the days of Molech. And they preach that the God of our fathers has lost interest in us. Even Baal and the kedeshah ladies will no longer bring fertility." I took a mighty breath before blurting out, "They want us to sacrifice a village child!"

Hosi was shaking his head, clearly unimpressed, so I gave him the top of my voice, hollering, "No baby, no rain!"

They stared open-mouthed. "The whole souk is full of it, and traders think this will be only the first child."

I had been too young for the slaughter of infants in the last dry season, but I had often heard the callous gossip of street lads who had more summers than I. Nothing was left to imagine about an ogre god who demanded plump babies offered in flaming ovens so hot that some slow-moving elders of Molech's priesthood were often burned alive. The first baby was always a sacrifice of repentance for forsaking Molech in times of plenty. Only when rich-robed priests had extracted enough tears of remorse did the main sacrifices begin. Then, only the best families must offer babies, better still a new mother who had tried for years for a family. Her sacrifice would especially pry open the heavens and drown the ground with divine blessings. Only once many rains had fallen and new crops were assured would Molech be washed back into the hidden gullies of life.

Hosi and Father gave mutual nods, apparently of acceptance.

"The old hags and traders laughing in the souk are more honest than you," I screamed, remembering callous stallholders digging out leftover fertility dolls from the last Molech revival. I fumed accusingly at my betters and added their latest hypocrisy to the lying years of my childhood. Both had always stressed the supremacy of the God of our fathers, yet now, at the first hint of drought, they were just like all the rest.

Bitterness welled up. I had been cheated. Following the Gomer trickery, all was a web of sticky, spidery lies. I burst into sobbing tears. Through glistening wetness, I watched my father and brother turn away to talk with each other—and I snapped.

"Why are you marrying into all this?" I brutally pushed Hosi into the blood reds and yellows of our roses, feeling triumph as the sharp thorns brought yelps. "And you, Father." I swung with snarling fierceness, yet still with enough little-girl respect to stop me from hitting him. "You teach me to obey the one true God of Israel. You mock those who chop down trees for firewood and then worship the trunks as totem-pole gods. You laugh as they sit on one piece of the tree and then pray to another part. You plot to marry yourselves to a whore of another god, and now you shrug off baby sacrifices ..."

I trailed off in utter disbelief. I passionately prayed that my face showed the inner disgust I now had for my weak menfolk, even though I no longer knew where to aim my prayers.

"We need to tell her, Father." My brother was picking a thorn as long as my little finger out of his thumb.

I looked up.

"Not yet, Son." Daddy shook his head. "Too young; she doesn't have to know yet." He turned toward the bakery.

"Too young!" My voice rose against his retreating back. "For what?" This time I did push him as I ran to overtake him. "Too young to do your books, to cook your meals, to clean the house? Too young to

115

swell your profits and still leave caravan customers smiling because they think they have a bargain?"

"She is right!" Hosi's voice came from behind my father, "and we should be the ones to tell her." Daddy Beeri seemed to shrink into his work clothes.

"Not me." He turned to me, shaking his old head with eyes that glistened. Hosi's large hand came to rest on Father's drooping shoulders.

"What?" I whispered, "Please!"

I hardly dared say more for fear that some fragile bubble of hope might burst into nothing. Daddy Beeri placed a hand on my cheek, his rough thumb gently stroking the wetness below my eyes. He nodded his tired face toward my brother and walked into the bakery.

"Tell me." This time I spoke in slightly more than a whisper to Hosi.

He took two strides toward me, wrapped an arm around my shoulder, and led me to the teaching stone. "Worry not about Safed's babies, little one. They are safe, at least for this season."

"But I heard them."

"No, you heard ugly lies of robbers in priest clothes."

"No, they were real priests." I was puzzled at "priest" and "ugly" coming together. "Traders gave them tributes for their sanctuary at Dan."

"Priests they were." Hosi waved for me to sit by the teaching table. "Holy men—never! False prophets! They serve no gods but their bellies. Their religion is the shekel, and their favorite commandment is 'thou shalt steal' so long as they are takers. They have two sides, two faces, like our half-baked loaves of bread, charred on one side and poisonously raw on the other."

"But why threaten our babies?"

"Tomorrow they will offer Safed a way out—for a price. They did the same a few seasons back. It is my, ah, belief," Hosi said, choosing his words carefully, "that they will demand that the sacrificial child should only come from Safed's richest families. The day after that, they will smile and reveal that an expensive ransom might be enough to save the victim."

"What, a purse of shekels?"

"Oh, nothing so crude. Perhaps a brace of pulling oxen, a fine bull or a few cows, or maybe even a drove of sheep or goats. When the thieves think they have squeezed all they can from us, then they will move on to threaten another town's babies."

"But you must stop them, Hosi!" I pleaded. "The traders should have beaten the thieving preachers and thrown them out of town."

"They are simple folk." Hosi sighed. "These rogue priests know that traders and villagers in the hill towns have much to lose. They know superstition will strangle any rebellion."

"What about the king? Surely he will help?"

"He has no real power. They would have him assassinated like all the others."

"What others?"

"This is what Father wanted to save you from. This world can be as rotten as week-old fig falls. You are of an age and need to know. For years kings have come and gone quickly. Our King Jeroboam has lasted longer, despite plots and assassination attempts. When he goes, the royal court will be a bloodbath."

"That's awful!" I held my arms open in supplication. "Why do we not protest?"

"Your father has spoken out long ago, and I am getting ready to add what the Lord is giving me," my sad-faced brother said, nodding.

"No!" I said firmly. Hosi shrugged. "Let somebody else," I wailed in sudden fear. "I won't let you." I grabbed his hand, the one still oozing blood. "There will be far worse than this if you speak out."

A sad smile hovered. "This warning will be played out as well as spoken about."

"How?" I glared at him.

"This is why I will marry Gomer."

"You scare me." My glaring turned to bossy intensity. This coming from somebody still short of her thirteenth summer might amuse some, yet all sisters know the deadly-serious business of bringing a big brother back to sanity. "How can the marriage of a baker's boy in the remote hills of Galilee possibly affect the affairs of a gang of unholy priests and cowardly kings?"

He shrugged. I carried on glaring. He continued to avoid me, gazing distantly into the cloudless blue sky.

"Hosi!" I sought to call him back to earth. "Please!"

CHAPTER 16

Marriage Made in Heaven

"It is time for your final examination, little sister." Hosi pulled himself back to earth and smiled. "Life will change with marriage and children, and time is fast running out on your education."

"This is no day for lessons." My face hardened. "Do you not understand? Right now I am hanging by a spider's thread to all my past. Why so many secrets? Why the betrayal and—"

"First, what do you remember about Israel's marriage?" I was shocked. Not only did he ignore my points, but also now he dared me to review the very heritage I suspected. I stared back with the contempt I usually reserved for spitting camels. I turned on my heels, picked up my skirt, and marched away.

"You answer me and you will find your own answers." I slowed, fighting conflicting instincts. "Humor me, little one, and you will smile with knowledge." I stopped. It was an offer hard to refuse.

A soaring mountain towered in my mind's eye. "The Sinai Israel marriage, you mean?" slipped out of my mouth before my mind had made a decision.

"Goood." The elongated praise warmed me, as a disgusted voice between my ears scolded me for caving in so easily. Yet the offer of answers pulled, and I did so love to be tested, especially on things which my heart and mind had long fed.

"First, tell me how we got to Sinai and Moses."

"Easy." I circled the stone, the show-off me marrying my sad eagerness to please even in the face of betrayal. "Long after Noah's Flood, Abraham was the only friend God had in a sad, bad world. He promised through his son Isaac and grandson Jacob that the family would eventually be as numerous as the grains of sand on the seashores.

"Forty generations ago," I said, now gathering speed, "he settled them a bit further south from where we now are, later taking them to Egypt during a famine." By now I was in full flow of our epic past.

"They were saved by Joseph, the favorite son of Jacob, otherwise called Israel. The eleven brothers hated Joseph because of the special treatment he got from their father, like his multicolored coat. After trying to kill him, they sold him as a slave to travelers heading for Egypt. Here, Joseph rose from being a slave and a prisoner. With the Lord's help he became second in command under Pharaoh, and during a great famine he provided everybody, including his lost family, with food. He then sheltered his kin in Goshen, where the Nile flows into the Great Sea."

Hosea nodded in encouragement, wanting me to continue.

"We thrived so well that Egyptians became afraid, and murdered a generation of our babies to stop us from growing. One of them, Moses, escaped. Eighty summers later he became our rescuer. Moses and the Lord plagued Pharaoh to let us go, and we escaped through the exodus sea. The Lord walled it up on either side of our fleeing ancestors, drowning the pursuing Egyptian army before they caught up to us. After all that, we came to rest at the foot of Mount Sinai."

"And now go on to the marriage, little one."

"What's all this got to do with you and Gomer?" the disgusted voice within rallied.

"Success puts one foot in front of the other—"

"And failure jumps to wrong conclusions," I said, finishing one of his regular chants as I pulled a face.

"So?" My brother smiled. "The mountain and the marriage?"

"The Lord often promised to love and keep us safe, starting with Adam, through to Noah and beyond to Abraham, and onward to us." I rattled it off like a pipe player who has forgotten the beauty of an old tune. "There was a covenant or pledge for God to be our God if we agreed to be his trusting people. For our part, we promised to keep our side of this agreement by loving, cherishing, and obeying him at Sinai and beyond. To mark this, he gave us, as his bride, precious stones on which were Ten Commandments to make our marriage work."

I slowed down as a possible marriage link popped into my head. My eyes widened and I filled with bubbling energy as the heart of our history once again captured me.

"We then spent forty years consummating the partnership and getting to know our new husband while honeymooning in the wilderness. He carried us across the threshold of Jordan's river and into our promised homeland, overflowing with all the good things of life. It was the area he had originally given to Abraham, Isaac, and Israel—the place called Canaan."

"What did the bride keep doing?" urged my brother.

"Cheating, you mean?" Hosi nodded. "Well, she kept running off with other lovers, such as Baal. She thought the local god had better farming talents because it was already a land of plenty. Also, this god didn't bother worshippers with Ten Commandments and only expected his followers to offer their, er—"

"What? You were doing so well."

"Did Baal followers really have to, er, well ..." I bobbed a couple of times into a half-sitting squat. "You know what!"

"Come on, Sister." His eyebrows arched in gentle mockery. "It's not like you to be shy. Spit it out."

"Stuff." I grimaced, waving a hand behind my lower back.

"Stuff?" I could see he was stifling a grin.

"You know!" I exclaimed accusingly, having reached an age when this sort of thing was embarrassing. "Stuff!" I held my nose between finger and thumb.

"Okay." Hosi released his laugh, a soft one. "Go on with what else Baal asks of his followers."

"Oh, he expects all the men to have sex with the temple priestesses to bring new life and fertility."

"You really are funny." Hosi laughed out loud. "You have no problem blurting out all the sex stuff, but when it comes to Baal followers offering their own dung, you get all tongue-tied."

"Your fault," I defended loudly. "And you never told me why, just that they went up on Baal's mountains to do their, er, what you said."

"Man manure?" Hosi asked with a straight face. "Back to God's marriage to his people on the mountain."

"Why?" I tired of my big brother's forever expecting me to follow where he wanted to go.

"Remember the day we went out to meet an important customer on the caravan trail and we passed Mount Peor?"

"I remember." I giggled at the word Peor, remembering what else it meant. "It was so far away that we had to camp overnight."

"Well, Peor is where Baal worship started, and from your grinning, you seem to know that p'r in our language is linked to, er, shall we say, products of the lower body. Baal Peor means 'Lord of the Opening,' and so nakedness and feces were all part of worship. The weather god Baal provides the manure, rain, and sun to make the plants grow."

"Glad you are not a Baal prophet." I wrinkled my nose.

"Now," he said, breathing, although it may have been a groan, "your next step is my marriage. See any links, little one?"

"Well, I can see two marriages ..." I trailed off, seeing no chance to show off or even make sense. Silence seemed better at the edges of my ignorance.

"God told me to marry a prostitute, just like he had done on Sinai!"

"Israel, a prostitute?"

"God says so." Hosi's face slipped more toward grief now, yet what bothered me most was the word he had used for prostitute. God had told him to marry a zonah, a street-corner girl, rather than the sacred temple kedeshah, the ranks from which Gomer was now retiring.

"A common zonah?" I queried.

When he nodded, I exploded. "But that makes no sense. First, why not tell the people that what they have done is wrong and then urge them to give up their false lover? Why go and ruin your life and ours?"

Hosi's wispy beard shook as though it were an almighty effort for him to go on. "Prophets have warned with words for years, and still our men go to Baal sex services. Little Sister, the Lord wants me to love a zonah in the same way that he has loved Israel. He wants me to go on loving her even though she will do evil in our marriage. And, if you are still confused, know that while I may be marrying a retiring kedeshah, Gomer will end up a zonah one of these days, just as Israel has been faithless in her marriage. God then wants me to do something terrible to Gomer as a warning of what one day he will do with his bride. It is then that she will become a zonah."

"You mean that little madam will then get what's coming to her?"

"All in good time, Little Miss Want It All Now; the Lord needs my marriage to be a living warning to his own bride. As he has loved his bride, so I must love Gomer."

"This is madness. How can you possibly love a stuck-up harlot?"

"Sister." Hosi had that smiling sadness. "I have loved Gomer ever since God told me of his plans, before she and I were betrothed."

"You..." No useful words were available. The old feeling of betrayal silenced me.

"I know, I know." Hosi nodded his head before me, a slight look of guilt flashing across his eyes. "Little Sister, you had not even seen seven summers when my betrothal was agreed. I was on the verge of manhood, which is when, as you know, betrothal takes place. I knew even then that she was to be trained for the temple. Equally, I knew that I loved her. I saw beyond the 'royal madam' act. I looked to what she might be one day with divine help. That is how God looks at his bride, even when Israel is

127

making love to Baal. That is how God looks at you and me."

There was a moment of silence. Hosi wanted me to take this in before he delivered his next shock.

"I need your help."

"What can I possibly do?" I was amazed.

"Father is supporting me, even though it goes against everything he has ever preached and ..." Hosi's voice trailed off, and then he seemed to inhale new energy. "Father believes it is from God. He understands that the whole nation needs to see this as a real marriage, no play acting. Do you understand?" I nodded.

"Terrible things will happen in this marriage, just as terrible as the things happening between God and his bride. Will you join hands with Father and me and show the world we are one in this?"

I was appalled, terribly disappointed with the betrayal of it all. Hosi knelt before me and searched my eyes as if trying to read the thoughts behind them. "I am so sorry for the past. I want you fully involved from this point on."

"No." I was trembling from shawl to sandals. "In any case, what can I possibly do?"

"Be Gomer's first virgin."

I looked at him as though he were mad.

"Will you be chief marriage maid to my bride?" he asked again.

CHAPTER 17

Journey of Memories

Dave, having collected his own car, now tried hard to focus on the Luton-to-Oxford route.

He shivered at the thought of somebody suddenly stepping out in front of him while he was driving without due care and attention—absent from consciousness. Perhaps he should have stuck to the motorway, but the quaint lanes of southern England were an attraction his American heart rarely resisted.

He pulled into a lay-by after spotting a stall advertising bumper triple cheeseburgers with giant fries and a free bucket of diet Coke. He eventually settled instead for the friend to all drained drivers—a regular americano.

He tried the mobile again. His wife had still not answered. It looked increasingly like he would be dining alone once again. Colette had been living at Bridie's for much of his time in Israel, but he knew she regularly returned to their college flat. He was now less than an hour away, and so he texted once more in memory of his last unannounced return and the kitchen table affair.

He then fuzzed, deliberately concentrating on a cow on the other side of a five-barred gate at the rear of the lay-by. For some reason, it returned his steady gaze. Its tail then lifted and its staring efforts gave birth to a steaming stream that formed a new cow pie to his rear.

Americano-fortified, Dave was back on the road, this time driving more slowly so as to avoid any country-lane jaywalkers. His slow crawl through rural Oxfordshire also enabled his unoccupied brain cells to take a safer trip, down a dark and painful lane in his memory.

This time fuzzing was no longer an option, he willfully decided. This time he would, once and for all time, deliberately analyze how he had ended up at this dismal crossroads in his marriage. He decided to get the worst over before he changed his mind and honed in at the most painful junction—the showdown.

Dave, in his mind's eye, now faced his icy wife across their cramped lounge.

"Colette, you ..." He hesitated, wanting to avoid confrontation while recognizing its inevitability. He struggled for the right sentence, perhaps for a right sense of what the next sounds might fashion or, more likely, crush.

The cold academic in him sifted the evidence for the prosecution, which had been extracted since he'd found her entwined with her ethics-spouting lothario on the kitchen table. That cold academic examined Colette's words and actions, and already knew the crisp judgment Dave was now to pronounce. Still, his aching heart screamed for mercy and even clemency, and within he pleaded a dozen unlikely explanations of what was plainly evident. The head ruled. Eventually he finished his sentence.

"Colette, you love him."

As Dave drove, he gasped oxygen to fill the seeming void left by such enormous words. He had made it a statement, though he did briefly consider hinting at adding a question mark. Amid the agony of this memory, Dave suddenly had to screech the car to a standstill as the gates of an unmanned rail crossing threatened to deroof him. He had missed all but the last flashing warning lights.

In the stillness that followed, one of those "if only" moments engulfed him. If only that counseling session had not been delayed; if only he had answered that stupid God question of Llewellyn's; if only the meeting hadn't further been postponed and then completely overtaken by events; if only he hadn't had to go off and leave her; if only he'd loved her more, paid more—

"*No!*" he shouted to stop himself from completing the last thought just as a freight train trundled before his windscreen. "This is not my doing," he muttered at the blurred train. "This is down to her and that ethics guy who had forgotten his right from his wrong."

In his inner mind, he was now back glaring at Colette, who had turned away. He waited for her response. Her back stiffened. He knew from past confrontations what was coming—defiance, defense of self, deflection from herself and her actions, accusations about his conduct. This time it would be worse than usual.

She had been drinking. The stench he had grown to hate hung about her, so pungent that a day's production of sugar-free mints would have failed to camouflage it. The conversation now pending would be between him and a bottle rather than his bride, and usually such a futile exercise would have made him walk away. But now, that was no longer possible. Too much hung on words that could no longer remain unspoken.

He had once worked out why she drank. It was not just an illness. It was more than the stress of miscarriages, and only partly was it genetic. He remembered that her mum's mouth cancer and early death had been drink-related.

Colette's glass of Irish gold simply delivered that which she most craved: pure, precious self-containment. Self-assurance was at the bottom of the first drink, and after that she needed nobody and nothing, save a second glass, and then a third, the multiplying milliliters in the blood raising her frail self with the surety and security of a float on tidal water. Alcohol was not her primary addiction. The heady power of self-confidence that accompanied it was what she really craved.

Her mother's own baby torments had been the genesis of Colette's angst. A stillborn baby boy was followed by a miscarried male fetus, and then along had come a daughter. Disappointment was rarely obvious. Colette daily breathed it in through resigned sighs. Mother's evening whiskey sometimes descended into a sentimental mush about the lost might and prowess of the lost O'Hara males. At such times, Mother's withering looks in her direction caused Colette to flee.

Ma O'Hara had then uncaringly left her for a different world on her seventh birthday, and without even any good-byes.

It was felt that Colette was too immature to face terminal illness. In her ignorance, she had simply skulked on through her Madam Brat stage: old enough to cheek her parents, but too young to mourn the loss of one of them. Her exclusion from the funeral had only underlined the certainty that she was not needed and of no value. What's more, she was wholly to blame for driving her mother to drink and an early death.

Dah O'Hara had left within weeks of the lavish and cheerful Irish wake, having placed his daughter with an aunt in Dublin. He had explained that he needed to seek the Lord's will in England via the medium of a junior tutor's post at a London theological college. But Colette knew the real truth. Her father could not stand to live with the one who had caused his wife's early death. She was blamed and bereft.

When they were eventually reunited as father and daughter, four years had passed and Dah O'Hara had all but forgotten how to be a father, if he ever had possessed such knowledge in the first place. He had little idea of the dreams and needs of a preteen girl, and therefore he left her in the less than capable hands of a succession of part-time housekeepers.

In due time, Colette was more than happy to escape into the residential halls of St. Brendan's Teacher Training College. To some extent, she recovered a little confidence in a classroom full of need and dependence. Here was a place she could control, a place where she was wanted, an environment where she could grow in the esteem given to her by adoring four-year-olds. It was this confidence that had enabled her to make short forays into the world of adulthood, supported by what she called her stiffener. It was the occasional glass at first. Later, when life's complications increased, so too did the intake of the precious liquid gold.

Dave's amateur psychology had concluded that the drink was all down to upbringing. It was done, dyed as an indelible habit. Such damage could not be undone by a mere man. He was no miracle worker. He did have a stab at praying, but the bottles still kept appearing in the hiding places where he always found them, and they had emptied just as quickly as before.

On a rare occasion, it had crossed his mind that a strong and positive kind of husband might try to undo some of the negatives of her childhood. Perhaps giving his wife more time, understanding her, and listening to her would do wonders. Maybe if he focused on her when at home, to the exclusion of others and their issues, then maybe her self-worth might blossom. But then the others and their issues—his students and the ever-present crisis of a fading college—would take over.

These made considerations of Colette so rare that they failed to affect his actions. In any case, he had concluded in more practical moments that anything he might do would hardly ripple the ocean of premarital neglect. And, in any case, the stronger, selfish side of his mind would occasionally snap, *At least her mother gave her a home and didn't abandon her on a fire hydrant in the middle of New York City!*

A four-by-four's horn blasted Dave's daydreams.

He immediately jammed the car into first, released the hand brake, and raced under the now raised level-crossing barrier, waving apologies into the rearview mirror. Within a few hundred yards, he slowed to let an irate fist-waver pass him so he could continue his meander through the Oxford countryside. He gave his mind permission to turn down memory lane once again.

The mind immediately flashed back to showdown night.

"But you left me long before," Colette's voice quietly accused. This was her response to Dave's accusation that she had emotionally abandoned him for the love of Caractacus Llewellyn.

He remembered his surprise at her tone. It was cold, if slightly slurred—almost sober. It was not at all like the usual illogical rants that were fueled by the fire she had consumed. The following conversation replayed as though it were happening there and then.

"I'm nothing to you, am I, Dave?" Colette glared into his face. "I'm like those Old Testament women you go on about. I come fourth or fifth in priority. They were runners-up behind male children, the family camel, work, and anything else the husband desired. I play sixth fiddle behind your precious God, his college, your Old Testament studies, the students, and your own sex drive."

"That's totally unfair," Dave immediately hit back, "And I didn't leave you. Let's get that straight once and for all. You know why I had to work away in Wales for a while. You know it was for our future. We agreed it was best, didn't we, Col?"

When no reply came, he saw red and snarled unkindly, "And what's that got to do with what I caught you doing on the kitchen table with Llewellyn?"

"You just don't see it, do you?" Colette matched his snarl and pushed past him with a roughness he had not experienced previously. She slammed the door shut as she ran back into the kitchen.

Dave slumped down into his chair. Colette was being totally unfair about his work trip to Aberystwyth. He seethed. He had every right—no, more than that, every duty—to leave her for that short period. It was his responsibility as a loving breadwinner to provide for their future.

"She knew this!" he shouted, throwing a cushion at the far wall, wishing he had chosen a heavy glass or vase that would shatter and show her in the kitchen how vehemently he felt. He slouched further into his chair and sulked.

Another horn sounded.

This time, the driver of a Mini Cooper was peeping at him for going too slow in the narrow lanes. He pulled over at the next lay-by and waved on a queue of cars and even two tractors. He abruptly sobbed, grasping tightly the still steering wheel. He was surprised. He was not one of life's criers, but his frustration suddenly felt it needed to escape.

Such was the showdown nightmare that was on a constant loop running around his head whenever he forgot to fuzz, whenever he was caught with nothing to do and nothing else to think about.

CHAPTER 18

The Kitchen Table

When Dave felt sufficiently recovered, he began to replay the lead-up to showdown night, which then led on to the day he flew out of Colette's life to join his college's dig in Israel.

He was not feeling particularly rugged as he dried his tears, yet he had to get things straight in his mind. As he replayed events, he wondered if he could have done anything differently. Could he have been wiser in his choice of words? Had he been too hard? Had he been too soft?

He had isolated the point of no return on the downward slope that brought him to his present marital pit. It had begun with a smart rap on his college study door the morning after that aborted counseling meeting. It was only hours before he was due for the rain check. Dave had spent the morning trying to puzzle out how he, Colette, and Llewellyn could meet, and how he could deal with the Welshman's impertinent questions.

This time of self-examination had not been voluntary. It was the consequence of a hellish night before with a drunken, weeping wife who blamed him for his uncaring and eternal toilet trekking, his slowness in answering "perfectly sensible questions," and his rudeness to an honorable visitor from Wales who had given up his precious time to try to help a couple frustrated by death and treble miscarriage.

Dave had come to the conclusion that they should meet that evening, that he should honestly answer Llewellyn's silly questions, and that he should really take control of the situation to win back his wife to the relationship they once had in courtship. All this was settled in his mind when Dean O'Hara knocked on his study door.

"We're in a spot of bother, Dave," he had announced upon entering. "Aberystwyth has been hit by some virus, and they want Llewellyn back sharpish. I don't have to tell you what a mess that will leave us with. I need a favor, a big one."

"Ask away, Dean." Dave felt lifted by the news of Llewellyn's imminent departure and the likelihood that he could now legitimately dodge this evening's counseling.

"If we lose him, there's nobody to take his students, some of whom are only weeks away from their finals. Frankly, Dave, it couldn't be worse, for them or the college's reputation. You know we're already several students down this year, and I have to tell you that the next intake isn't looking too bright at the moment. We have nobody to teach at his level. I was so desperate that I made a rather rash offer."

"And that was?"

"You, Dave." The dean smiled nervously and rushed on. "Apparently, Aberystwyth could cope if they could get an Old Testament chap like you. That would give them room to move teaching staff around—"

"Stop right there, Dean." Dave held up both hands in front of his chest. "There's no way—"

"Let me finish, Dave, before you say another word."

"A sentence, two at the most."

"You know my specialties, and so I can adequately cover your OT classes here. Ah, to be sure, certainly not to the standard of your good self now." The dean smiled with lips that had actually kissed the Blarney stone. "But I can promise that your students will not want for anything. And in any case, as you know, quite a few of them are doing their dissertations and are later booked for a field trip to Israel. Also, we would continue to pay your full salary into the bank, and full expenses will be met by Wales."

"Dean, this is not a good time. Your daughter—"

"Now, haven't I saved the best for last, my son-in-law?" The dean grinned without a trace of shame for playing the family loyalty card. "And I can promise you that my lovely colleen will think you're the apple of her eye."

"You've won yourself another sentence, Dean."

"Aberystwyth will also pay you a salary for the six weeks you'll be away. If you take over their chapel services and oversee student pastoral responsibilities, they will double the salary as a bonus. This, of course, is in addition to your present salary here. Come on, Dave, think it through. You'll have that deposit she's been going on and on about for her cozy hideaway by the canal. I promise you that my lass will love you even more for it."

Dave looked into the dean's beam of triumph and pictured a matching smile on his daughter's face. Colette's facial muscles seemed to have forgotten how to produce one for too long a time. Also, both of them had been cooped up forever in the cramped rented campus flat. Admittedly, it was one of the better ones on the ground floor, with both lounge and kitchen looking out on lawns that swept down the Thames. They could open the frosted-glass kitchen door and within minutes set up a picnic by the river. Yet his wife had yearned for distance between her and the college.

In particular, she had her eye on the quaint first-floor maisonettes in fashionable Jericho, overlooking the canal, near the Swan and Royal, where they already enjoyed socials and quizzes with university friends. They had noticed a For Sale sign only last week.

"A little over a month," Dave had later told Colette, hitting the right time of the day as she got home from class and before the teatime tipples began. He quickly added, "And then we can get our very own place."

"Fine."

That was it. That's all she had said, a flat, emotion-free, single word. No tears. No drama. No elation at the good news. No "Great, Dave, we'll be snug as a bug in a rug in our own place." Not even a complaint about missing that night's counseling session. Just a level, disinterested acceptance.

"Worrying," Dave had muttered at the time, and yet he acknowledged that he'd be more bothered if he didn't know how badly she wanted this new place.

"We can take another rain check on this evening's counseling and do it when I get back," he added hopefully.

"As you wish." Her voice had been quite cold.

*   *   *

Dave's drive from the Marriott Hotel had now ended.

He had still no word from Colette about the evening meal. He did not even know if she was home or at Bridie's. He sat in his parked car outside the college block of flats and, quite suddenly, found no way to stop his memory from going into multicolored overdrive as he remembered the early part of the fateful showdown night when he had parked up in the same place.

It was the night he had returned from Aberystwyth. He had eventually arrived home to discover that counseling was no longer an option. It was all too late.

The short task at Aberystwyth University had stretched to two months because of the Welsh germ's virulence. He had texted Colette frequently in the first two days and received few replies. He had sent three to her one. Also, hers were in marked contrast to his romantic themes. He had just received facts, nothing fancy. He had e-mailed but gotten no reply. He had rung but knew that she stuffed her leather-encased mobile into her deep handbag, where not even London's Big Ben could be heard.

Colette's texts had majored on the practical, such as, "R u doing car taxx?" He'd idly wondered if the extra *x* could qualify as a kiss. "Cred. Card bill here! Wot i 2 do?" There was not so much as a "Luv, C."

Guarded phone calls to mutual friends in Oxford confirmed that his wife was fine; she was out and about shopping, even seeing friends, and was in a regular evening group "led by that cute Mr. Llewellyn."

Toward the end of Dave's secondment to Aberystwyth, a sick staff member turned in one morning laughing about "a miraculous recovery." By late afternoon, Dave had tidied his affairs, had packed the car, and was on the road.

Passing Llandrindod Wells, he thought he might pull in and text Colette, but he drove on, relishing the surprise. Around Cheltenham, he pulled over for a quick burger to get food out of the way of homecoming celebrations. Anticipation pleasurably increased as he drove slowly between the darkening spires of Oxford that soared on either side of sodium-yellow-lit streets. He listened to the seven o'clock radio news headlines and swung into the college grounds.

The first thing he had seen was Llewellyn's car.

Flaming jealousy flushed him with anxiety. He had sat grasping the steering wheel, entertaining ideas previously set aside as unworthy: the odd coldness that had crept into their relationship; the matter-of-fact texts; the resigned

acceptance of his Welsh secondment. Without a conscious decision, he was out of his car and heading down the side of his block of flats to the riverside lawns.

Logic and civility began to wrest back control from an inner raging torment as the river came into view. *This really was stupid. This was cowardly. It was untrusting.* He had turned into a snooping spy on his own wife.

He turned on his heels and retraced his steps, suddenly stopping to smash the palm of his right hand on a wall as his jealousy reignited. The next thing he remembered was standing outside the frosted glass of his kitchen door watching two shadows passionately embracing. It was when they swung around toward him and stretched out across the kitchen table that he roared.

Colette he had recognized immediately. Llewellyn he guessed. The figures had immediately jumped apart. Dave raced around toward the front door. When he was halfway around, a moment of coherence slowed him. He should have shoulder-charged through the frosted window and caught them in the act. *Too late,* he thought, as he raced on to the front door, key in hand. He was reaching for the handle when Colette opened it.

"And you can put that down," he had snarled, pointing to the front of her skirt, where the hem of the heavy fabric remained turned up on itself, making it kink outward and upward like a tent.

"We love each other." Llewellyn had stepped protectively in front of Colette, enraging Dave even more. His wife, fearing

144

what was about to happen, had pushed her lover roughly to one side and then stared with a blank expression at Dave.

The look had stopped Dave from advancing. There was no guilt and not a trace of shame, just defiance. The odor of alcohol was double what it normally was.

There was one more shocking thing: he wanted her. That he did not understand, and it slowed him. How could he still feel this? Was it a caveman thing? Wanting to repossess that which had been stolen from him? A pitiful macho reclaiming of lost territory? Was it his grief at losing something that suddenly seemed more precious than his own life? Was this love? Or hatred? Some of the rage buckled with the indecision.

"Get out!" he had snarled past her at a cowering Llewellyn.

"Go." Colette nodded.

"I love her!" Llewellyn bleated again before scurrying into the night.

*   *   *

Dave now sat like a dummy in his parked car, partly wishing he were still on his journey from Luton. This arriving was proving too painful.

Tears ran down his cheeks. His face had melted, and his cheek and jowl muscles fought for control. His chest and stomach leapt up and outward as he stifled sobs. He so badly wanted to take his wife in his arms, to look into her eyes, to go back to the beginning.

The mobile gave out its two-tone warning. His heart jumped in hope. In one quick movement, he wiped his face, took the phone from his shirt pocket, and flipped it open.

"Not 2nite, Dave. Meal tomorrow poss. In Dublin visiting kin. Soz."

He now sagged, emotionally exhausted. He struck at the steering wheel. The horn blared in protest.

"Why do I do this?" he roared at his face in the rearview mirror. "Fuzz, fool! Fuzz!" The longing of a love realized too late was far too painful, and revisiting the kitchen table scene in such detail robbed him of any trace of control.

Now, he fuzzed with every ounce of energy. Some might escape into finger-tapping computer games; others might take refuge in drink or drugs. He now reached for his scroll of salvation.

Unpacking could wait. So could a flat empty of his love. He desperately needed clothes free from excavation sweat and sand. A loaded washing machine would have been a logical next step. But escape was now Dave's top priority.

146

CHAPTER 19

To Kill or to Trust

Day 59

Our ninth Sabbath and I break our rules to scribe. I must set down my doubts, for I am fit neither to be a mother to my precious ones nor a friend to Isaac, and especially not to Magdalen.

Also, my Masada leadership role has become laughable.

Is it really right to kill my five precious ones? I can hardly believe I am writing this. Can I really let Isaac kill me? Is Magdalen right after all?

I know this diary should just stick to Masada essentials and the sister's story, yet if I can just set things down as they pour from me, maybe then I can find peace to carry on.

My head whirled like one of our desert dust storms as I sat with the women at morning worship. It was Uncle El's fault, speaking so powerfully on why we worship. I find it odd that the one who won us over to a death pact should now sow doubt.

"Why does our Creator want worship?" Uncle El's rhetoric thundered. "Would we not be tragic souls if we insisted on the whole world bowing down to us?" We looked at him and then at each other, nonplussed.

"Worship is giving worth," Eleazar said, beginning to unknot his questions. "We do this by giving our attention, our love, and our tributes. So, why should our Maker demand this?"

Again he let silence underline the dilemma. I relaxed knowing that "Uncle God" had all the answers.

"First, your Maker worships you." His eyebrows were raised, his mouth a wide grin. "Each of you is the apple of his eye, says our sacred poetry. He gives you worth, especially high in his sky beyond the reach of the foe. He gave us worth by creating us and by giving us our freedom and treasures, and now he spends every day sustaining us." Nodding heads were smiling in approval.

"Note his grace in bringing us here. Does this salvation not mirror how he plucked our ancestors from slavery in Egypt?" Again heads nodded. "He gave us wise commands for successful lives. He fed us for forty years in the wilderness and then gave us the Promised Land. He is here now in our high haven because he worships us!"

Cheers erupted, the joy coming from our knowing ourselves to be in heavenly hands that are far stronger than any enemy throughout our history.

"I ask you, my friends." Eleazar's arms stretched out toward us. "Is it at all unusual to return this worth, this worship? Is this not how relationships work? Is this not what happens every day of our lives in our families and friendships? We give worth, and worth is given back to us."

Now I joined in the loud cheering, but I stopped abruptly, halted by an inner voice. "Do you really give worth to your precious ones by cutting their throats?" I gasped and stinging tears pricked.

"What?" Magdalen looked sideways at me.

"Worship," I lied. "It just got to me."

I moved away quickly as Uncle El finished, craving quiet to manage this inner vortex. Now at home, my mind is quietening as my understanding dawns. Pure panic! Nothing more. I had let down my guard.

My Isaac's wise words seep back as I sit alone, the children still at their own Sabbath groups. I replay the arguments he gave to Magdalen: no escape possible; no mercy expected; we were treasure for the enemy to plunder, merely auction fodder, or a shapely wench or innocent child to satisfy their lusts. Of course I cannot hand over my loved ones to be slaves. I have no doubts.

I think ...

Day 60

Magdalen was subdued late this afternoon. Abigail, whose son found the escape cave, is choosing to remain on Masada. "We will be caught," Abigail had sobbed. "Far better to be dead." This has spread ripples of doubt among the other escape widows. Magdalen remains unwavering, so much so that I lost my temper.

"I am not a silly ass," she said, quietly answering my "stubborn donkey" jibe. "We will be kept safe, just as he has always protected Israel."

"Safe!" I had exploded. "When the Romans sent us scurrying from Jerusalem in fear of our lives, were you not also running? What has changed between then and now?"

"Me."

She hardly sounded the word. When I continued to glare, she elaborated. "Me, Mary; I have changed, and we will be free. Of this I am now even more certain. These last few weeks have made me sure, and my friendship with you, Mary, has helped."

The last words punctured my swelling indignation. I had no clue as to what she meant, but my temper collapsed in uncertainty. I also remembered all that Magdalen had done for me and the children. Maybe what we now needed from each other was not rage but a little kindness. I also suspected that my outburst was caused not by Magdalen but by my closeness to my earlier dithering panic.

"How have I helped you, Magdalen?" I matched her quietness.

"These last days have shown me that you will not judge me too harshly, even if I tell you the truth of what and who I am."

I stayed silent, remembering yet again that I was totally ignorant of her past. It was blank before running into her as we fled Jerusalem. Some of us had rounded a corner only to find Magdalen struggling with a donkey harness twisted around the shafts of her cart. She looked exhausted. I felt I had to help her alongside my children. Both Magdalen and I ended up in her cart, together with young Gad, whose short, stubby legs were weary. The other four ran ahead, and so we soon caught up with the main flight group led by Eleazar.

I had arrived safely on Masada with all my children, mainly thanks to Magdalen. She had repaid my small help a hundredfold. Despite her advancing years, she had continued to devote her limited reserves to protect, marshal, and amuse my brood. I think I loved her as a friend before the first week was out.

I had often shared my past with Magdalen. I recalled my first meeting with Joseph at our betrothal and related how I had been proud to be promised to a well-regarded youth, how we stood strong against Rome's domination, especially eight summers before, when he helped to plan our first war against the Romans.

"What about your family, Magdalen?" I had asked more than once. She had subtly sidestepped my curiosity, though she had let slip that she had been married with two young children. Something in her manner told me they had not survived. She had arrived alone in Jerusalem the year before our flight.

I also knew she was not like other Jewish women on Masada. She could certainly detail her Jewish lineage, but her attitude toward our rules and laws was shockingly relaxed, even while she was more devout in other ways. She always took a full part in our Sabbath, yet with extras: she smiled a lot in our services, and the interminable readings from the old scrolls made her ancient face light up.

"Of course I will not judge you, my dearest friend." I had smiled with encouragement, though I still wondered if I really should leave well enough alone.

"I should have told you long ago, but I could not risk it." Magdalen was solemn. "We were thrown out of our synagogue once, and they whipped us. Some even wanted to stone us to death."

"What had you all done to be judged so?"

"I then lost my children." Magdalen went on as though she had not heard me. "Then my husband was burned alive. They coated him and some of our friends with tar one afternoon and hung them on walls in rich men's gardens. Once the sun set, one after another they were set on fire to illuminate evening orgies.

"Mary." She had looked at me with gentle pleading, asking for understanding. "This all happened because we told people what we were, and this is why I always ignored your questions about the past. At times you must have thought me most rude."

"Of course not." I ignored the shadow it cast over our relationship. "But what could you have done or been that was so terrible?"

A voice called, "Hello, inside." I almost screamed in frustration. Much as I was growing to love the man and much as I was always glad to see him, Isaac's timing could have been better.

"Later." Magdalen had smiled and then left as Isaac entered.

CHAPTER 20

Rapping and Doodling

Dave Jackson viewed his embryonic Old Testament doodle in the top left-hand corner of his clean white blotter. It was vital that he finish it before the end of the day.

Genesis, Exodus, Leviticus—they're the first three.
Then comes Numbers, and already
we're at Deu-ter-o-no-my.
They're pillars of foundation,
Tales of Israel's formation,
Consecration of God's special nation
To be a worldwide sensation
As a light to every other nation.

His filing cabinet bulged with other squiggles of ideas that, for him, were scribbles of safety. They were his secure retreat from the messes of life, those happenings that hurt too much to dwell on.

Last night was one such forgettable occasion. Colette had texted in the afternoon from the airport to say she would be free for dinner. It had been wonderful to see her after so long. He had high hopes for the evening, but nothing took off. In fact, the reunion had fizzled out on a hopeless low. Now, Colette teased or tore at his mind. There was only so much of that he could tolerate.

"Now, where was I? Ah yes." He spoke into the still air of his study and then carried on scribbling halfway down the blotter:

<blockquote>

So, hit me again from the top.
I mean the Pentateuch.
That's the Torah—a God-sent law book.
Genesis equals beginnings;
Exodus, escaping and law-giving.
Leviticus is rituals for a people sinning.
Numbers gives God's chosen ones healthy living,
Winning wars led to their Promised Land winnings,
And right back to Deu-ter-o-no-my.
I said
Deu-ter-roan-o-my,
Due to Mose, you see.
That's Moses to you and me,
God's Superman doing his last big preach;
That's Deu-ter-o-no-my!
Big Mo's last will and testament, see?

</blockquote>

He says, "Here's how to be,
This is how it is to be,
So that God's OT people may stay free,
To cross more Jordans and Exodus seas, see?
"To be or not to be"
Is not to be an Israelite query.
God leads them through a dried-up sea
To be no team B, man.
In a Promised Land, they're to be the cree-am!

"When I'm with you, Dave, you're never with me."

Colette's cold accusation echoed in a distant recess of his mind, even as he wondered if his English students would dig his use of "cree-am." Half his mind conjured a frosty picture of his wife across last night's dining table, while the other half recalled the "don't give up the day job" jibe from a student who had sampled one of his previous biblical raps.

Colette's titian-framed loveliness had eventually burst through to command his whole undivided attention. Once again he mourned her loss. Her absence from his life hit him afresh. Gone was any chance of scrambling back into his safe mental haven.

"Oh, you're there in the flesh, Dave, but your mind is—" his beautiful wife had shaken her head in frustration—"God knows where."

Then came a litany of blame: "Your eyes look in my direction, Dave, but never focus on me. You look right through me at times as though I'm nothing. We talk face-to-face and your attention is on some nameless ghost, six feet beyond me."

Dave had amazed himself at that moment of the restaurant conversation. Drifting into his mind's eye was a promising student's essay he'd noted in his college pigeonhole. He immediately raged inwardly, *Now is the time for your gorgeous wife, you raving great academic numbskull!*

It was becoming a regular inner self-rant reserved for those times when he most despaired of himself, of his childish inability to shut down the academic to make room for the equally vital domestic.

No, idiot! He caught himself arguing within again. *To make room for the* more vital *domestic hmm, yes that sounds more correct.* Dave never had majored in self-honesty, but as he had gazed at Colette at that moment, he could truly say she was the most important focus of his mind.

It had been more than three months since he had walked out on her. He had lost count of the months before that without any closeness, save for a disastrous coupling halfway through the night some months back.

Dave had enjoyed it immensely. They had touched as each turned over at the same time. She had sighed with passion in the old familiar way, and he had instantly responded. So too had Colette, with more sighs, much to his amazement. He could smell the Irish gold on her breath, but the touch of her was heaven.

It had been an extremely brief coupling thanks to Dave's enforced abstinence. At his shout of exultation, Colette had suddenly awoken and exploded from the bed, grabbing the quilt for cover.

"How could you?" she had screamed. Her sobbing anger included shouted words and phrases like "disgusting" and "hateful" and "being used all over again!" The following day he had arrived home to find two single beds.

At the reunion meal, Dave had gazed at her across the candlelit table, and again he loved the silky roundness of her cheeks. Her cocktail dress was full and flowing and hid her figure, but that was no problem. He could always remember her figure's lines and delicious curves. His gaze burrowed into hers, and he slowly felt they were really seeing each other in a deep and meaningful way. He had smiled with warmth, with wide-open eyes penetrating hers.

"Oh, for God's sake, Dave, grow up and stop the play acting!" his wife had flamed into his face. She had shot up from table, sending her napkin flying over the romantic candle, and then flounced off to the washroom.

Now, with his Old Testament rap well and truly on hold, Dave winced. He recalled gazing after her longingly, and then scrambling to dowse the suddenly flaming napkin on a blazing red tablecloth. Surprised diners watched with open mouths. Once again he glumly felt the guilt and injustice of the memory. For once he had really tried. He'd entirely blocked out that student essay. Sure—maybe a bit late, but, for heaven's sake, cut a bloke a bit of slack. Give him a bit of credit. He was trying.

Dave wanted to kick himself, but instead he fuzzed, willfully blotting out the incident with his blotting-paper doodles. Momentarily, as he sat now in his study, he thought he should spend more time perfecting the translation of his Masada scroll. It still needed much editing and polishing. There were still a dozen questions that needed his undivided examination. This, after all, was going to be a huge part of his future. This was going to make his name and reputation, without a doubt.

But then the blotter in front of him was filling up satisfactorily. He did have to get this rap finished for his next class.

All starts, would you Adam-and-Eve it,
In Genesis. You're a wise one to believe it.
Fallen humankind in a garden called Eden,
Ruining God's beautiful and complex creation,
Turning perfection to dirt and mud,
Causing—yes, you've guessed it—
one almighty mucky flood.

A new start out of Noah's ark, then Abraham, né Abram,
Followed by Isaac, Jacob, and son
Joseph, his dad's favorite man.
An amazing Technicolor trip down into Egypt,
Followed by slavery under a pharaoh's whip.

Moses to the rescue,
Through plagues of pests you

Just wouldn't like to know,
Like frogs and hail-like snow,
And bloody rivers, as you well know.
"Let my people go!"
proclaims the Big M-O,
Right there before the might of a stubborn old pharaoh.

"I'm leaving!"

Colette's voice had broken the harmony of the doodled composition. Dave was immediately in the restaurant once again.

He remembered her last sentences almost word for word. Suddenly, with Colette's farewell announcement, he remembered starting to concentrate hard while simultaneously realizing he was years too late.

"But where will you go?" he had blurted out, trying to win more time for his now focused mind to dream up a miracle.

"Well, now there's a surprise, to be sure," his wife had mocked. "You can actually hear things on the first asking? Sure, and here's me thinking that all this time you're in need of a hearing aid or two."

"Okay!" Dave put up his hands. "Point taken. So—where? I mean, who will you go to?

"Bridie has a spare room."

Dave had sat hunched in on himself, desperate for an attack or defense, or even a sentence that would put off what now seemed inevitable. All he had eventually managed was, "But we're married."

"Dave, I'm married to you, but you're not married to me." Her face had sagged in sadness, the red eyes slightly puffed and wet. "I speak to you and you're too busy talking through a lesson in your head.

"I kiss you, but you're making eyes at your job. And how do you think that makes me feel, Dave Jackson? Like a jealous God widow, that's how! You've turned me into a green-eyed monster coveting what belongs to the Almighty!" She spat the last words in bitterness.

Dave had racked his addled brain, feeling less Bodleian by the moment. Surely there must be a solution, some pastoral sentence that would explain this problem away. His futility still raged as Colette resumed.

"I tell you what's happened at my school, but you're lost in your college. Even tonight, you've hardly looked directly into my eyes, into me, into the wife you promised to love and to cherish. The only time in our marriage when I have your undivided attention is when your sperm counter reminds you of my existence, and even then it's rarely my eyes you look at."

His recollection of her walking toward the restaurant exit was so real that he shouted out his plea again: "No, Colette, I can change. I will change. See, I'm looking at you right now."

She did not falter, and walked off over the night lights of Oxford that were shining in the wet pavement.

"*No!*" he now shouted across his study, and screwed up his eye. Fuzz or fear? Fuzz or grief? He fuzzed, and then he doodled to distract himself.

And in any case, his well-practiced inner defense lawyer pleaded, *this Old Testament rap ain't about to finish itself in time for your next lecture.*

Callous cad! another inner voice shockingly screamed at him. *How can you swap from heart to head in an instant?*

He knew the answer. He had done it ever since his Brooklyn fire hydrant days, when the scream for his lost mother reverberated for hours within his soul. It was so painful that he had learned to slam a mental steel door shut to imprison his emotions at the first hint of hurt. The door took the form of his head getting busy with diversions.

He picked up his rap pen. He was forever seeking to give his trainee pastors usable tools for parish life. All those readying themselves to be "revved up" needed to rap through their history, or "his story," as one God commentator had coined it. All should know, by heart, the great divine romance at the heart of a tragically fallen universe, its Number One Person eternally in love with a host of self-appointed Number Ones, too caught up in their own selfish desires.

His inner voice echoed an ironic, "And what about your own romance?" But again the head took control, and his pen cooperated.

So runs a divine romance with few human morals,
Insults galore, and many, oh so many, a quarrel.
In Joshua, Judges, Ruth, and double Samuel,
Through the lists of Kings and Chronicles,
toward a promised Emmanuel.

Emmanuel—that's God with us, a promised messiah.
But long after Ezra, Esther,
And that Jerusalem-wall-building chap, Nehemiah.
God tries poems in Job, Psalms, and Proverbs—right on!
Even in Ecclesiastes and the Song of Solomon.

Isaiah, Jeremiah, and Lamentations
Are major prophetic protestations.
Then there's Ezekiel's environment,
And young Daniel tossed into a lions' den.
On and on rolls this divine romance,
Mirrored in Hosea's marriage to Gomer going askance.

Joel and Amos give other stern warnings.
And you couldn't accuse Jonah and Micah of fawning.
Nor Nahum, Habakkuk, Zephaniah, and Hagg-a-i,
Plus old Zechariah and that young Mr. Mal-a-chi.

Well, that's all for now, folks; that's all we've got.
But, of course, it's just the intro to
the almighty divine plot,
To save you and me from a fate worse than death,
Emmanuel—God with us—and you and me
Heaven blessed!

Not only did Dave want a usable rap for his students, but also he wanted to remind his charges that the Old Testament was the greatest of all love stories—*hesed* in the Hebrew.

All of his students turned up at college thinking that the old part of the Bible was crammed with wrath, wars, and floods. They had overlooked the overwhelming never-say-die, cruel-to-be-kind, disciplined kind of hesed loving.

"This tale of love," he was always impressing upon his students, "is the positive answer to all the world's negatives."

Now, the rap was done. His students had another tool.

"And what will you have, Dave?"

"Eh?" He swung around in his study. The question was almost audible. There was nobody save him, and a glowing laptop illuminating his doodled rap.

What indeed? his inner voice replied.

"Land of Hope and Glory" blared from his shirt pocket. He reached for his mobile without looking at whom the call was from, "Hi. Dave Jackson at your service." He tried to sound more cheerful than he felt.

"I'm expecting." Colette's voice was without emotion.

Dave stared coldly ahead, his mind immediately invaded by ugly scenes all centered on a kitchen table. An unfuzzable jealousy allowed only a strangled sigh when he actually wanted to scream.

"It's *yours*, Dave."

Still he could say nothing. Still the awful scenes flickered. Something in his chest wanted to explode outward and upward. He began rocking to and fro, trying to hold it down and in.

"Did you hear, Dave?" Colette's voice was edged with concern. "His wife back in Aberystwyth made him have the snip years ago. He can't have any more kids."

Dave still could not trust his voice. More, he could not trust his words, save one.

"Really?"

"Do the sums. The night before we got single beds? Remember?"

Dave's mind counted slowly. It faltered, and he started again. Finally, it absorbed an astounding possibility. Colette seemed to realize she needed to be quiet. Her husband's "really" had sounded hesitant, heartbreaking.

"But—" Dave exhaled with a silly grin that broke into half a giggle, still not having the faintest trust in anything he might add. He basked in the moment, thrilled that she had come back, if only on the mobile.

"I'm pretty sure I'm now in my—"

"Are you sitting down?" Dave blurted, his doubts buried as he suddenly remembered their problem pregnancies. "I mean, are you okay? You know, erm ... Oh my God, this is—"

"Dave, I'm well into my fifth month. You've been in Israel for three of them. We've passed the previous danger times, and so far, God help us, all's well. I didn't want to say before now in case ..."

"Yes, yes, of course."

"And last night in the bistro, you were just so infuriating that, well—" There was a pause. "Dave, we need to meet. We need to talk again."

I might score zero as a husband, thought Dave after they'd fixed a date and Colette hung up, *but fatherhood's a whole new ball game.*

He grinned at his reflection in the study mirror and then gently rocked to and fro. This time he was not fuzzing. Now, he dared to savor the role he had come to accept would never be his. Successive miscarriages had eroded the hope he had never voiced, hadn't been able to voice, in case it made Colette's suffering and loss even greater. He had had to be her rock, and in the end he began to act like one, unfeeling, cold, and unresponsive. Again, it was a way of escaping from feelings too tender to toy with, too sharp and cutting.

Now, he risked moments of dreaming of what possibilities lay only a few weeks away: his own baby gurgling in his arms, him smiling as the little one suckled on a well-scrubbed knuckle while teething.

He found himself reaching for his scroll with a strange thought. Yes, he had to distract himself. He couldn't get his hopes up too high. His daughter still had to battle for survival in a womb more used to failure than success. And yet set against this was the more hopeful thought: he needed to clear the diary, deal with the unfinished, make way for a new responsibility. No. He had to make way for the family responsibilities that he had ducked, make way at last for a mother who was his wife, his other half, whom he was falling in love with all over again.

He unfurled the scroll.

CHAPTER 21

Consummation

Ten of us wait at Gomer's gateway. We are all virgins, dressed in white with matching posies, all with gold-streaked lilies and irises woven into our tresses.

The immense stone gateposts marking the entrance to the kingdom of Diblaim boast plump purple figs carved in clusters with stalks delicately picked out in gold.

A distant Galilean mountain swallows the sun's last rays, and evening drops on us abruptly. Our lamps are topped with oil, ready to illuminate the path of the expected bridegroom. While we wait and gossip, we trim our wicks in the light of a newly lit flaming torch of tar.

We stand or sit in small groups of twos and threes, the young ones giggling and the older ones teasing and joking, leaving little for virgin imaginations to wonder about the activities that will soon occur beyond the garlanded front door at the end of the long winding path. Our task is to greet the groom and ceremonially light his way to his love. I stand a little apart as first virgin with the responsibility of official greeter.

"Flee!" I will want to scream as soon as my Hosea walks into the light. "Come within, you who seek your love," is instead what I have been persuaded to primly utter. This follows days of heated domestic argument and not a few mutterings on my part.

We will then light our lamps from a single torch and escort my brother down the path to a fate I would not wish on my worst enemy.

I still burn with resentment over my imposed ignorance of the ketubbah. The deceit that Hosi and Gomer have been legally paired in betrothal for years still stings, especially whenever I recall the scornful looks and the dismissive "You!" aimed at me by an insufferably superior Gomer.

How could she address me with such disrespect? What sort of woman would so mock her betrothal sister? Would she not rather have tried to make friends? It hardly makes sense. Was it jealousy because I lived with Hosi and she did not, or little-woman pride in knowing something that I did not know, or simply thinking she was a class above me? Maybe that small, pretty head behind those beautiful tresses has something wrong with it. Or did she detect from our earliest days my obvious dislike of her pretend-princess act in the court of the fig king Diblaim?

Whatever it was, I have now played first virgin to a girl who has only a distant memory of what a virgin is, and I had to officially present my dearest brother before eyes, which, quite bluntly, I would prefer to scratch out.

Much as I disliked missing the ketubbah betrothal, I now hated even more this evening's chuppah, the second stage in our marriage traditions. In this I was a small-part player, though still with some significance. This particular uniting or consummation was an insult to our beliefs and also to my brother. What was the point of uniting in one flesh with one man when this thirteen-year-old madam had done precisely the same with practically every other male in Safed?

Even as I fumed, a trace of guilt nagged at my exaggeration. First, she had only been known by worshippers at the White Temple and, as a young virgin, probably by a select few—more likely just the priests and leaders, who had first pick of the young ones. Finally, she had been in service for only a few months as her personal sacrifice to her fertility god.

In more generous moments, I did allow that many a young girl within the Baal community dreamed of becoming a famous kedeshah. Every year prepubescent girls would flock in their finery and with their parents to join winding queues waiting to parade before four assessors looking for perfect candidates with the right aspects.

The blame, I had to admit, did not rest entirely with Gomer. However, generosity of thought is rare for me when my brother's happiness is in danger. Most of the time, I resented her with a savagery that even I did not fully understand.

What irked me most as first virgin was my attendant role as witness. I was expected to join with observers of both sets of parents to stand outside the bridal bedchamber, awaiting the bridegroom's emergence and his triumphal presentation of the bloodied proof-of-virginity cloth. In a normal marriage, we would then have examined the item so that we could report evidence of consummation, and of the bride's purity, to both sets of parents at a later hour. The viewing of the cloth would have been followed by a ceremonial procession to return it to the bedchamber for the bride to keep safe as her trophy of proof.

In this sham of a marriage, there would be no virginity cloth. How could there be? Consequently, for this special situation, my role had been downgraded to the distasteful alternative of detecting evidence of completion. Following the act of consummation, I was to enter the bridal chamber to examine the bedding and then to exit with a detailed description, including the state of undress and demeanor of both bride and groom.

This, I had been assured by Daddies Beeri and Diblaim, would be sufficient to indicate that chuppah had been achieved and that Hosi and Gomer had passed from the nonsexual status of betrothed to becoming one flesh in chuppah, fully and absolutely man and wife.

Stage three of the marriage ceremony, beginning tomorrow, will also be hard to endure: escorting bride and groom from the rich realm of Diblaim to the more humble domain of our bakery rose garden, where the wedding feast is to begin.

Not only will it be a day's slow trek over or around steep hills, but also we will meet many who will accuse us of polluting the faith by marrying into a fertility cult. Remote villages still keep strictly to the God of Abraham, Isaac, and Jacob, and are prone to stoning prostitutes and those who associate with them. Of course, I will remain on my best behavior and lead my fellow virgins with put-on gaiety. Behind, the happy couple will attract an increasing procession of guests, previously invited to the wedding feast.

"The wedding must be believable for your dear brother's sake and for his God-given ministry." I again hear Daddy Beeri's oft-repeated insistence to me.

"But it is dishonest!" I had exclaimed in sulky righteousness. "It is not worthy of the One we follow."

"Not dishonest, little sister," Hosi spoke sternly, having overheard our words. "I love Gomer with an everlasting force, and I will do so until the day I die. This love is commanded. It is my act of will. It is my obedience, and it is now, after all these betrothal years, something within, a thing of the heart." He tapped his chest with gentle fingertips. His look told me that I had said more than enough.

The celebration feast will last from one Sabbath to the next. On the first day of our arrival, we will be welcomed by the whole village of Safed, plus assorted friends and extended family dotted about the Galilean hills. The second day, and overnight into the third day, will be for specially invited customers and business friends of both families. Our new fig and date cinnamon bread will take center stage, one of the main reasons for both families uniting through marriage.

"Are we not Jews?" Father Beeri had once again challenged me when I questioned why we were using Hosi's wedding to promote business. "And has the good Lord not blessed his people with sense and skill to make the most of what he has bestowed upon us?"

"Old prophet turns in a bold profit!" Even as it rushed out of my mouth, I knew I had gone too far. Unamused, Father sent his truculent bookkeeper to bed.

Days four and five will be set aside for religious and community figures, often one and the same. They have been celebrating the marriage ever since Diblaim descended on Daddy Beeri, rejoicing in it as a "deeply meaningful and wonderful celebration, not only of fertility, but also of our unity in worship and faith."

"Perhaps," one of our priests had said to Daddy Diblaim after one Sabbath meeting, "we may have no need to trouble either Baal or the Lord of Sinai for some considerable time. We all take great delight in such an auspicious marriage between leading figures of our two great religions."

I remembered being numbed at how easily this leading priest of Israel could bend our faith and culture just to suit the world around us.

"Too long have we been critical of each other," the high priest of Baal's White Temple had declared the day the wedding had been announced. "It is long past the time that we should have united our faiths and gods and become one. Together, we can more powerfully influence the fickle forces of nature, and with this happy union we can persuade our gods to assure fertility for our crops. Apart, we will die of thirst and hunger and famine. Together, we will prosper in the lap of our pleased gods."

"See, Hosi," I later challenged, "this marrying a prostitute will do nothing more than bring together the things you seek to keep apart. Now, even more of our people will queue to worship Baal and his child prostitutes at the White Temple. Do you not see that we are now making gods in our own image, carved out by our own selfish desires?"

Hosi had shaken his head. "My marriage, little one, will confirm what already now exists. Our people mixed the manna of our true God with the pagan yeast of Baal long before I was born. God has sent me as their last chance to return to him and stay alive as a nation. This is life or death for our nation.

"In this marriage and in the way that it is played out is the clear message that Israel's only hope is to return to her husband. If they reject the message of this marriage drama and refuse to return to their own husband, a terrible force will descend upon them from the North. They will be beaten and exiled from their promised homeland before being scattered across the world."

At the time of hearing those words, I had doubted.

How could my sixteen-year-old brother know such things? Why would a simple baker's son foretell such events when business was booming, with our combined date and fig company now beginning to rule Galilee and the hill country?

Certainly, Hosi might face up to towering mother bears, but could he really stand against the might of corrupt kings and courts and powerful robbers dressed in religious robes, not to mention a people happy to invent false deities just for an extra drop of rain?

I was soon to learn how strong my brother was and how wrong I was.

CHAPTER 22

"Stone Him!"

Life could not hurt more than betrayal and my holy brother's marriage to a prostitute, or so I, now in my thirteenth summer, assumed.

I was wrong. I have now learned that they will kill my brother as soon as they catch him. It is all because Gomer has given my Hosea a son and me a delightful nephew. The world beyond our ever-rising bakery is scandalized by the name he has been given.

People I have known all my life have begun to pick up jagged stones and weigh them in their hands under my nose.

Daddy Beeri is not helping. He mumbles promises from the psalms, a sure hint that our earthly father has run out of human ideas about how to protect his family. I chide him.

"No, Daughter!" he answers. "This is good! We are only strong when he"—and here Daddy reaches upward—"is at the center and we rely on him. We are weak when we act alone, thinking we know it all, when we are merely ignorance on legs, guided by fickle feelings."

I am most certainly still at the feeling stage, so I storm off in disgust at these pious words starved of action. They seem about as flat and useless as my father making bread without dough. What precisely I want of him I have no idea, but it is most certainly more than his present mumbling about nothing.

Sometimes, I do secretly wonder if I am that much different from Gomer. She felt she could twist her god to her way by flashing her eyes and giving her body to men. I feel I can, with a flash of emotion and by applying sheer willpower, whip my God into line to do exactly what I want. My will be done. Both Gomer and I seem to make mini false gods in our own image and according to our own feelings. If all this makes you think I am ranting like a budding preacher, then blame my teacher.

Right now, I want a supergod bigger than all of us, one who will swoop down and make things right. Most of all I want him to protect my brother from his own stupidity. Hosea has put himself and maybe us in great peril with his months of highly critical preaching all over Galilee. He has blasted the corruption of priests and kings from Lake Kinneret, or Galilee as they are now beginning to call it, up to Dan and the border with Syria. He has also ridden, and sometimes hidden, up by Lebanon and Phoenicia and the Great Sea.

Naming his son Jezreel was the ultimate insult to royalty and religion. As a direct consequence, he has now become Israel's most wanted villain.

Even as Daddy mumbles his spiritual poetry, I do understand that all good Jewish girls should share their parents' faith, especially in the great psalms of the past.

"Have we not a thousand and one poems and stories of divine rescue from raging waters and wildernesses?" my father asked, chastising me. "Has not our Maker rescued us countless times when we were outnumbered by hordes of wild tribes who wanted nothing less than our total extermination?"

And yet my father seems to forget that this danger involves my beloved brother. It is his life on the line, maybe ours too. I still want to scream back at Father that it also includes a Lord who has commanded my brother to stride into death's presence with a message and a marriage that both threaten to topple every pillar of Israelite society. Since the wedding, increasingly I find my faith stretched. I do secretly wonder if this God of the Israelites knows what he is doing.

A week ago, chariots brought men with swords and spears from the royal court. Long-bearded priests came with them, brandishing scrolls to prove beyond their own doubts that my brother was a false prophet whose words and actions were endangering the whole of Israel.

"Treason!" they kept shouting when Daddy Beeri tried to explain that his son was only passing on what he believed had come from the Lord. "Drag him out and stone him!" But Father politely explained that such a course would be difficult, as his son was on a preaching tour of the hill country toward Lebanon.

"Hosea cannot be allowed to jeopardize our unity," one of the priests said, waving his heavy scroll. Silence blanketed a growing and growling crowd. "We have worked long with our Baal friends to ensure rain for our crops. Are not our barns full, and do we not enjoy a land overflowing with much milk and honey?"

"We do!" yelled a mob of stone carriers.

"And are our purses not also bursting with our hard-earned shekels?" A roar of approval rose up. "We live in open-minded times when we can all work together and create our own prosperity. Each of our ways is valid; each of our religions strives toward the same truths. We cannot allow close-minded prophets to endanger our future."

The crowd clapped their stones loudly, their minds so open that they were eager to close any other that disagreed with them.

"My husband is not here."

Silence fell. I was amazed that Gomer had emerged from the bakery to face such a hostile crowd, especially holding her tiny son, the cause of their anger.

The second surprise was that she still held such power. Seasons had passed since her short kedeshah reign, but still she commanded respect. Insulting a temple maid was the unforgivable sin of abusing Baal, as good as waving good-bye to future rainy seasons. My amazement was mixed with something I had never before felt concerning Gomer: gratitude.

When "You," as I mischievously had started to call her after the wedding, came to live with us, we survived with an absence of outright violence. Just. Our eyes remained bright and unscratched, though they were occasionally dampened in private frustration. I was expected to share my kitchen with a prostitute who still thought she was a princess, so royal she did not know the difference between boiling and baking. I was not happy.

"You!" she had continued to call me. On one occasion she had actually used "You, first virgin!" In my own home! I do not know to this day how I kept hold of the stewpot that I was carrying.

It was my right to put this fourteen-year-old madam firmly in her place, which was definitely nowhere near me, no matter the stern looks from Father and Hosea. And here was my main irritation: Hosea treated her like he had once treated me, only better.

I thought he loved me. But no. It turns out he really does prefer this strange creature he has married. He treats her not as the princess she thinks she is, but as the queen of our house. Every moment he is not away preaching, Hosea talks and listens to this madam, laughing at her jokes and following her silly gossip. He puts her first and foremost, even before his own flesh and blood. And Gomer loves it. She blossoms and beams before him. I hate it. I hate her. I detest Hosea for demoting me below a prostitute.

Gomer and I had kept up our sullen insults for many months, until the evening an emergency stopped us once and forever. Her enormous stomach lurched visibly, making her scream out my name in panic. I felt elated. I had won. I was supremely satisfied with this great name-game victory, almost dancing around our stone oven in delight.

181

Half a dozen happy hops later, it dawned on me that this ecstatic occasion might also be imperiling my unborn nephew or niece, so I eventually rushed to help Gomer in her doubled-up agony.

That night I tended to Gomer's every need, purely because of the precious contents within her. We were two frightened girls clinging to each other by necessity. She lay in the glow of several torches on the bear rug draped over my teaching stone, just as my mother had done. I cursed my brother for being away, trying to convert the city of Dan singlehandedly, while struggling to recollect his description of my birth at this very spot. I tried desperately to recall what he had done to ease my passage into this world.

I sobbed with mixed emotions: fearful I might kill my own kin with a wrong move, yet weirdly nostalgic over my own birth and gulping inexplicably over the loss of my own mother. Then, finally, a flood of total joy burst over me as my nephew slurped out of the writhing, screaming Gomer. My bloody waiting hands cradled him and placed him on Gomer's chest. She and I grinned at each other in sheer relief.

A new civility was born from that enchanted moment.

"Hosea will not be back for a week." Gomer now stood unblinking before the stone-carrying crowd who were baying for a target. I was amazed by her confidence. She hushed the rabble by her princess determination and her past status.

"No doubt, it is my son's name that brings you?" She turned inquiringly to the soldiers, who were shuffling with uncertainty. "Please go from this place." The charioteer commander stood firm. I could see the toe of his left sandal begin to tap rapidly. He seemed to be winding himself up for action.

This one will never leave, I thought. How could he back down now?

And yet indecision did delay him. Should he ransack the place as a lesson to all who challenged the king? Would that offend the gods and the priests at the home of a still-respected former priestess? What would best bring success to his mission?

The hush stretched out. Gomer and soldier glared, their stares as fixed as the teaching stone between them. The eyes showed nothing more than the flickering yellow torchlight. No crowd had ever been quieter; there was neither a shuffle nor a cough, nothing but stillness.

"Perhaps," he finally jeered, "I should take the traitor's son who dishonors us all." An audible intake of breath made the commander flinch. More uncertainty added ticks to his face. He knew he had gone too far. The standoff continued.

"Enough!" the commander eventually snarled, and then swung on his heels. "We will be back!" he barked over his shoulder. Gomer and I stood together, hardly believing. Stones tumbled out of hands. A leaderless mob shuffled and began to turn away.

"What about the name?" I whispered to Father as the last soldiers, the chariots, and the crowd were lost to the night.

"Jezreel was not the best choice," said Gomer, overhearing.

"But it's such a beautiful valley. All our wheat and barley is grown there, and—"

"Shh." My father waved toward the bakery. "The night has eyes and ears. Do you want to hear this, Gomer?" my father asked in a loud whisper as he closed the door.

"I will hear your version," she answered, gently settling her sleeping bundle in a manger by her bed.

"My son is now in an extremely dangerous position," Daddy Beeri said, nodding. "By naming his firstborn Jezreel, he is telling King Jeroboam II that the his royal days are numbered."

"That's treason!" I exclaimed.

"More than that." Daddy Beeri sighed. "He is foretelling that Israel is to be destroyed by a powerful invading military."

"But how can my nephew's name kill my brother? The whole thing is madness."

"You have to understand that Jezreel is a bloody blot on our history," Father answered. "This is where our royal family once lost their crowns and their heads after encouraging Israel to run off with foreign gods like Baal. God commanded an army general called Jehu to remove the royal family, but Jehu went too far. He chopped off many more heads than he should have, and then waded through a bloodbath to seize the throne. Once in power, he ignored the pagan god problem, allowed the shrines of the vanquished to stay in business, and ran Israel as his own.

"In God's eyes, Jezreel stands for all that was rotten in the state of Israel, a constant reminder of how faithless Israel has been as his marriage partner.

"Kings and people had turned their backs on him once too often. God therefore commanded your brother to prophesy through his firstborn that the divine marriage would one day end because of Jezreel. The bride would be thrown out of the Promised Land."

"Do you see why they want Hosea silenced?" Gomer interrupted gently.

I looked at Gomer and wondered what was going through her mind. This former priestess of a foreign god was quietly nodding her head to a tuneless hum over her son. I wondered yet again how she coped with her fall from near royalty in Daddy Diblaim's palace to become the wife of a wandering preacher.

"What about you, Gomer?" I asked hesitantly. "How do you feel?"

"I will be lost." The words were flat, giving no hint at her feelings. "I will be a widow with a child to support." It was something to which she was already resigned.

I think it was this day that Gomer decided her future, one that did not include us, or her husband, and certainly not our God.

CHAPTER 23

Emotions Run High

Day 61

Tragedy has struck. There is no time for anything beyond supporting bereaved families. We lost seven of our finest young men last night.

Many feared this as our youth increasingly demanded action. More and more they hated the ban on playing near our new defense wall, especially with increasing noise of construction echoing up from the other side.

A few evenings ago, we celebrated the coming-of-age of our thirteen-year-olds, in what has become known as bar or bat mitzvah, meaning "son [bar] or daughter [bat] of the commandments [mitzvah]." It marks the moment the oaths of our offspring become legally binding, and when our youth become men and women answerable to the law.

Two of our bar mitzvahs were involved in the group of boys whom we had sworn to secrecy in our early days on Masada. Impatient with old ones doing nothing, they and others had descended the Snake Path to spy out the land for a possible attack.

That is all we know, thanks to one bar mitzvah who had stayed on Masada. Lookouts saw the group descend and then heard the cries of a short battle. It is certain they are either dead or captured.

If only they had spoken up, we could have saved them. Some of our strongest and fittest soldiers had tried the route and found that the path ended up in the middle of enemy tents. I cannot write more tonight. I am too exhausted from dealing with bereaved parents.

There was no time to seek out Magdalen to see why she has been so afraid to share her past with me. It must be something awful. There is no time even to add to my Hosea story. With events like today's, I pray God will provide time to finish it.

Day 62

Emotions on Masada run high. Waiting for death makes us weary, and the loss of our young men brings our own deaths to the fore. We held an emergency meeting today of all available adults, and Eleazar spoke with courage. He was on fire for our cause, stilling many dissenting voices. I suspect it will not be the last time he has to do this.

The meeting settled on an oft-debated subject: how best to kill with loving-kindness. It seems a crazy sentence to scribe, but we have to be practical. Many have approached the leadership, anguishing over how to carry out the lightest of evils.

"With children, we think it is best done either when they are in their deepest sleep or, if that is not possible, in a tender embrace," my executioner Isaac had explained at the meeting. "If it is during the day, take each of them aside so that you are unobserved. Give them the longest parting hug, and when they are relaxed use your sharpest knife hard against the neck. Kill swiftly with all the strong love you possess."

This is so hard to scratch on this scroll. I will have to do this five times with my precious ones.

Some parents continued to be anxious until another instructor partnered Isaac in a demonstration, using a blunt baton. It all seemed distasteful, and yet, amazingly, some were not satisfied until they had practiced on each other with sticks.

"My friends," Isaac finally advised, "when it comes to your wives and other family adults, you must talk this over between yourselves. Some may wish to do it in a tender embrace, as with the children, though there is greater difficulty with strong adults. Even though our minds accept what must happen, our bodies and emotions will struggle hard for survival. The leaders strongly recommend a well-honed sword well swung. This is the least painful and swiftest method. If you cannot do it to your beloved, you may call on the leadership, which includes expert swordsmen."

This was followed by lessons on the best use of the sword, exercises that eventually led some to break down in tears. Many needed all the emotional support we could muster. It was most distressing, and yet, strangely, many found it helped. Knowledge and practice appears to have given them confidence about the lightest of evils.

This evening, once my children had retired and before I started scribing, Isaac and I strolled over to the new wall to look down on our enemy. Their many fires and torches appeared to reflect the host of shimmering stars in the blackness above.

"We should talk of how we will do it," he said gently, though his deep voice cracked on the word it. I knew my answer. It should come in a gentle embrace. No: I must be honest in this diary. I also want a long and lingering kiss before the final act. There! I shock myself even in the writing, but this is no time for conventional modesty.

The truth is plain. In the two months since Isaac became my executioner, I have grown to love him as I once loved the precious father of my children.

It is a different emotion. Isaac is a unique man, and the situation we are in is unmatched by anything I have known. Even I am a changed person. Yet it is love and it is deep. It seems strange to scribe in view of our circumstances, but I cannot envisage the rest of my life without him in it, even though it is now measured in days and hours. I would not want a life without his presence, his words, and his ways. He is a blazing beacon banishing my darkness. He makes me laugh, even giggle, and that is so precious at this time.

Of this he knows nothing. He behaves with faultless kindness, still my husband's best friend. Oh, I so wish he were more. I so desperately want to tell him, with a warm and loving smile, that I want to die in his arms.

"Perhaps," I said, smiling up at him and feeling the dishonesty in what I was about to reply, "we should think on what we have heard today and then talk another time."

I could do no other. Isaac seemed strangely disappointed. Yet how could I go on and burden

him with the embarrassment of having to fend me
off after all he has done for us?

Day 63
A great day!

A huge cheer and much whooping filled the high
plateau as we spontaneously and rather unwisely
expressed great joy that there had been a collapse on
the northern ramp. It is a massive stay of execution,
giving us maybe another month. Of course, wisdom
should have muted our response, because our
youngsters were immediately eager with questions.

"The games!" was Eleazar's swift response. "We are
going to find the champion boy and girl of Masada."

All adults close by immediately caught on. Within
an hour it had developed into something that would
rival the coliseum games of our enemy, or even the
Phoenician Greeks and their Olympic efforts.

"You will draw it all together, Mary, will you not?"
I looked at Eleazar. Quite suddenly, the reprieve lost
its shine.

"Is it not good to know that we shall live longer?"
encouraged Isaac later as I grumbled under a full
moon that needed no help from torches. I glared
at him for not understanding my extra workload.
He simply shrugged with a wry grin. "Who knows,
the exercise might finish us all off and save us the
trouble. If not, then we shall at least die healthier."

I grimaced at his black humor, but my reply was immediately stifled by his next comment, which was what really made this day great.

"There is something I, er, need you for." Isaac paused awkwardly and took a deep gulp of the dry heat. "Well, not just for me. Er, maybe it would help you also, erm." His face uncharacteristically reflected indecision. I waited and wondered.

"Sorry, Mary. Not making much sense, am I? Would you … er …" A word-stumbling Isaac was new to me. "Mary, I know Joseph was …" Again he faltered. I leaned forward, smiling upwardly with wide-open eyes and nodding encouragement.

"Oh, Mary, this is such a mess. Look, I will say it, and if it is shockingly wrong, then forget it." He took a huge breath and blurted out, "I love you. I think I always have."

Half my mind had been thinking of how to plan the games. All of it now focused on words that I thought I would only ever hear in my own dreams.

"Will you be my wife?" I was shocked, delightedly so. "Say yes, Mary, and it can happen tomorrow."

Day 70

There was little time for scribing once Masada cheered our news.

Soldiers, death pacts, and even Sicarii vs. Zealot infighting vanished amid wedding celebrations.

We Jews adore our love feasts, where normal life and, yes, even death are banished from conversation and consideration. True, metal and stone could often be heard clashing as Rome's ants scurried to rescue their collapsing ramp, but this cheered us all the more.

In bequeathing this, my tale of love, to a mad world, I never suspected another's love might also save me. This diary already has enough of my affairs, so I simply report that Isaac's arms and bed and manly strength have greatly changed me for the good. We are promised until death do us part.

Of course, that is now a few short weeks away, and again I must fulfil my vision. The sister's story must go on.

CHAPTER 24

"Not My Children"

The day Hosea named his third child Not Mine was the day I came closest to hitting him very hard.

"Well, he is certainly my nephew," I screamed at him. "How can you treat such a precious bundle so cruelly and still preach about hesed? You and your heartless God know nothing about the true meaning of love."

Jezreel I had come to accept. He might be a reminder of Israel's godless and murderous royal court, but he also had the name of a pleasantly green valley—and he was the nearest I would ever get to having children.

My chances of giving birth were nil now in my nineteenth summer. Baker and accountant with much to inherit I may be, but my face is as plain as our flour.

Offers had come. A wrinkled Ethiopian silk seller wanted to add variety to his concubine tent. I was invited to make free with his silken bolts, but I declined. Daddy Beeri was delighted to retain his bookkeeper and cook.

In Safed, with the young men all either betrothed or married off, the best I might attract is an old man looking for a servant-wife to keep him clean, cropped, and free from constipation, or maybe a poor young male on the lookout for a rich catch and a kept life. The first would probably have given me no children, and the second was a price no woman should have to pay.

Being an aunt would be the nearest I would ever get to mothering. It was possibly this that generated a special disgust at the manner of naming my nephews and nieces. Even now with them grown up, I find it hard to understand, let alone forgive, my brother.

After recovering from Jezreel, my brother named his second child Lo-Ruhamah, meaning "unloved." She was a beautiful, cuddly bundle with black curls and deep violet eyes. How could he do that to my little niece? The breaking point for me came when

Hosea disowned his last son outright by calling him Lo-Ammi ("not mine"). He made me doubt once again all he had ever taught me.

By then, I was in complete charge of the bakery, with father's ailments multiplying and Hosea's preaching taking precedence.

I firmly believed I had seen the real world far more than had my brother, with his head constantly buried in sacred scrolls. He had even dared to scribe a few divine thoughts himself, claiming that they came from the God of our fathers. He was now calling himself, and acting like, a prophet, one of the most exalted callings in our society. Prophets can be stoned, spat on, and even sawn in two. However, they and their words commanded grudging respect. An oracle who had consulted with God is many steps higher than a baker. My bread feeds mere bodies, whereas prophets provide the food of God.

However, this head-in-the-scrolls preacher-brother of mine had to be told in straightforward words that he was in danger of losing the audience he most craved.

This, I believed, had become my exalted calling—keeping my brother's feet firmly on the paths of earthly Safed. I told him straight that once the people realized how he was treating his own children, they would simply stop listening to him.

"Not so," Hosea had once calmly replied. "I know exactly what I am doing, and so would you, my sister, if you allowed your mind to rule you instead of a silly heart."

"Silly!" I shouted back. "You call it silly to disown your children, silly to make them feel unwanted and—"

"You are wrong."

"What about, O mighty one?" I was no longer his little pupil.

"They ..." Hosea paused as though too full to speak. "They are not mine!" I was instantly cold. I glared at a brother who was becoming a stranger.

"Have you gone mad?"

"The children are not my flesh and blood." Hosea was speaking calmly, his wretched eyes pooling around as they looked unblinking into mine. "At least not the last two."

My mind floundered with jumbled half thoughts. Not their father. So did that mean I was not their aunt? I was now shivering. Half ideas wriggled and nibbled at the edges of my memory, insistent for attention. Then, quite suddenly, Gomer's words rushed to the center: "I will be lost."

That was it. No thought for Hosi on the night we feared he might be killed for criticizing the king over Jezreel. It was all about Gomer. Her position! Her suffering! Gomer once more putting herself first.

"I will be a widow with a child to support," she had added. Lost in her own selfish world, had she begun to doubt her husband and a future with him? Had she gone further and acted upon it, done something beyond being his wife?

More substantial suspicions that were previously subdued now thrust themselves into full-blown allegations. Gomer's trips back to Daddy Diblaim during my brother's preaching tours had been questionable. Some had even claimed to have seen her around Safed at those times. Had she always gone home to her daddy? I had often quenched such anxieties, being only too delighted to look after Jezreel and, later, my niece.

"Sorry, Sister." Hosea's quiet voice startled me. "Perhaps I should have been gentler."

I nodded, but my mind reeled around Gomer's absences, her prostitution, the children, angry kings, and the night they had come to get Hosea. Nothing was making much sense.

Gomer had a husband who doted on her and treated her like royalty, much to my annoyance. Of course he had to travel away from time to time, but when he was at home Gomer was his focus and his first love. He was her ever-patient listener, her caring husband. She never wanted for anything. Many was the time I walked away in disgust from just watching him hang on her every word as though she were the most important person in the whole of the Levant.

What made a woman who had everything decide she needed so much more?

"You look lost." Hosi smiled at me. I nodded. "The children tragically have a part to play. Their names may even save our nation of Israel!"

"How?" I spat out in loud distrust, my natural defenses immediately rallying around my nephews and niece.

"Remember the divine marriage on Mount Sinai?"

"Your precious God betrothed to Israel!" I sneered.

"Yes, and then the bride running off to play around with other gods?" My inner whirl slowed as I forced myself to concentrate on familiar territory. "I also explained that I was commanded to marry a prostitute and live out a drama that would teach God's bride what she was doing to her heavenly husband. Well, is it so difficult for you to see that Gomer and the children are part players in the divine drama that illustrates Israel's adultery?"

"What!" I cried out in disbelief. "Using our little innocents to …" I halted, so appalled that words deserted my fogged mind.

"…To save Israel!" Hosea said, finishing off my sentence, though not with the words I had in mind. "It is the hesed of which we spoke. Hesed equals tough love. Hesed is a divine husband's love. Sometimes strong love must do hard things to prevent further evil. Sometimes the lover must be hard in order to protect a wayward loved one."

"Play games with your fancy words if you must," I said, acting as icy as the waters of Safed's cascades in winter, "but surely not with the lives of our innocent children."

"Not games, Sister!" Hosea seemed he would burst into tears. Then he shouted, "This is my life. It could mean my death. This involves the woman who is my life, who is about to be torn from me."

"No, Hosea!" My reply was untouched by the tears spilling by his nose. "This is playing with people's lives. Worse! You and your God are abusing defenseless children."

"Hesed!" pleaded Hosea. "God is taking desperate steps to get the bride's attention, to provoke a loving response before she is lost forever." I turned away, and he pursued me. "Sister, the terrible truth is that our country is heading for disaster. For generations, she failed to hear words of warning and acted deaf and mute. Prophet after prophet was ignored or whipped out of town. Maybe Israel will see the truth if it is acted out under her nose in a real flesh-and-blood family."

I stood my ground, blind and deaf to anything but the welfare of the children.

"This is so wrong, Brother. This is the old flood-the-world deity," I snarled back, unresolved doubts of childhood exploding to the surface. "This is the God who brutally drowns everybody, save for Noah's family, to teach humans how to obey him. This fire-and-brimstone deity destroys towns just because their people ignore him. His spite flattened Sodom and Gomorrah. This God of yours has killed off thousands for daring to worship a golden calf at the foot of Sinai."

"Come on, little sister, we have often studied this, and—"

"Don't you 'little sister' me. This God of yours has slaughtered thousands in rescuing us from Egypt. This murdering monster then told us to invade the land promised to us and wipe out every man, woman, and child. He sends plagues to punish and sickness to whip his people into submission."

"Would you rather he—"

"He loves his violence!" I spat venom like a viper, giving little chance for Hosea to answer. "This God's *hesed* story is all about using us humans in his games, and this time he has gone too far. And you, my sad, deluded brother, are this maniac's mouthpiece on earth." I stood panting and sobbing. All the old questions and doubts I had ever entertained rushed in as I fought for my nephews and niece.

"Today I am going to tell Gomer to leave," Hosea said flatly. No emotion. Amazingly, it was as though he had not actually registered one word of my rant.

"What? Just throw her out?"

"To show Israel what she as a nation can expect. Remember, I warned that her divine husband would throw her out of the promised homeland if she kept flirting and having affairs with other gods."

"What of our children?" I wailed.

"They stay," he said quietly, yet he looked at me with appealing eyes. "I was wondering if you would step in to look after them?"

"Why don't you throw them out as well?" I hurled the sarcasm into his face.

"I am not the monster in all this, Sister. Please!"

With a suddenness that shocked me, my anger melted into peace—a selfish peace. The children were going to be safe! I was going to be able to mother them.

I immediately felt like the she-bear that Hosi had faced down in the shrines. The mother bear suddenly realized that her cub was safe and that she had all that she wanted. I stayed quiet. I simply nodded acceptance lest I betray my elation. Not daring to show the smile, I beamed within. My brother's face was open and grateful before he turned to walk away. He had taken half a dozen steps when he turned back.

"*Would you really prefer a God who did nothing to stop babies from being sacrificed in blazing fires?*" I said nothing, wondering where he was going. "*Are you happy for him to stand by and let priests lob infants into the flames?*"

"'*I am not!*" I snorted with shock.

"*Well, then, perhaps you are content for God to allow our young girls to be turned into prostitutes and raped every day in temple worship?*"

"*That's a horrible thing to say.*"

"*Should our divine Lord smile and do nothing as priests become thieves and as kings rule the land that he gave them without even asking his opinion?*" Hosea waited for a reply. He looked to see my expression. I turned away.

"*Sister, do you think God should let his priests line their own fat purses and rob the people of justice? And if this God did absolutely nothing to stop all this terrible evil, would you not then criticize him for being the very Devil himself?*"

I shook my head. I was in no mood to play obedient student. I stormed away, happy at least that the children were mine.

I never did see Gomer before she left. It did cross my mind that I would have liked to tell her that her children would be safe, even though I was not at all sure she cared.

CHAPTER 25

The Bride's Fate

Ten summers were to pass before I next saw my sister-in-law. She was tied to a slave trader's stake in the middle of Safed souk.

Thankfully, none of the children were with me to see how their mother's pretty looks had faded. Her skin was yellow and bruised, and many of her teeth were missing.

Safed's women mocked this madam who had entertained their menfolk. "You!" they screamed, splattering her face and tunic with rotting fruit. One or two ex-customers, pretending to be buyers, prodded and felt her as though she were a suspect vegetable. All reveled in the downfall of this princess of the Diblaim dynasty, remembering how her father had disowned her after she opened her backstreet brothel.

Before long, I spotted my brother standing on the other side of the square. My chest swelled with emotion as I tried to imagine his state of mind while watching the final degradation of the wife he had never stopped loving.

"You are well rid!" I had often scorned into his mournful face. "You should be truly grateful that the wretched woman is out of our lives." If I am truly honest, I must say that as we both watched Gomer from our different positions, I swelled a little with pride at being proven right. Now, he would at last see what I had seen in Gomer all along.

What happened next whipped the tongues of gossips into a headlong gallop. For days it became the first and only topic of conversation along the highways of a scandalized and mystified nation.

After his and Gomer's five years of marriage and a further ten separated, I fully expected Hosea to turn away or maybe join in the fig throwing. Surely she deserved to be left to decay in her own mess, if only for all she had done to her children, my precious ones.

I could never have predicted what happened next.

Hosea walked slowly toward the slave stake to stand gazing at Gomer with a sad smile. It was a soft look, gentle as the love I had for the children, even when they were naughty.

"I'll buy this one," he said. I felt my legs buckle under the shock.

"Ooh, very smart buy for you, that one, Your Honor," an oily trader groveled. "I would be giving her away below fifteen shekels." The trader, wringing his hands, quickly added, "In silver."

For a normal, healthy female slave, the trader would have started at fifty shekels, grudgingly resisting being bartered down to the going rate of thirty. There was nothing normal now about Gomer. Whoever bought her would probably soon have to bury her. A ten-shekel price tag would have been robbery.

Gomer, to her credit, looked as shocked at Hosea's words as I was. Her husband touched her cheek as lightly as a passing butterfly and then whispered something to her. She quickly nodded and whispered back.

"Hey!" The trader stepped between them. "No talking. No pawing the goods either." He pushed my brother back, sneering. "Buy, or be off and waste somebody else's time."

Gomer tried to croak something from her parched throat, but the trader raised his whip high, only for

Hosea to catch hold of the flails and wrench the whip from his grasp.

"You'll pay extra for that," the trader said, snarling. "You want her? Then add a homer and another half of barley."

"Done." My brother nodded and, with this, threw the coins before the trader together with his whip. Then he beckoned one of our bakery workers to come forward with a large sack.

"The price paid in full." Hosea smiled as he withdrew one of our sharp baking knives from his robes. The gathering crowd immediately gasped, and then rumbled in loud murmurs as Hosea swung away from the trader to face Gomer. She cowered, whimpered, and pulled away to the end of her tether, choking as it tightened about her neck.

"Go on," cried an old woman in the crowd. "Finish her off, holy man. Miss High and Mighty deserves all she gets."

"Yeah," shouted another, "slit her scrawny throat!"

Hosea reached up to Gomer and, placing a hand behind her neck, drew her to him and back toward her stake. A swift upward stroke cut her free. He threw the knife on to the pile of silver and barley. He swept his bride off her feet and turned to survey the crowd of open, silent mouths.

"My wife!" He quietly smiled and then picked his way in my direction between shocked neighbors and souk traders. He looked happier than I had seen him in years.

"Come on, Sister," he called upon catching sight of me. "It's been a good market for us today."

CHAPTER 26

Lunch with Colette

Early for his midday date with Colette, Dave strolled across a newly painted bridge spanning the last reaches of the Oxford Canal in Jericho. He gazed down through its latticed sides at a green and red sixty-footer gliding beneath him, and he idly wondered if the man leaning against the stern rail, his left arm draped casually over the tiller, had the same domestic problems as he.

Dave's eyes moved to the woman he assumed was the boatman's partner. She proprietarily fussed at a healthy crop of geraniums in a shiny copper cauldron on the prow. Around it, neatly and safely wrapped, was the front mooring rope. He wondered if she had ever been unfaithful enough to tend another man's flora.

These days, he mused, *everybody's at it. Why should I expect to be so different, so hurt and jealous?* But he was. This was personal. This was not wayward impersonal society reveling in extramarital affairs and making a profit from them on its small and big screens. This was about his heart, his life, and now his precious child.

He wondered about building a sermon on the subject. *Idiot,* he thought, immediately scoffing at himself, *forget work, why don't you? Mind in wife mode!* he mentally commanded. His ill-disciplined head still amazed him. He could easily understand Colette's claim to be married to the lodger, in and out without much communication or commitment.

His mind now firmly fixed on his own love life, or lack of it, he quickened his pace off the bridge, cut through a cobbled courtyard between the fashionable maisonettes, and rounded the corner into a street of age-stained Victorian terraces. He was still ten minutes too early for his rendezvous, yet there was his wife standing across from him outside the Swan and Royal and looking in the opposite direction.

He grinned, thrilled that she too had made the effort to be early. He looked for signs of a small bump but was disappointed by her coat loosely flapping in the early autumn breeze.

"Silly chump," he chided himself aloud. "Only five months gone and she's three hundred yards away!"

He had not rehearsed precisely what he would say, but he was pleased with the general gist of his thoughts. He would be measured and appropriate in mentioning his hurt, though he wouldn't speak of it too much. He feared another angry walkout.

He would certainly include his willingness to forgive. There would be an offer to start again, this time with perhaps a little courting and quality time thrown in for good measure. Again, he would try his coup de grâce: the prospect of their renting or even buying a two-bedroom Jericho property in Canal Terrace, just yards from the Swan and Royal. With a child on the way, surely she would be eager for the best nest.

He would again express his delight at the baby. This would be genuine so long as discreet enquiries regarding paternity were answered convincingly. Perhaps a DNA test. Hmm, that would be sensible. He was surprised at how quickly he had arrived at this rational approach to a most difficult situation.

No longer did he care to dwell on the nightmare negative. Fading these days was the "I'll kill her" nightmare—well, at least in his conscious moments.

Approaching Colette with warming anticipation, he now recognized again a number of surprising truths. He had missed her more than he ever thought possible. His three-month absence had proved this to the satisfaction of his analytical mind. His heart was very much in agreement. In fact, he had reached the stage where he could not imagine life without her. He had grown accustomed to her words, her presence, and her face. He almost hummed this last thought, quietly chuckling at the thought of being a modern Professor Higgins, anxious that his missing Eliza Doolittle was no longer his fair lady.

Dave was convinced that all would be well so long as he kept his temper, was gentle about the past, and remained positive about the future.

He had one more security in the deeper, more devious vaults of his mind: divorce would be a messy alternative in a theological college, even in these enlightened days. Of course, unchivalrous thoughts would remain locked away, never to emerge, lest coercion or manipulation be suspected. However, it was there. He was content to let it remain in quiet repose for the time being.

"Hello, Colette," he cheerfully called out to her back as he drew near. She turned and nodded. No smile.

Poor girl's obviously distraught about being with child but without man or home. This assumption made him feel generous, especially because recent events allowed him to be so. Ethics Man was even now packing his bags, as he was no longer required for an autumn term that had sadly attracted far fewer students than anticipated. Caractacus the adulterer would soon be a hundred miles away, battling for the ethics of Aberystwyth.

Dave noticed how sad and uncertain his wife looked. His heart expanded with affection. As she turned, he reached out to embrace her, but she carried on pivoting toward the pub door, saying, "We'd better go in before our table goes." Dave, wrong-footed and off balance, almost teetered into the gutter.

"Trombone table?" she called over her shoulder.

"Fine," he called back as he struggled to recover his poise, before meekly following her through a bar lounge mounted with dull, unpolished ancient musical instruments. They were trophies hunted down in countless car boot sales by licensee George, who boasted of once being lead bassoonist "up north" in the Manchester Hallé.

"I think we should try to make another go of it." Colette suddenly looked up from the menu after settling. "Mine's the lamb rogan josh; the meat's so tender here." The adjective did not describe her clipped tones. His list of topics now in disarray with Colette taking such an unexpectedly masterful role, Dave stared back.

"Your mouth's open." She at last smiled, but with no warmth. "Have you seen your favorite, the mixed korma?" Dave glanced back at the menu. She added, "Well, it makes sense, doesn't it?"

"What, the korma?"

"Keep up, Dave." Colette sighed. "In a little over three months, we're having a baby. For her sake, I believe we should make another go of it."

"*Her sake!*" Dave leapt to his feet. "It's a girl!?" The trombone above him could not have blared louder. "I'm going to have a daughter?" This last sentence was delivered an octave and a few decibels lower as Dave responded to his wife's cringe of embarrassment.

"Is that good news I hear?" George popped up from stacking mixers under the bar. "Did you hear that, everybody? A great booming voice has just announced the patter of tiny feet."

The odd cheer went up from some regulars at the other end of the bar, drowning the scattered disinterested applause of visiting diners. The couple nodded awkwardly. Colette glared at Dave, while lunching businessmen and others quickly returned to their plates and purposes.

"Well, it was shock!" Dave hissed as he at last resumed his seat. "Is the tiny one all right? Are you okay? What's the due date? Will my little one cope with a Rogan Josh?"

"Now my turn." Colette impatiently slanted the large menu in her right hand to tap his lips. "Look!" she said, sliding a black-and-white grainy scan across the table with her left hand. "She's fine. I'm fine. The Rogan will be fine when my body's dealt with it. And before we go on, we need a few ground rules."

Dave nodded in agreement, aching as the widening grin on his face competed against other emotions that threatened to crumble his facial muscles. Even his eyes had moistened at the corners.

"The single beds stay."

Colette's voice was hard and her face straight. "We're doing this for the baby we have created and for no other reason."

Dave's facial muscles now united to tighten his jaw. He no longer felt like crying.

CHAPTER 27

A Drunken Mother

"This child," Colette said, jutting her chin toward him, "will grow up knowing she is loved, knowing that she was, and is, desperately wanted."

"Of course, but—"

"You don't love me, Dave." Colette obviously preferred monologue to dialogue at this point. "And even if you do have feelings for me, your precious Old Testament students and college come first. You have made that abundantly clear over the years. You use our home like a hotel, with me as the receptionist. You pop in to eat or change or sleep before rushing off in a new direction. Well, you can make love to your other mistresses by all means, but not to me as well. The single beds stay, right?"

"I do love you and—"

"Words, Dave, just words." Before he could contest this, she called out, "George, two diet Cokes with lemon on the rocks, plus a rogan and a korma, plenty of hot naan. And we'll be after having a generous tub of your delicious mango chutney." She answered a couple of George's menu queries and then swept back to Dave, who was wondering what had happened to Colette's Irish whiskey. Had pregnancy put a temporary or permanent cork in it? He was framing a mild query on the subject, but he ran out of time to ask.

"And there's one more thing you need to know, Dave. I've changed."

"I can tell that already." Dave smiled back. "As far as I can see, you've changed into, erm, well a—"

"Christian!" Colette stuck her chin out in a familiar take-it-or-leave-it pose. This defense mechanism he knew well. When she offered something suspect or open to challenge, she always led with her chin, defiantly inviting anyone to have a swing.

"Er, you're already one of those," Dave punched back, following up with, "Don't we go to church? Don't we say our prayers? For God's sake, Col, we're in a theological college, teaching others how to be Christian pastors and minsters."

"A proper one, I mean." The chin still led. "A real one."

"You're not making sense." Dave's voice had lost its edge. Now it was tinged with nervous concern.

"I had some long discussions on the subject and—"

"With...?"

"Erm, well, with friends who know—"

"Caractacus?" A fleeting hesitation confirmed Dave's worst fear.

"Yes." Again her chin was leading. "He was telling—"

"*No!*" The word came hard and commanding. "There is nothing that man can teach me about Christianity after what he has done to us. I cannot believe you are actually quoting him."

Silence reigned, save for the clink of distant plates and utensils and the low hum of neighboring conversations. Colette stared down at her place setting. "God's inside now!" her tiny voice whispered.

"What?"

"Dave, you can truly be sure that this is nothing to do with him." Her voice was soft. "Look, I just got to the end, so I did." Whenever emotions rose in her, so too did her Irish brogue, and the old idioms and phrases of home increased. She took a deep breath, knowing that more would be needed to alter the red and angry face before her.

"I looked over my life and it was like gazing down on a bomb site, so it was. I had a drunk of a mother who loved her dead baby boys and a bottle more than she loved me.

"She knew exactly what she was doing when she chose death instead of looking after me. My useless dah then flitted to another country and ended up further away than even my ma in her grave. Then, to top it all, I ended up sucking the same shameful bottle as my mother, all because I married a brain as big as the Bodleian Library that couldn't even figure out that a simple Irish colleen just needed to be loved and cherished and listened to.

"Look." Colette's face creased with concern as she saw Dave bristle at her last point. "What happened shouldn't have happened. And, yes, I feel as guilty as hell itself. For what it's worth now, Dave, I am sorry I have hurt you. I truly am. Believe me."

There was a standoff silence, mainly because Dave could not trust himself to say anything helpful at that moment.

"You must know that I drank because I was hurt," Colette continued. "Every relationship I've ever had branded me as unlovable. I drank when rejection churned my insides to quivering jelly. At those times, a tipple of Irish was my only anesthetic. It flooded me with confidence to the point where it no longer mattered what people thought of me. I was me. I could be mean. I could be nice. I was free to be whatever I wanted to be, to be myself. Everybody else was free to be what they wanted to be, and they could go and hang if they didn't like what I chose to be.

"The drinking slowed when we started seeing each other. There was hope, real and beautiful hope, Dave." She was pleading, her voice cracking with the emotion. "The way you looked at me at first was wonderful." The voice rose with the last sentence as she squeezed her throat to stop a sob.

"I felt cherished, truly loved. But then it slowly and painfully dawned on me that I'd married a carbon copy of my parents, someone who loved just about anything and anybody before me."

Her voice had fallen to a whisper and she juddered to a halt, trembling a little. Visibly shaking her body, she added, "To you I was a—oh, I don't know. I really, really don't know." She shook her head, gazing into her lap, and then rallied. "To be sure, I don't know what goes through your big useless brain most days."

"Well, I don't think that's—"

"And then this wreckage of a marriage exploded all over again, this time with my stupidity." Colette talked on, seemingly oblivious of his attempted interruption. "I took pity on a charming Welshman who was old enough to be my father, because he listened to me, Dave! He actually cared about what I said and thought. He looked into my eyes and it was me he was looking at. Somebody cared. I counted as a human being in somebody else's life. Suddenly, incredibly, I was significant. Can you not imagine what that felt like?"

"And what's this Christian thing?" Dave barked, trying to move the subject on to less personal areas, selfishly hoping for something less stressful.

"You were off in Israel digging or something. You had left me mentally before you physically vanished altogether. Oh, I didn't love Carac. Not like I'd loved you." Dave flinched at the past tense of the last phrase.

"I was flattered that he cared. I was sorry for him being far away from his family. I was on my own, he was on his own, and most of the time we were tippling and chatting.

"One night after Carac had left, I was so desperately unhappy that I did what probably most others would do. I cried out for somebody to help. God! Anybody! I even shouted out, 'If you're up there and real, now would be a really great time to do something to show it.'"

"And ... what?" Dave's half chuckle sounded hard. "You saw a sudden blinding light?" He winced at his stupid cynicism.

"Nothing." His wife looked up at him. "Nothing at all happened." Dave saw that her chin was now less rampant. She seemed more relaxed, even happy.

"I fell asleep. I woke up the next morning smiling. No hangover. Somehow, I knew I wasn't alone. I knew there was more than me in the room. Between me falling into that drunken stupor and me coming round, something had happened, and it, erm, he, hasn't left me since."

"What? Who?" Dave listened intently, fearing what was coming.

"I am loved, Dave." She smiled peacefully.

"Who loves you?" Now Dave's jaw jutted forward. He was immediately on the wrong wavelength.

"The One who made me." Colette smiled, nodding her head to encourage him to get his mind on the right track. Dave merely shook his head. His wife rushed on. "He offered me all the quality time I never found on earth. Guess what I said, David Jackson?"

His answer was a worried frown. He cleared his throat, slightly embarrassed at such talk of a personal god.

"I shouted a very loud yes and asked Jesus into my life."

Dave's discomfort was now complete. He had never appreciated people using the name of Jesus in what he

considered to be an overfamiliar way. It sounded weird and a bit over the top.

It was the same every time he came across this holy lingo, a regular occurrence in theological colleges, especially with every intake of new students. Always, the "born-againers" were out to show everybody within earshot that they were saved and had guaranteed lodgings in the mansion Jesus had gone ahead to prepare for them.

He had even had some of the same secure feelings himself as a kid after going forward to give his life to Jesus at the Captain America Church. But then, the drug-running days followed. Belonging to the Brooklyn Brothers' street gang somehow seemed more important than staying loyal to his Jesus brothers. As the gang's only white, he'd had to beat up more than his fair share in lower Brooklyn—both in and out of the gang—just to prove he was worthy of membership.

When the judge gave him his second chance, assigning him back to care of his church pastor instead of jail, Dave had given God his second chance. He read the Bible, said his prayers, and attended church, but he never again felt Jesus had saved him. How could he, after doing such terrible things? How could his record simply be wiped out? Not even his mother loved him enough for that. She didn't even love him enough to stick around. Could a heavenly father do more? Born-againers and even some parts of the Bible claimed he did. Somehow, Dave had his doubts.

He had reckoned from then on that any acceptance could only be earned, whether in the church, among his mates, with the Captain America family, or anywhere. He had to deserve love. This was one gift that wasn't free. Doing stuff about God's Old Testament book had seemed a surefire way to please him. Dave, working his way to God, was just thinking how he really disliked these Jesus-loving, happy-clappy born-againers who had salvation and heaven all sewn up, when he suddenly became aware of Colette talking again.

"And what I mean when I told you that God's now inside me. Before, he was outside. Before, I was my own small god and alone: scared of death, scared of living, scared to be unloved, terrified of loving." Colette reached across the table to touch his hand, but Dave withdrew it.

"I was the center of my own world, and it was scary. When he came in, everything began to fall into place. He took center stage. I could let him take over. Things you and others have preached about, God's Son, Jesus, forgiving Mary Magdalene's adultery; him dying on the cross to pay the penalty for all my rottenness; him crying out at the end, 'It's finished,' just before he died on that horrible cross. He'd finished the job he came to do. He'd paid the whole penalty for my wrongs, for what all of us have done wrong. That's how much he loves me—"

"Great." Dave tried to sound reassuring, attempting to conceal his worry. "Glad you got something out of my sermons, but I wonder if you're not taking things a little too literally and—"

"And if he's paid for my sins," Colette said, her excitement overriding his interruption, "that means I know I'm going to heaven to be with him when I die."

"So that's what all this is about!" Dave snapped, hearing an echo of what Ethics Man had tried on him the first night when Colette had invited him for a chat.

"That fella's been filling you with his own weird brand of theological garbage, and you've fallen for it, just like you fell for him." Dave was now towering above her with surrounding diners looking nervously in their direction.

"Here we are, my hearties." George abruptly appeared from the kitchen with two steaming plates. "Who's the Rogan?"

Dave swung away, marched past George, and stormed out of the pub.

CHAPTER 28

Of Women and Death

Dave shot out of the Swan and Royal, turning right onto Canal Street.

Long before he reached the latticed bridge, he was running hard and had scorched a mile of towpath before his lungs complained of ill-treatment, another of his strange ways to fuzz. Physical discomfort could always mask deeper pain.

Gasping lungs reeled him to a standstill. He reached out to steady himself on a berthed narrow boat. His legs, cramping with lactic acid, lowered him to his knees, which in turn collided with the taut mooring rope so that he lost balance and rolled flat on his back, fighting for more air.

"You all right, love?" a pleasantly flat Northern voice asked from above. He looked up to an incredibly tall figure

with her head up near the clouds. "Wait there, dear," the voice commanded kindly, "and I'll be down to help."

He then realized it was the narrow boat's geranium lady he had seen before his pub lunch. She had paused in concern while mopping her roof.

"No!" Dave gasped. "No, really, I'm okay … run too far … carry on … thanks all the same." By this time, Dave had scrambled back to his knees, in which position the strangest of temptations struck. Looking up to Mrs. Mop, he wondered if she might share the secret of precisely what drove her mysterious gender.

God made woman from one of Adam's ribs, so the Good Book had informed him. Dave wondered if this was why woman now had a driving need to reorganize the other 99.9 percent of man. And if Adam was, as the Good Book also stated, set over woman, then why was new man forever looking up to her? Why do men pray their wives will never change while women prey on husbands until they do, and then have the nerve to complain that they're no longer the men they married? Dave was sure that came from an Albert Einstein quote. And if Einstein didn't know the ins and outs of the opposite sex, what chance had Dave?

The mop lady, propped up with both hands resting atop her handle, was now looking at him with serious concern. He heaved himself up, quaintly touched finger to forelock, and smiled his farewell.

Women had always been a mystery. During his fire hydrant vigil in New York, he had watched women go by and marveled at their assorted shapes and sizes. He had had accidental lessons on female anatomy while putting to bed his befuddled ma, especially when things that he didn't have flopped out—and one or two things he did have seemed to be missing from his mother. He had no idea if this was unique to his family or if all females were minus essential parts. His only certainty was that such wisdom wasn't to be had sitting on a fire hydrant.

Gangs and high school eventually corrected or further corrupted his knowledge of biology, but the sum total of his varied upbringing gave him few clues as to what drove this increasingly attractive yet puzzling half of the human race. Colette had been his first real dating girlfriend, and he had married her without much preparation and thought. He knew as much about getting on with women as the Western world at that time seemed to know about mating Chinese pandas in captivity.

His reverie stumbled as his foot jabbed again against a towrope peg. Recovering, he realized he had already passed Worcester College Lake. He broke into a trot across Walton Street and continued trotting toward Balliol College and the Bodleian Library.

Bodleian brain. He shrugged at his wife's crack echoing in a memory chamber. "How can a Bodleian brain not see that pots don't climb from work surfaces into dishwashers on their own?" or "Why can't Bodleian Brain see we can't afford a new car before getting a decent apartment?"

He promised himself that he would one day undertake a doctoral dissertation on the mechanics and mysteries of the opposite sex. This problem pigeonholed, Dave turned to another urgent matter—Colette's father and his demands. His college boss had ordered him to focus on far more urgent matters than attending to his wife, O'Hara's daughter.

"Planning the next two years and saving the college's bacon" was, according to Dean O'Hara, the only appropriate occupation for their minds.

"To be sure, Dave, are we not sitting on a gold mine in literati terms?" Dean O'Hara had enthused in his study two days before. "Your team's find in that faraway cave is going to help turn around this college's fortunes, and you, my dear Yankee son-in-law, are just the man to do it for us."

"Your daughter, Dean, is not with you or me on this."

"No worries, Dave." He had waved aside the issue. "She'll soon come round with a new home and a baby to occupy her. What you've got to do, my lad, is concentrate on first-rate research into these scrolls."

"It's not that easy, I'm afraid."

"Nonsense!" the dean had butted in. "I'm cutting your work schedule to make it easier."

The dean was in full arm-waving, man-management mode, brooking no argument. "I'm working on our falling numbers, and you and your find form a big part of our strategy. We need first-class, well-publicized scholarship on these scrolls. We need you back out there in Israel ASAP. The most important tools for textual critics are the original manuscripts themselves, not computer images. You need to double check your translation—"

"That's not going to—"

"No! Hear me out, Son," commanded the dean. "A couple of months may be fine to get the general gist of the scrolls, but from what you have given me, your work is too hasty. We need accuracy. We need good scientific work that will stand up to ruthless scrutiny by our peers, and I'm going to make sure you have all the time you need."

"Dean, there's much more to it than easing college schedules." Dave had taken a slight pause for breath before launching his full counterargument, but the dean had jumped right back in.

"As you know, other experts are tied up with the main Dead Sea scrolls. There's still a massive amount of work to do with those, even after half a century or so, and, to be sure, they're not about to hurry on to your discovery. Your scrolls are going to languish for months, maybe years, in Israeli vaults, awaiting some graduate student hunting for a juicy thesis, especially so because the scrolls are not related to the Bible like many of the other finds.

"What's more, we urgently need to counter the skeptics. Can we take this scroll seriously? Is written anecdotal female evidence acceptable when there is so little record of women's previous involvement in this area? Could the scroll be, in fact, a more modern venture? What of date testing?

"Dave, you've got to go back to where the original manuscripts are. We might not be able to test-date papyrus accurately, so you need to go on to the fallback position of examining the way the text is written.

"You and I both know handwriting changes within cultures. You'll need a good paleographer working alongside you to compare your scroll with others that have known and accepted datings. At the very least, we can hopefully place your scroll within a century of its being written. Get that done, plus a more accurate translation, and you, my whiz-kid son, will have a new book plus a PhD, and the college can greatly enhance its glitterati."

Dave, having lost a chance to step in when the dean momentarily paused, was quietly wondering why he had, all of a sudden, become the dean's "son." Why had "in-law" been amputated? He was about to raise the issue of Colette again, but he was too slow.

"Two years from now," his boss said, beaming, "we'll have students queuing down the drive." Dean O'Hara's arms were raised toward his ornate study ceiling for the crescendo of his argument.

"Dean, do you want an unhappy and divorced daughter, or do you want more students?" The dean's arms waved downward in disgust. "That's your choice, father-in-law. You sent me off to Wales with your college loyalty argument. This time, that's not going to happen."

"You can't seriously turn your back on all you've worked for, Dave." The dean's hands had now balled into fists. His next sentence was menacing. "This is not why I took you on in the first place."

The Bodleian Library was now far behind as Dave recalled the colorful language that had boomed from his father-in-law's office as he left.

Despite standing firm against the dean, Dave found that part of his boss's argument still tugged. Academically, he should be well advanced on plan A, ascending smoothly toward the heady heights of literary fame: one book already acclaimed, and now the fruits of two scholarly years on the scroll to establish further recognition.

"Dave Jackson, PhD" had a fine ring to it.

Emotionally, plan B had now gained the upper hand. Colette and a baby girl ignited his passion as nothing before had ever done, despite the Caractacus thing and even that recent pub row. Handling crumbling scrolls somehow didn't compare with cradling a newborn daughter or with the possibility of once again embracing his Irish colleen.

And there was yet another influence.

Just as a lion is the product of all the lambs it's digested, so Dave saw himself as the end result of all he had ever read and experienced. Even so, he was still surprised at how an ancient scroll had impacted his modern soul in just three short months.

His inner being was being reshaped, or maybe *repaired* would be the better verb, he thought. Already, he was aware of looking back with less anger as he recalled his fire hydrant days and a mother who barely qualified for that title. The cynicism born of his survival-of-the-fittest trek through Brooklyn's jungle of gangs and drugs was also softening.

He was now even regretting storming from the pub. Maybe he had overreacted. Perhaps his wife's amateur theology was not just a parroting of the lothario lecturer. After all, much of what she had said of a new relationship with Jesus chimed harmoniously with his own childhood experience at the Captain America Church and the beliefs of the pastor whose love rescued him from his fire hydrant hell.

Even the scroll echoed his wife's beliefs. It unfurled a kind of loving that had no strings attached. It was pure, actual love, not love wearing a selfish masquerade. Hosea, for example, actually loved a wife who ran off with other lovers. He loved because he could do no other thing. He loved because a God of love was his model. And as far as God was concerned, no matter what this human bride did, Hosea could not help himself.

Actual love loved. It could do no other.

The god of Dave's upbringing actually didn't love, or so he had come to believe. His god only loved him if he deserved to be loved, if he behaved himself, if he kept the commandments. Maybe Col was right. Maybe the real God did love no matter what.

One thing was becoming certain: pre-scroll, Dave knew himself to be a loser. Oh, he could pass a few exams and had a book to his name, yet he was a junior tutor in a failing college with a disaster of a marriage who couldn't even father children successfully. He also had a God he didn't like: an Old Testament taskmaster who expected him to meet his standards of excellence. In this, especially, Dave was an abject failure.

Post-scroll, well, actually, he was still trying to puzzle it out. Certainly, if actual love—hesed—was right, then Dave was actually loved and accepted. He was truly—

"Excuse me, sir." Dave suddenly became aware of a little old lady with an angel towering over her left shoulder. She was smiling apologetically and clutching a bunch of drooping autumn sunflowers. "I don't suppose you carry a penknife?"

Dave patted his pockets, knowing full well that he had never carried such a thing in his life, and noticed that the stone angel had wings outspread and was carrying a black marble tablet with gold inscriptions. He realized he had wandered into Headington Cemetery, just by the North Circular Road.

"Sorry, no." He smiled back. "What seems to be the problem?"

"My arthritis can't cope with the florist's knots."

"No problem."

As he worked on the knots, some of his wife's earlier words of life and death came back to him. They seemed to tighten up the eternal knot that was forever within him, and his new surroundings didn't help. Death was a fear that had always gripped his innards. *Have I done enough? Surely turning my collar around might stand me in good stead. Have I helped enough old ladies to cross the road or to untie their knots? Have I pleased the One I'll have to face eventually after this life?*

Immediately, he was back in his love-with-strings god. He thought how he had used people, had abused Colette, and had never really given himself fully to her or others, always standing apart, comfortable with his own company on the fire hydrants of life.

A sudden, overwhelming envy caught hold. He coveted Colette's belief that all her sins were dealt with and paid for in full. He wished he too had a divine light that could wipe out his dark side. Headington Cemetery, he thought, must be such a peaceful place for those with no fear of death. This old lady had a peace. Death appeared to have no sting for her. He handed back the untied bunch of flowers and cheerfully waved away the old lady's thanks.

As he strolled, his scroll's characters again came to mind. Hosea walked with God and had no awe of death; Magdalen likewise. Maybe Colette after all had the right, victorious approach to death. Maybe he needed a rethink. Maybe.

He walked out of Headington Cemetery the same way he had entered it: not much wiser, though wondering if the scroll's characters and their stories really did have some guidance for him. He rehearsed yet again in his mind the time Hosea and Gomer had been reunited.

CHAPTER 29

Sorry

"What did you say to her?" I pressed my brother again after he ignored my first three similar queries.

The slave market was far behind as we reached our rose garden. He was still cradling a frail Gomer in his arms, and I was simply showing sisterly concern as to what each had whispered to the other on their first meeting after ten long summers apart. When I quizzed Hosi in this way, he often suggested that I risked losing the most prominent part of my Jewish face by sticking it where it did not fit.

"I asked her if she wanted to come home," he replied, humoring me.

"And she said?"

"She began to cry. She nodded and then kept mumbling 'sorry' over and over again."

"But how did you know she would be sold today?" I pressed him as he tenderly lowered his now-sleeping wife onto their old marriage bed of goat skins. How could he possibly know? The bakery took his days when he was not off preaching; he never listened to gossip and rarely went to market.

"An inner voice mentioned it." Hosea spoke as though this idea was as normal as breathing. He hummed to himself, obviously satisfied with his morning's work, and then added, "The same voice that first told me to go and marry a prostitute." He kissed Gomer on the forehead and then folded a soft kidskin to tuck beneath her bedraggled head.

"Go again and show your love for a woman caught in adultery."

My Hosi hesitated, as if remembering the exact words. "You must love her just as I still love the people of Israel."

"How do you know it was God?"

"Am I not, my nosey sister, a well-practiced prophet?" His pleasant face wrinkled into a teasing smile that tugged his beard to one side. "This is my job. You mother your nephews and your niece, and I mother Israel for her divine husband."

A ghost of a groan rose from Gomer. Tired agony was etched in the weathered crevices around her sunken eyes. Words must wait. We had a patient close to death. For the remainder of that day and the next two, we fought to keep life within a wrinkled skin containing bones and little else. We shared the nursing over the next two weeks. Even Daddy Beeri helped when his aging bones allowed.

Occasionally, my niece would peep between me and Hosea to gaze upon the frail frame that was her unremembered mother. She giggled when I first told her that she looked just as pretty as her mother had on the day I had been her maid of honor. I had renamed this precious child Ahuva; the one Hosea had originally named Lo-Ruhamah (Unloved). My name for her meant the exact opposite. I loved her as my own.

My two nephews, Jezreel and Not-Mine (later I renamed the second one David—meaning "beloved" and, therefore, "accepted"), showed as much interest in their mother as Gomer showed about life itself. She spurned much of the food, though she did sip our mixture of goat's milk, honey, and figs enhanced with delicate herbs and spices.

Outside the sickroom, life had never been more vital. The whole village, and people from beyond, streamed by our rose garden daily with necks at full stretch. The shelves of our bakery shop were bare of all but crumbs by midmorning. For once the fame of our breads took second place to the crowd's expectations of a long-overdue public flogging, perhaps even a bloody stoning.

"No respectable Jewish husband is going to forgive and forget the Levant's greatest-ever scandal," one old woman cackled as she passed by.

"He wants revenge," another called back. "You mark this: there will be a public thrashing in the souk before the week finishes."

In the humdrum sameness of our hills, this was the biggest news for a generation. The shocking saga was packed with royalty and power, played out against the backdrop of the late King Diblaim's still mighty fig industry. There was money and pretend-princess Gomer's adultery, subjects guaranteed to keep campfire gossip aglow long into many a night. This was also payback time for a holy man who constantly threatened others with divine punishment for their sins. Some even came in caravans of camels from neighboring towns to see these greats of Galilee tumble in disgrace. Surely there would be at least some public punishment.

"If your dog misbehaves, you beat it, but you slit its throat for a repeat offense," one scavenger shouted down our bakery path.

It was a whole month before the baying crowd got answers to their gruesome speculations. It came the day Hosea left the bakery and began to walk toward Safed souk. Gomer was nowhere in sight, yet still the neighbors followed. Long before he reached the market, word of mouth had swelled Hosea's following to crushing proportions.

Disappointment swelled in the crowd as Hosea took a left turn away from the stoning pillar. Apparently, Gomer was not to be dragged out and flogged this day. Murmurs of excitement took over as the prophet walked up toward a fresh batch of slaves tethered at the same post from which he had redeemed his wife.

"The Lord has an accusation to bring against the people who live in this land," he roared out across the crowd. An embarrassed, sandal-shuffling hush descended. Curious whispers swept from one to another, mainly led by a gaggle of priests who seemed offended that somebody not of their cloth or calling was preaching.

"Listen, Israel, to the One who brought you to this land, who gave you everything you now have. 'There is no faithfulness or love. The people do not acknowledge me,' says the Lord. 'They make promises and break them; they lie, murder, steal, and commit adultery.'"

"You vomit words," screamed out one of the priests, "like the back end of a camel spews." A roar drowned out the heckler as the crowd's anticipated entertainment appeared to deteriorate into a religious gathering.

Hosea raised his arms. Perhaps, after all, there was still hope of fun. A reluctant quiet hum blanketed the people.

"What shall I do with my wife?" These shouted words were immediately rewarded with complete silence. "Some of you want me to hand her over to be stoned to death. Others want her stripped naked and flogged. No doubt some would then be happy to throw her to Safed's wild dogs." Hosea paused, letting his words ring around a crowd of leering, nodding heads.

"You see justice in that." Hosea's head turned to take in the throng. "It is what she deserves, so you claim. But let me ask you this: what of your adultery, my friends? What do you deserve?

"What does justice demand should happen to you? What of the bride of God who runs away to other lovers such as Baal? What should he do when you offer your newborn babies to the greedy flames of Molech?

"What should your husband do when you talk to the trees instead of him? You chop down a cedar to make furniture with one half and then build a wooden god with the other."

A low rumble of dissent rippled out from where he was standing.

"Let no one accuse the people!" Hosea shouted, and suddenly the rumble subsided. He had won another brief reprieve. "The Lord's complaint is against you priests." A thousand heads turned to follow Hosea's pointing finger.

"Yes! Flog the priests," one man screamed.

"Preach it loud, Hosea!" one woman called out.

"They cheated me of everything when my husband died," called another. And with this, cheers mixed with jeers echoed about Safed market. Hosea again raised his hands, asking for silence.

"'Night and day you priests blunder on,' complains the Lord. He says that you priests have refused to acknowledge him and rejected his teachings, and so the Lord rejects you." Another great cheer went up. "The more of you priests there are, the more you sin against God. You grow rich from the sins of my people, and so you want them to sin more and more."

Even I joined in the cheers from the edge of the crowd. Moments before, I had feared for my brother's life, and mine too. Now, suddenly, he was the people's champion.

I knew from bitter experience the unholy rackets of the priests. Whenever we went up to Dan or down to Bethel to offer sacrifices, the animals we took were refused. The priests ruled that only perfect specimens could be sacrificed to a holy God. Only their animals were given the stamp of perfection. One moment they sold a cow or pigeon for a fat profit, and the next the buyer was handing it back to them for sacrifice free of charge. The robber priests then killed the animal on the altar, threw a token chunk onto the Lord's fire, and then sold the remains for another fat profit.

"The Lord says he will punish you," Hosea said, his voice rising magnificently, "and make you pay for the evil you do!"

I thrilled in the ownership of my brother. I almost nudged a nearby woman to boast, "He is mine," but she was a villager and already knew. They were seeing him as I saw him. My hero was becoming their hero. If Hosea kept this up, they would be carrying their new champion shoulder high around the souk.

Again my brother's hands went out, and again the crowd swept into them and hung in silence for his next words. They were disappointed.

"Wine is robbing my people of their senses."

The silence held. I looked around and saw some people nodding. They knew they had to shoulder some blame. It was as if my brother had won the right to comment. This defender of the people, this scourge of profit-pocketing priests, had deserved his hearing. He even got away with the next words.

"A people without sense will be ruined. The people of Israel are under the spell of idols. They ask revelations from a piece of wood. After drinking much wine, they delight in their prostitution."

"What about your Gomer?" a brave lone voice cackled. The silence that followed prickled my neck.

"Gomer was like you, my friends. She ran to other lovers. She did not trust her husband." Hosea smiled across the crowd with his arms wide open, as though wanting to embrace all who stood before him. "She thought my life would not last very long, especially after I had criticized the king for the nation's shame at Jezreel."

I was thrilled to watch my neighbors' faces recognize this truth.

"Gomer felt I would not last long enough to provide for her and her children. She needed more security, just as you did when you suspected your divine husband would not be able to provide your rains and crops. She ran after other lovers, just as you, the bride of God, did."

"Stone her!" a solitary man's cry went up from just in front of me. All eyes swiveled in our direction, many of them widening as they saw me.

"Then stone each other!" cried Hosea. A crowd of widening eyes swung away from me and back to my brother. "Yes. You see it, don't you? Should we not all be stoned for what we have done to our heavenly husband?"

The man before me stayed silent. I sighed with relief that a thousand eyes had turned away from my direction. Once again my hero and his authority had come to my rescue.

"Gomer has paid for her adultery," my brother called out. "She was exiled from her home and spent ten years in her wilderness. There will be no stoning today. There will be no flogging to satisfy your lusts, for Gomer is back home and loved and accepted."

Mumbling and grumbling swelled.

"And all that has happened to Gomer will now happen to you, Israel." Voices were again angry. Hosea shouted over them, "This is what your God says: 'The Promised Land will dry up, and everything that lives on it will die. My bride would never acknowledge that I am the one who gave her the corn, the wine, the olive oil, and all the silver and gold that she used in the worship of Baal. So, at harvest time, I will take back my gifts. I will strip her naked in front of her lovers, and no one will be able to save her from my power. I will put an end to all her festivities, all her religious meetings. I will punish her for the times she forgot me.'"

By this time the voices of anger were drowning out my brother's words. Again, I feared for his life, and still he stood his ground. Still he raised his hands for a hearing. The crowd's hero of moments ago had once again become their prime enemy.

"That's not fair," the loudmouth in front of me yelled over and over. It was taken up as a chant, and soon the whole crowd was yelling. In the midst stood Hosea, his raised hands ignored. It seemed futile.

Then Gomer walked past me. She glided with grace, her back straight, her head held high, aglow with traces of her old beauty. By the time she had reached her husband's side, Safed was soundless once again.

"This is what the Lord says," Hosi spoke over his smiling wife. "'A time will come when Israel, my bride, will once again return to her husband. She will receive my good gifts. I will make her my wife; I will be true and faithful; I will answer the prayers of my people, Israel. I will make rain to fall on the earth, and the earth will produce corn and grapes and olives. I will establish my people in the land and make them prosper. I will show love. I will say, "You are my people."'"

A roar of approval rose up. Hero yet again, Hosea stepped down, took Gomer by the hand, and walked off through the parting, cheering crowd.

"How do you stay alive?" I whispered as he passed me.

"This is nothing, Sister." He grinned. "Tomorrow, I will set out to tell the king he is to lose his throne and his life."

CHAPTER 30

A Sister's Puzzle

The big question remains unanswered: just how did Hosi last so long? We have now reached the most dangerous time of my brother's life, and perhaps this is the right moment to try to unravel this puzzle.

Bothersome people could disappear without a trace in the ravines, caves, and abysses of our wild hills. Those who defied thieving gangs, especially of the religious variety, risked shorter life spans or were later found without useful body parts like tongues, eyes, or limbs.

Galilee, and especially its well-worn tracks plied by rich caravans, was largely lawless. Unprotected travelers easily fell among thieves. Life is rarely as precious as somebody else's property, and it is not too hard for disgruntled priests to hire lawless hands for their unholy work.

I began my saga by telling you of my God-and-me moments. Hosea's survival is another example. This time God comes out on the plus side.

Of course there are human explanations for my brother's fifty-five fit years. He had natural allies. Much of his preaching punched the well-off, most of whom had gotten rich by robbing the rest, downtrodden folk who regarded Hosea as a hero. Many of these also knew where their daily bread came from, especially those in poverty. Our Safed bakery always had spare loaves for the needy. Many supported a prophet who attacked those who attacked and robbed them and were consequently more than happy to pass on any hint of danger.

My brother could also disappear on a preaching tour of the hills when enemies drew close. When he did travel, he was accompanied by disciples who, though a poor match for determined foes, would be witnesses to any foul play—and priests never liked awkward questions.

But these human explanations stretch only so far.

If the rich and powerful wanted rid of a nuisance, they had their efficient ways and means to make that happen. The powerful and corrupt hated parting with money and profit to please moral mouths, and so I have days when I almost convince myself that my brother's survival was beyond the mere human.

If Hosi is God's mouth for our times, then it does seem reasonable that an all-seeing, all-powerful God would keep the mouth not only open but also healthy and loud. A few pestilent priests and puny corrupt kings were not going to stop the man whose protection team belonged to the King of Kings.

I prayed this was true the evening we arrived safely home from Safed souk. Hosea's whispered words as he passed by still echoed in my head. Telling a dictator that his time is up is as good as signing your own death sentence.

Priests are petty criminals compared to power-hungry princes. In the cruel dictatorship that often controlled Israel, mightier men than my brother, and even kings themselves, had been silenced by their tombs. Tomorrow, this lone brother of mine was to take on his biggest bear yet. This time I feared that his authority, and even its divine source, might not be enough.

"This one may not amble away," I called out quietly that night as he passed my curtained-off alcove. His footsteps faltered.

"If this bear has the right ears," Hosi said, popping his head into my area, his eyes twinkling over a crooked smile, "then he will hear and will be grateful."

"And if the ears are wrong?"

"Then he will lose his kingdom, we will lose Israel with an invasion from the north, and all of us will lose our freedom or even our lives."

"With you as the first casualty!"

"Your chin is in the attack position." Hosea grinned, and then quickly ducked out as I ran toward him. He was too quick and bolted into the kitchen.

"Peace, Sister, peace." He faced me, holding a finger to his moving lips so we would not disturb the others.

"Peace," I whispered hoarsely, "when tomorrow you go to war against the royal court in Samaria?"

"I know, you worry." He was suddenly solemn. "You think of my safety, and for that I am pleased."

"Then listen to me, Brother!" I stood with balled fists hanging from rigid arms by my side. "You will walk into a pit of assassins. You know it. You taught me this. I was born under King Jeroboam II, but Zechariah killed him off. King Zechariah enjoyed a few weeks on the throne before perishing at Shallum's hands. You know they did not even have time to fit Shallum for his crown before Menahem lopped off his head. Then, King Menahem also fell before the sword of Captain Pekahiah of the army. Menahem lasted only months before Captain Pekahiah aborted his reign."

"Top marks, Sister. You remember well."

"Now you go to face King Hoshea, the latest in a long line of cold-blooded killers and the one who beheaded Pekah. Hosea vs. Hoshea! Your names both mean "savior," and you battle for the soul of Israel, but can you honestly expect that this king-killing king will allow a baker from the hills of nowhere to tell him his time is up?"

We were face-to-face, I fuming, he assuming that all would be well.

"How many times have I been killed?"

"What?" I whispered.

"How many times have you and your tormented head had me dead and buried?"

"I worry!" I sobbed.

"Sister," he spoke gently, "what keeps me alive when the powerful priests and an almighty royal court both want my head?" I guessed where he was going, but I was reluctant to follow.

"Your lessons are long gone. But think! Your education gave you knowledge to help you make decisions of life and death. You have seen how God turned up time and again for Israel. He saved us from slavery, from an exodus sea, and from a Jordan River. You know our enemies have always outnumbered our tiny tribes. You've seen how he has protected me, and maybe how he has protected you also. You know that all we see and experience in this world is no accident. Just as a loaf needs a baker, so a world needs a maker."

"And your education," I quickly retaliated, "tells you of assassin kings and crafty gangs of priests, and still you insist on marching into their killing courts."

"So." My infuriating brother smiled. He held both hands out, palms up. The left hand rose higher than the other as he said, "Mere weak men who want their own way." His left hand dipped, and up came his right, "The Number One Person of the universe and his mighty power." Both hands balanced like our bread scales. "Your choice, Sister. Today's dangers completely dissolve when you realize that strong hands hold you."

Hosea took one look at my fixed face and stooped to kiss my clenched cheek, whispering, "See you before I leave. I am taking a couple of bakery workers with me, but you should still have enough help here."

I accepted the kiss. Under my breath, I said, "More than a couple."

CHAPTER 31

To See the King

"And where are you going, Sister, dressed like that?"

Hosea looked me up and down as I emerged into the rose garden, where he and his helpers were packing one of our donkeys. The sun was yet to rise on Safed's hills. Pitch-soaked torches cast a false dawn, illuminating my travel clothes.

"You have an extra disciple on this trip."

"No, Sister."

"I see no reason why I should not come and encourage my big brother. Besides, it will be pleasant to see Samaria again. I have never seen the royal court and a real-life king in action."

I chattered on about my assistant managing the books, and I explained that the children were becoming more relaxed with their mother. I stressed it would be good for Gomer to have time alone with them. She had overheard last night's conversation and was looking forward to being Mother on her own.

"You are not coming." Hosea was firm. "Far too—"

"Dangerous?" I said innocently. He nodded. "Has your faith so quickly fled?"

"Meaning what?"

"Who is in charge as we go before this tyrant king?" I felt a satisfying mischief rise within. I formed scales with my hands under his nose. My left hand rose as I said, "Power-hungry men." Up came my right as I said, "Or the Number One Person of the universe and his power." Both hands mimed the act of balancing. "Your choice, dear Brother."

"I trust you slept as well as you scheme," he said, his look as dark as the predawn sky.

"Do not forget, my wise brother," I said, unable to stop myself, "that today's dangers dissolve when you realize in whose hands you rest." At that moment, a golden Levant sun peeped over a faraway peak and Hosea shook himself into action.

"Get it tightly packed," he called to the donkey packers. He issued a string of other orders and completely ignored me from that moment onward.

We were halfway through our trek south on the second evening before he next spoke to me. We had tented on a plain of low scrubs. Our glorious overhead canopy was charcoal-black parchment splashed with countless stars and occasional shooting silvery trails.

"You won't see a real, live king in action, Sister." Hosea spoke as though our argument had never happened. "Hoshea is merely a puppet monarch whose strings are pulled by another."

I said nothing, but my face must have shown amazement in the fire's glow. How could such a thing be in an age of revolts and assassinations?

"Bears come in bigger sizes than Israelite kings," my brother said, shrugging. "When I taught you the facts of rulers, I left out the mighty emperor of Assyria, Tiglath-Pileser III. He is based at the other end of the Fertile Crescent and hates any power but his own. His victory over Israel helped him to straddle the world's greatest crossroad. Whoever possesses this land bridge rules the world."

"But you taught me that the King of Kings called us as his special people to live with him in the middle of his world," I blurted out.

"Exactly!" Hosi nodded. "You remember well, Sister. Carry on."

"You want to turn me back into your pupil after all these years?" I laughed into the fire without malice.

"Humor me." Hosea chuckled. "Anyway, if you insist on facing another ferocious bear alongside me, the more you know, the better our chances of survival." He looked expectant.

"You mean how our heavenly king guided and ruled us?"

Hosi smiled, content yet again to be teacher. "Well, around twelve generations ago, he guided through various judges like Samuel and Samson. But our ancestors wanted strong kings like other nations had, strong leaders who could be seen.

"We were warned that human kings would demand high taxes for gold-plated palaces, but we eventually got our own way and crowned Saul. He was a good king to begin with, but jealousy flamed over one of his army chiefs, David, who eventually took over. This second king started badly by stealing another's wife and arranging for the husband's death, but he finished with an empire stretching down to Egypt and up into Syria."

Hosea lay back against a camel saddle, nodding in contentment.

"David's son Solomon was said to be the wisest man on earth, yet he foolishly treated his subjects like the slaves they once were in Egypt, insisting they build lavish palaces and the temple in Jerusalem."

"Go on to the great split." My brother was firmly back in his encouraging role, and my excitement at showing off had resurfaced.

"When Solomon died, our ancestors promised to crown his son, but only if he reduced slavery and taxes. Prince Rehoboam did the opposite, so our ancestors, led by Jeroboam, rebelled. Ten northern tribes of Israel made him their first king and set up their capital in Samaria, our present destination," I said, finishing with a beaming flourish.

"Finish the tale," my brother commanded. I looked blank. "Ten from twelve leaves?"

"Ah." I grinned. "The last two tribes, Judah and Benjamin, around Jerusalem, chose to stay with the rightful heir and crowned Rehoboam. They called themselves Judah, while the others became a shrunken Israel."

"Fine." My brother nodded and then stood to take up his teacher stance. "Hoshea is Israel's nineteenth king since we split. All of them faced external enemies who wanted our strategic land bridge. For the last three generations, Assyria has been dominant, more so since Tiglath-Pileser became emperor.

"Israel had a choice when Tiglath's troops threatened Israel. The bride could go to her heavenly husband and ask him to deal with Assyria, as he had defeated previous enemies. However, the bride once again ran out on her husband, and went to settle in Tiglath-Pileser's bed.

"The emperor was more than happy to let us join his harem, and he quickly plundered much of our wealth and gave the crown to one of his supporters. So, Israel no longer rules herself; she is merely a vassal, one of Tiglath's slave nations."

"But that means, er," I stuttered, searching for the right words, "that your God is nowhere near Samaria and we are walking into a tyrant's killing courts with no armor, no weapons, and little protection. Actually, it is worse! You think you can simply stand up before the world's biggest bear and just shout, 'No'?"

Hosea nodded. "I have one or two other words as well, but yes, as usual you are proving a good pupil, except for the God bit. He will be with us here, as always."

"Madness!" I cried. "You will walk into the king's court and shout out what you can before he chops off your head. Is that it? Have I missed anything? And once your head stops rolling across the courtyard, they will come for mine."

"Has your faith deserted you?" Hosi smiled wickedly. "And in such a short desert trek, Sister?"

"Do not dare!" I advanced toward him.

"Who is in charge?" He sprang away to mimic our two-pan balance scales. "Mere weakling bears or the Number One Person who made them?"

I grabbed both his hands and held them in mine. I suddenly wanted them around me as a cold fear gripped me.

"This could be your last bear, Brother." I looked up pleadingly. "Will we really die?"

"Two more days, Sister, and we shall find out."

CHAPTER 32

Turmoil on High

Day 99

Our spirits can soar higher than our castle in the sky, as with my wedding celebrations. At other times morale plunges as low as the arid valley below. As I scribe, our spirits barely skim the sluggish salts of the Dead Sea.

No longer is there a common agreement shaped by a clear purpose. Conflicting visions clash. Sicarii daggers have been seen to flash in the high sun, with tempers almost as hot. Should daggers or Zealot swords just once draw in red, I fear we shall be carved into divisions beyond healing.

In the midst of discord, my own spirit now soars toward life rather than the bloody end of our death pact. But with this comes anguish.

I must soon tell Isaac, my dearest husband of the last thirty-three beautiful days, that I no longer wish him to be my executioner. Deep betrayal conflicts with the joyful heights when I think of why I should tell him this news.

But first, the communal discord.

Sicarii, Zealot, and Essene living in union is a miracle. I cannot describe it any other way. A thousand Jewish souls working as one is rarer than a herd of three-humped camels. Two Jews in discussion always produce three opinions. Our nation was born out of argument: tricky Jacob quarreled with God one night and ended up with his hip and nose out of joint. This, as we have noted, was when he became Israel, one who strives with the divine. As Israelites, we have not stopped quarreling since.

Our hundred days of relative unity is so unusual that our leadership has called for a celebration. My Isaac had been selected to organize it, even though newlyweds normally are left to themselves for the first year. Up here, tradition and time have loosened, especially with the latter ticking down to death.

"Five hours of raging argument," Isaac had fumed after a recent meeting, "and still no decision on how many shofar horns will be needed for our fanfare of unity!"

"It is all off," Isaac had cried a few nights later, "and so are your children's games."

"What now?" My concerned expression hopefully masked my relief about the canceled games.

"We spent three hours discussing whether we had enough unity left to celebrate, and nobody could agree."

He sat clenching and unclenching his fists. He tried a smile, but his mouth twisted into a scowl and his eyes brimmed with tears of frustration. Bless him; he was battling to be pleasant with his still-new bride.

"Remember the father of that dead bar mitzvah boy?" I nodded, wondering where Isaac was now taking me. "Well, he joined our planning group to take his mind off his son's tragic end. We were at last making headway on the fanfare when he suddenly screamed out against the lightest of evils. He claimed the parents of the other dead boys were also in revolt. They had had enough killings and were not going to see any more of their children dead."

"Oh," is all I could manage. The topic was too close to the conflict burning within me.

"And another problem," Isaac carried on. "As you know, we have had several deaths in recent weeks, mainly elderly heads of families. Most were to be family executioners, and now all is endangered. We should have taken early action to help grieving families choose others to carry out the lightest of evils. Masada is now full of muttering critics, and some have been careless. Now, even the youngest children have guessed what is planned; hence, there is no need to hide the truth through the games you were planning."

Isaac had every right to expect comfort from a supportive wife. All I could do was hug him. I could not trust words. I could not speak falsely in the face of death, nor could I bring myself to voice my own change of heart.

"Isaac," I would have said had I possessed the courage, "we have a new life to consider."

I would have gently explained that when we had married, the day after his proposal, I was just entering my most fertile time. I would have reminded him that my present brood proved I was not slow when it came to producing babies. I would have explained that my monthly cycle was as predictable as is the sun and moon and that not even Joseph's terrible death or the flight to Masada had delayed it by more than a day or two.

I was now many days overdue. I would have finally added, "Isaac, this precious baby of ours makes all the difference. Please, I cannot kill this tiny life within me."

How could I begin to reason about this new life? I barely understood it myself. This was not a matter of my head. This was a passionate scream within. I could hear it, yet not with my ears. I could feel it with every square inch of skin. My body parts were leading this violent inner revolt, and I knew beyond a doubt that it would never allow me to lie in an embrace of death with Isaac. I knew with the same certainty of my love for Isaac that I would also become his executioner if he tried to kill our child. I would fight for the life we had created.

This was the joy and betrayal that made my spirit dip and soar toward life.

Tomorrow, I will test this with wisdom greater than mine: with Magdalen, my bridesmaid. Perhaps I will also ask about the mysterious thing that screams within her soul. She has still not told me why she fears to tell people who she really is.

I would like to make two small points before I close this evening.

First is that the enemy has more than made up for the collapse on the ramp. We constantly seek cover now that we are only an arrow's arc from each other.

Second, my girls kept asking why they fall asleep to the sound of reed scratching papyrus. As a result, they are now enjoying Hosea as their bedtime story. I describe the evils of the times in lighter ways, and still they demand another episode. It seems to be more than escaping sleep and the extinguishing of torches. I rather think their young hearts have fallen for Hosea, who, of course, was only a few seasons older than they when our story first began. They laughed so much when Little Sister scolded her daddy and her big brother over the betrothal secret, but they grew serious as they wondered about their own futures.

"Are we not to be betrothed?" the eldest had asked, suddenly alarmed by her young years rushing by without any sign of a prospective bridegroom. I promised to talk with other parents, and the girls then began scribing a list of virtues for their ideal candidates. With the rapid progress of the ramp, I knew events would soon overtake us, one way or another.

CHAPTER 33

"Tell Me, Please"

Day 100

I spotted Magdalen in the angry morning crowd and threaded my way to her side. She greeted me with a guarded look. My return smile was as friendly as I could make it.

"I am with you, Magdalen," I whispered. Uncertain eyes narrowed; otherwise, her weathered face was blank. She needed more.

"We want room in your cave."

These last words were mouthed more than whispered, and I was rewarded with a beam that doubled Magdalen's wrinkles yet produced an expression of beautiful peace. Tears welled in her smiling eyes.

An hour later, we walked away through a crowd stripped of its anger and buzzing with fiery zeal. We picked our way past friends, avoiding all eyes except each other's. We hoped all would respect our bowed heads and not ask our opinion of Eleazar's latest rallying cry. The eyes are the traitors. We might lie with our lips, but neither Magdalen nor I have eyes that will collaborate with anything but the truth. They would betray our opposition to my uncle, and that would not be good.

We were now a tiny minority after Uncle Eleazar had skillfully turned the mood of the morning's emergency meeting. I marvel at how he continues to paint masterpieces in our minds with only the rising-and-falling cadences of words. I could use identical sounds yet leave all unmoved. He declares, pauses, shouts and then whispers, adds half smiles, and then scowls. Sometimes he flows with the sweetness of warm honey, and then he jolts with the acid of lemons. Within minutes his protesting audience were reduced to murmurs and then to the smiling silence of approval. Once more his listeners were preparing to lay down their lives for the cause.

He met the major fear head-on. The failing scheme of family heads executing their own was replaced with an efficient drawing of lots, with all executioners fully trained to swiftly perform the lesser of evils. He had then repainted in vivid adjectives precisely what a heartless enemy would inflict on those they caught, demonstrating yet again why the communal death pact truly was the only way to escape a future worse than death.

"Could you ever again call yourselves Zealots if you simply surrendered to a cowardly enemy? And could you Sicarii surrender your daggers so easily? Could you smile while slavishly serving everything you have always fought against? Will you each bow before your new masters' whips, and contentedly look on as they use your babies and abuse your children for their own wicked pleasures?" The gratuitous barb of this last arrow pierced through any remaining opposition. The crowd had burst into a flashing uproar as hundreds of daggers blazed with the reflections of a climbing sun.

Magdalen and I were thankful to escape the frenzy without drawing attention. We watched as a group peeled away from the melee and ran, heading for the wall overlooking the enemy ramp.

"Look," I said, anxiously motioning to Magdalen, "Isaac's leading them." A few days ago I would have pointed with pride. Today I felt sad. He was on his way to shout his defiance at an enemy that was now completing its ramp, and still I had told him nothing of my change of heart.

267

"Why?" Magdalen ignored my last words.

"What?" I swung away from my running husband.

"After all this time, why do you suddenly want to come with me?"

I stopped and stood looking at Magdalen. I had lots of words, but their exit was suddenly blocked. My chest and airways were fully extended by a rising passion and pride, and a small smile widened into a fat grin on my face as my hands went to caress my middle. Magdalen needed nothing more. She enfolded me in an excited embrace and kissed me profusely all over my now wet face.

"How?" she shouted, and then burst into laughter at her silliness. "Oh! Praise God that you are with me. This is unbelievable. What of Isaac?"

Now Magdalen was crying. We both dissolved into the happiest of huddles, forgetting for a precious moment husbands leaping on ramparts and Uncle El's earlier terrifying description of what would happen to those captured.

This issue still haunted me, yet strangely less so after a season of scribing the powerful story of divine actual love.

Had Hosea quit life so easily? If he could survive fifty-five years of stoning mobs, then was there not a glimmer of hope for my family? He believed himself to be in the hands of a power greater than his enemies. Why should I not share in that?

And another thought: does not this whole Masada death pact contradict all I have written in the last hundred days? Are we Israelites not once again showing our lack of faith in our husband? Is killing our children and each other not giving up on our Protector? What would have happened had our ancestors done the same before a hundred previous battles? Were we not now rushing into the arms of death just as our ancestors ran to other gods or stronger nations?

Is the leadership of Eleazar ben Jair right? Is it time for me to grow up and stop treating Uncle El as Uncle God? Why follow a mere man who has no more idea of life and death than any other human creature does?

Hosea had reminded me that our long history was supported by almighty life-giving hands far stronger than any human ones. Had he not parted mighty exodus seas and Jordan rivers while exterminating whole armies that pursued and opposed his beloved people?

Or is all this just wishful thinking working overtime to defend the decision of my heart? All this jostled in my mind as I held Magdalen.

After a while, I felt her stiffen. Abruptly, she pulled away and looked fearful.

"What is it?" I reached out, but she backed further away. "Tell me. Please."

"You do not know me, Mary," she spoke flatly. "You have no idea who I am or what I was before that silly donkey harness of mine got twisted."

"I do know you, Magdalen. Have I not seen the good you have done, your words of wisdom, and your actions of love? I know that the heart that produced all this is noble, and I have no fears about coming with you. We would never have made it to Masada without your cart and your help. Magdalen, you have been my tower, my support, and my friend."

"You have known me for much less than one year out of my sixty-six. You need to know the rest before we take another step together."

I nodded. I feared more words from me might stop her words. This opportunity I was not going to miss after so many frustrations. I was convinced that her words would make no difference. It might help Magdalen to let them escape. Also, in honesty, the suspense of not knowing was stretching my curiosity far too much. I waited patiently.

"I told you I had to be quiet about my past," my friend began. "The dangers were very real. Had some known about me, I would have been dead long ago. We were born and brought up in Jericho, on a farm that stretched down toward the Jordan. I have occasionally climbed down to our lower terrace here on Masada, for on a clear morning, before the sun gets too high and the land dissolves in a shimmer, I have been able to see the eastern tip of our land.

"This was where my older sister was stoned to death as a prostitute." She let that statement hang for a moment, as if awaiting condemnation. When none came, she carried on.

"Father and I were forced to watch as they buried Sarah up to her breasts. The leader then read out a scroll declaring her crime and punishment. He reminded the mob that their stones must be small enough to ensure that death did not come quickly and so allow a punishment to fit her wickedness. However, they had to be big enough to break the skin. All the time Sarah was struggling to get free and crying out for mercy."

"No, Magdalen," I said, interrupting more for my sake than hers, "you do not have to tell me these things."

"I do," she sobbed. "Yes, I truly do." She quietened herself and continued. "My father was huge and cruel. When we were younger, he struck Mother in a wild drunken rage. The next morning we found her dead. He buried her somewhere on the farm. He said she belonged to him and he could do with her what he wanted. He also made it plain that he owned us. Days later, he insisted that Sarah and I should take over what Mother had done around the house and in his bed. We did not want to end up like Mother, so we agreed.

"We were a normal family on the outside, always giving hospitality to passersby and still attending the synagogue, but then Father missed a growing season. He went out one day and lost our bag of seeds gambling. We were eventually left with no money and nothing to eat. It was then that Sarah started to go missing. She would tell me to look after Father and not to worry. A day or two later, she would be back home with bags of food to keep us going for another week. On the second occasion, she brought home some seed, and the following day we made sure it went into the ground.

"We struggled on through the growing season. The week before harvest, some Pharisees dragged Sarah up our farm track. They claimed to have caught her with a married man in the act of adultery in a cave on the Jericho road going up to Jerusalem. After the execution, a priest said he would buy our crop to help us. He brought a gang of workers and then disappeared without giving us a shekel." Magdalen was quiet for a long while.

She tried to continue, but the words did not come. In the end I took pity on her and gently offered, "So, you did what your sister did?"

She nodded. A fresh wave of energy seemed to catch hold of her, and she began talking rapidly.

"It was only what Father had done to me for years, and I found that a bit of wine numbed me enough to cope. Also, so long as there were no Pharisees or Scribes around, it was reasonably safe. It was even safer after my first customer. He turned out to be a robber. After we had finished, he took me back to his camp in a little-known valley, well back from the Jericho road. There, it was safe to give what I had, and his friends were happy to take what they wanted. In a single day each week I could make more than enough for us to survive. If only Sarah had found this safety. They told me I would always be welcome back."

I put a hand on her shoulder. "Magdalen, you had to do this so you and your father could—"

"Let me finish." Magdalen reached up to pat my hand. "Father died soon after Sarah had gone, and the farm was then too much for me. We had also fallen behind on the rent, which Father was supposed to have paid. So, when I next returned to the valley after the funeral, I stayed on. At least they made me welcome. I was soon found a spare cave. By this time, there were other girls there. There were plenty of robbers and shekels to go around, so one more girl made little difference.

"This went on for many summers, keeping the men happy, trying to forget my synagogue upbringing, most days drinking to forget Sarah's stoning and some of the things that some men demanded." Magdalen seemed to slump into herself as she reached this point of her story.

"I don't know what I would have done," I offered helplessly. I wanted to sweep her into my arms and smooth away her past. "I know a little of what you felt about Sarah. My Joseph's death was cruel and wicked. It haunts me now, even though I have married again." Useless words poured out of me as I tried to calm my friend, to reassure her, to say that it was all in the past and that nothing she could tell me would dissuade me or the children from coming with her.

"There is more," she said, abruptly interrupting my anxious flow. "Much worse, according to some." I stopped and wondered what could possibly be beyond what I had already heard.

CHAPTER 34

Human Torches

"Magdalen, I really do not need to know anymore."
I felt a fraud even uttering such hollow words.

I did need to know. I yearned to know, yet I did
not want my dear friend to suffer again through a
painful retelling. I was still sorting out this conflict
when Magdalen rushed on.

"They could have stoned me for prostitution." She
trembled, pausing for a few moments before taking
a deep breath. "For the next part of my life I could
have been covered in tar, hung on a post, and used
as a torch to light royal garden parties." She stopped
to catch her breath.

"Remember me telling you what they did to my husband in Rome?" I nodded and watched as her body rocked to and fro, fighting back tears. She eventually exploded with, "Some of our friends were herded before lions in a great coliseum, with the crowd roaring for their blood, yelling for the great beasts to tear them apart." She stopped with a small gasp. I was about to reach out when she spoke again.

"That is how I lost my two children."

Another long trembling pause saw her fighting for control. I took her hand to stroke it, feeling totally inadequate. Her chest rose and fell. Anger momentarily flashed across her face, and this seemed to provide her with strength.

"Another family ..." She broke off again, taking deep breaths and letting out each one rapidly and loudly. "Another family looked after the children while I was away. It was my job to deliver letters and things for the group I was with. When I returned to Rome with a long letter from one of the leaders, the family and my children had been carted off as entertainment for Rome's cowardly crowds." This time, the pause went on for so long that I knew she was elsewhere. She continued in a whisper.

"Even now it is not safe in some areas to be what I am." Magdalen shrugged. "That was why I was fleeing when you stopped to free my donkey harness."

"But you are neither Zealot nor Sicarii. Why would they want you?"

"They were rounding up all non-Romans, especially Jews, and with a nose and lips like mine, Mary, they would not need to use their imaginations, now, would they? They would have soon discovered who I was and learned that I was no ordinary Jew, and then I too would have been killed or sold into slavery."

"You could have told them any story, Magdalen."

"No." Magdalen shook her head so that her wrinkles wobbled violently. "No, I would have had to tell the truth."

"What truth?"

"The Way," Magdalen whispered. "I am a follower of the Way."

"You are a cannibal!" I shouted, and immediately let go of her hand.

I was as repulsed by my own insensitivity to a friend as I was by her dirty secret. I could have coped with any other evil, more prostitution maybe, even murder, but not the Devil's own church. Their leader had magic that only the Prince of Demons, Beelzebub, could power. It was a group that had always revolted me.

"That cannibalism thing is just an ugly, silly rumor," shouted back Magdalen.

"But you eat your dead leader's flesh and drink his blood," I hit back. "You say, 'This is my body ... this is my blood ... eat and drink in remembrance.'" I glared intensely at Magdalen, daring her to contradict me.

"Bread and wine," mumbled Magdalen. "Just symbols."

"And if what this Christ of yours says is true," I said, ignoring her interruption, "then what or who else do you eat as well? Children go missing all the time."

"You charge me without a hint of evidence." Magdalen was sharp. "You attack me with false rumors; you judge and pass sentence without any proof."

She stopped. I looked away. "Do you see why I kept quiet, Mary? I thought that if Masada does not kill me for one thing, it will kill me for the other. So, my friend, do you run to the northern wall to tell Isaac? Do you go straight to the top and tell your uncle? And when it comes to it, dear Mary, will you be throwing the first stone?"

I had sunk to the floor in despair. The Way and their so-called messiah we had crucified were so hateful to us Jews. For a generation, the Way had split or destroyed many of our synagogues across our Promised Land, despite the Romans and despite our whipping and jailing its leaders. Even attendance at our great temple had been affected.

It started with one of their number misleading a huge crowd in Jerusalem during a Pentecost celebration. He cursed all foreign visitors with a spell and made them believe his simple Arabic lies about the resurrection of their founder. We lost thousands that first day alone. Before that year was out, many synagogues had closed down because so many had been lost to the new heresy.

They met in Solomon's Portico on the eastern side of the temple. Half hidden by the long colonnade, they wooed Jews with tricks of healing, and then they bought the poor by giving away huge amounts of food. They deceived many of my friends by claiming that the Promised One of our scriptures had already arrived and that we had crucified him on Skull Hill.

They went through all the hundreds of prophecies of our writings and twisted them to show how their Jesus of Nazareth had fulfilled them all. They even struck blind one of our greatest Sanhedrin council members. Saul of Tarsus had been sent to Damascus to round up followers of the Way, but weeks later he was back in Jerusalem, fully healed and calling himself Paul. He then accused the Jews of killing the Son of God.

Even our Masada hell was their fault. Maybe if Jewish numbers had not been decimated; perhaps if we had been more unified; possibly if there had been no false Christ; then we would have gotten more respect from the Romans. We would never have had to declare war on Rome, and then there would have been no Masada. And maybe I would not now be groveling desperately on the floor, seeing the last chance for me and my babies dwindle to nothing.

"How could you?" I screamed up at Magdalen.

"I could do no other." She looked down with a sad smile. I wanted to wipe it off her stupid face.

"So!" I got up quickly, no longer wanting her to have the satisfaction of seeing my hurt. "Can you not see how this Way gang have bewitched you?"

We stared at each other. Both of us trembled, each for different reasons. Magdalen inhaled, lifting her shoulders and her head. There was no defiance, just a quiet steadiness.

"One of the valley girls came back from a week's business in Jerusalem. She told us she had seen Jesus and his miracles and then his crucifixion. Magdalene, she was called. I used to call her Big Dalene. She called me Little Dalen. It caught on with the rest of the camp girls. I used to say she was trying to be great, posing with such an ending to her name. She would playfully strut around like royalty, boasting that she came from the elegant

town of Magdala, whereas I was merely a Magdalen from nowhere in—"

"Why are you going on like this?" I snapped.

"Sorry." She flinched and then sobbed. "I'm nervous. My whole future is in your hands. I am afraid."

When I stayed silent, she raced on, trying to convince me. "Magdalene got caught doing her business and, terrified of being stoned, ran. Rounding one corner, she crashed into the arms of the Messiah preacher. Immediately, she felt he could see all her past and her filthy insides. She broke down in tears, and he prayed over her. Seven times she was thrown about by the evil in her before she eventually collapsed at his feet. She said she felt incredible peace; she felt like pools of poison had drained away each time the preacher had prayed. She felt fresh, clean as a new babe.

"When she came back to our valley, we could all see the difference in her. A smile had replaced her normal scowl. Her usual cursing turned to praise and laughter. She said that all the rottenness had been driven out, and I knew this was exactly what I had wanted for so long, Mary."

I refused to turn and respond to my name.

"You sell a piece of yourself every hour of every day." Now I looked up at her. It was strange how prostitution was no problem to me, whereas the religious thing was so repugnant.

"Your soul is a cake, Mary, and you keep selling small pieces of it—and soon you are just left with crumbs.

"You no longer know who you are. So many men have pumped their evil into you. You have drunk so much to cut off the horrors, the smells, the weird ones, and the notion that you are no more than a vessel to please men. And then there is the shame and guilt. There is boiling anger at those who smashed you to bits inside, and then simmering self-loathing for allowing men to touch you. My big sister did it to stop us from starving to death. I carried on to get money for food and wine, and then for acceptance and to be able to stay in the valley.

"When Mary Magdalene told me her story of this Jesus who released her, I desperately wanted his forgiveness and acceptance. They took me to a pool and pushed me under. Baptism they called it, and it was like a clean, fresh start."

A long silence followed. She looked at me, pleading for my understanding. I looked back at her, remembering the decimation of the synagogues, the destruction of Jewish life, and then the destruction of Jerusalem and our great temple.

"They tricked a gullible girl into believing she had a new life, just like that priest tricked you out of your first ever crop, Magdalen." I laughed. I sounded harder than I'd intended.

"No, Mary. You are so wrong."

"What is the difference?" I asked, cool and brittle.

"Mother!"

I heard the desperate scream from across the street.

"Mother, where are you? I was on my feet and running even as the second cry began.

"Jemima," I shouted as I ran into the street.

"Isaac!" She gasped. "Isaac!"

"What, Jemima?" I fell to my knees and took hold of her upper arms as her hands covered her face. She was still sobbing. I shook her to shock her into talking.

"Dead!" she cried. "An arrow." I fell back on my heels as Jemima dissolved into a heap on my lap. Others were now running toward us.

"I am so sorry, Mary." It was the wise man Rueben, breathless from trying to keep up with my daughter. "We pleaded with them not to go to the wall." He gasped a huge breath.

"Tell me, Rueben." I looked up. I was strangely calm.

"They were too near. When our men started shouting their defiance, the Romans loosed off a flight from their longbows, straight into the Masada sky. We lost three good men. Isaac was one of them.

"Mary." Again he stopped for air, tears rolling down his cheeks. "He would not have felt a thing. The arrow that killed him came down vertically into the neck and went through the cord of his back. He dropped without a sound."

CHAPTER 35

Winning Back Colette

Dave Jackson rocked to and fro with a thigh and a rear cheek perched on his stool, not too comfortable in case he fuzzed.

His hunched-over frame swayed backwards then forwards over his study desk, and a steadying right arm and hand held his doodling pen in readiness.

Every now and again, the rocking would increase as fuzz threatened to overtake focus. All the while his gaze was steady on something that only his inner psyche registered. To a passing stranger looking in through his study window, he would have appeared almost schizophrenic, incessantly soothing some inner hell. For Dave, it was merely a nervous habit to aid concentration.

Periodically, his efforts were rewarded with a fruitful brain wave that sparked a bittersweet smile and another bout of squiggling. This was serious business, he considered, more so than any he had previously undertaken.

This was D-day in the war to win back his wife.

It was a battle of the sexes that he must lose. Colette deservedly needed not only to win but also to be seen to win. Nor could this be a mere ploy. He had absorbed all her justifiable blasts and flare-ups, and only now were the impacts finally penetrating a thickness of skull that amazed even him.

How had it taken so long? And why had he forced Colette to wage war? Why was he so full of words yet devoid of action? Whatever he did today must center on strong acts of love. Whatever words he wrote must be peppered with mighty verbs. It might take months to prove he meant business. Correction—*years!* Justice suggested that it would take as long as he had known Colette. Fairness demanded that years of loveless, empty words could only be reversed by years of loving action.

It was midafternoon. The college was almost as quiet as the cemetery he had meandered through the previous day. Classes and tutorials were done, and students had dispersed to fulfill the college daily canon—"Work two sessions and play one." The afternoon was invariably downtime, and occasionally a faint sporting cry would echo from adjacent playing fields or a snore escape a nearby study.

Across the virgin-white blotter before Dave, an ornate doodle neared completion, with its intricate whirls, flutes, and squiggles. He felt he could have framed it as his work of art, enshrining his number one question of life:

HOW TO WIN A WOMAN?

The felt-tip banner headline bowed across the top of the blotter in blues, reds, and greens. Underneath, in black uppercase and lowercase, was the straight subhead:

Winning of Col—Pros and Cons

There was just one hastily scribbled exclamation under "Cons": "I am a pillock!"

He had chosen the crude word with care. In modern slang he knew it meant "idiot," yet it also derived from the Norwegian for "pillicock" (*penis*). It was appropriate. Initially, it had seemed sacrilegious to felt-tip the word on a holy college's blotter, but it was dawning on him that most of his thinking about his wife had been done with a part of his anatomy three feet lower than sensible.

Understanding was dawning that Colette was an affair of the brain and the heart, governed by the will. The heart mourned for his wife as a big-band drummer might miss his steady kick-drum bass beat. His head lacked motivation, and the gray matter identified little color in anything apart from her.

All of this had whipped his will into action. Dave now realized that the "I will" of his nuptials had been a mockery. What he really meant was, "My will." It was this that gave birth to the monster that was his marriage. The first promised Colette everything. The second added a quiet, "Only if I want to." The first loved Colette, and the second loved self. He'd won his own way and lost his wife in the process.

Only now was he beginning to grasp the truth; only now did he see what drove true love. He was amazed yet again at his own slowness, his own self-centeredness.

In love, "Will" took the wheel, even when the selfish "I" wanted to recline and be the passenger. "Will" disciplined its eye to take the right road even when "I" yearned for selfish detours. "Will" always paid close attention to the co-driver.

It was for this last reason that Israel and his academic future was now no longer on Dave's road map. Now, he belatedly realized that no destination mattered other than Colette.

A nightmare featuring a world without her had crashed him into panic and wakefulness in the early hours. He'd dreamed that he was running back to the Swan and Royal from his cemetery stroll to find his wife miscarrying once again and screaming that they were finished, that she never wanted to see him again, that everything was his fault.

The lackluster instruments hanging on the pub wall had comically begun to sound mocking raspberries down at him, while his pub mates cackled derisively at his stupidity. He had run from the cacophony in slow motion, only to find a horse-drawn hearse outside the pub ready to take away his beloved Colette. She lay in the back, arms crossed over her bosom. She was wearing a white dress, all framed with lilies. At this point, he had awoken screaming.

He had sat up, shivering in the autumn chill, and looked across at his wife's neat, unslept-in single bed. The emptiness of life was stark and painful. Colette was his starting point. She was also the terminus. He loved her. He was learning to cherish her more than himself, beyond his studies, over his reputation, before his future, and certainly over another study trip to Israel.

Pillock was exactly the right word for his crude behavior. It was the only word that summed up what he had been, no matter how sacred the blotter. To fly off now and leave his wife alone for months would certainly be the death of a marriage he now desperately wanted alive and thriving.

The remainder of the early hours had brought him to some sober conclusions. Now, hovering over his blotter, he applied the finishing touches to the blotter's main question: how to win a woman?

"No." He frowned. "That isn't quite right." He overinked the *a* to transform it into an insert caret. Above it, he printed "The." There really was no other woman and no other goal on his blotter plan than Colette and his unborn daughter respectively.

Fighting the fuzzing habit of his lifetime, he concentrated on Colette, retracing sad memories and reducing them to bullet points and explanatory comments.

Pillock was sufficient to embrace all the cons working against his marriage's survival. Now for the pros:

Marriage's Golden Rule

Treat Col not as I want to be treated but as she needs to be treated (keep in mind the dreadful honeymoon). Treating Col like I want to be treated meant sex anytime, anyplace, and in every position, initiating it with the instant speed of a light switch rather than an iron slowly warming to the idea. My Colette should be treated according to her needs, and that should transcend the merely physical. Closeness can be a kiss and a cuddle, not always a full-on fight to climax in every clinch. Let head and heart do the thinking, pillock!

Rebalance Life

The domestic outweighs the academic. Emotion is heavier than Einstein mind exercises are. Academic admiration is featherweight compared to the fullness of being well loved by the one I love. How stupid to think that brains trump the beauty of my beautiful colleen.

Concentrate, Not Con

"Sure, babe" is now a banned response. It's a scam. My "Sure, babe" wins me time to look right through Col to make eyes at a theological puzzle or a college problem. A woman needs to talk. A husband's job is to listen (and vice versa). If I don't, should I be surprised if a vacancy sign eventually goes up?

Dave doodled for some moments below this point on the blotter, using black shading around green forks of lightning striking downward. One prong pierced the black heart of a dragon—a red Welsh one. Another fork struck a dunce's cap held by a tall matchstick man with stray wisps of hair straddling an otherwise bald head. Dave lingered over his own stupidity.

He added a caption underneath the dunce:

Fancy abandoning one's most precious
jewel in a den of thieves.

He suddenly felt he should mark this moment of honesty in some special way. He scrawled a caption below matchstick man:

Stop pulling the wool over folks' eyes and your head.
Cut the con. Bald is the new virility.

He grabbed the offending comb-over, extracted a small pair of scissors from his desktop tidy, and snipped its way free.

Now ready to move on to another marriage lesson, he was amazed by what a walk by the canal and a sobering nightmare could achieve. He paused over the long trek from wedding aisle to marriage mayhem, and cringed afresh at what he had inflicted on his poor wife.

Arms, Not Alms

Buying my wife's quietness with a cute canal maisonette turns her into a charity case. Rather, my Col needs strong arms about her, especially given that her mother's emotional limbs had been amputated by shards of selfishness.

Dave abruptly rose to his full height and walked out of his study to stand, feet splayed, hands behind his back, looking out of his kitchen window and down toward the Thames. This took him by the kitchen table, causing remnants of anger to flare. Here was the reason he needed a break before setting down his penultimate point. This one was so new and raw that he still trembled with its impact.

At first, he thought it fanciful. Upon further consideration, he saw that there was no escape. This, more than all the others, may see an end to his stupidity and to his winning of Colette.

"And it has to be written here!" He spoke the words not to the sluggish, careless Thames but to the table behind. Here was where his folly had brought them. Not so much a scene of fatal attraction, it was more the culmination of his own fatal distraction from Colette.

He marched back into the study, gathered pens and blotter, and returned to the scene of what he had once viewed as a dark crime against him. Now, self-illumination flickered. This was the scene of his crime, not Col's. He had caused it to happen. He felt-tipped the next headline slowly and in capitals.

Who's Who?

Masada Mary's scroll reveals uncomfortable parallels between my marriage and Hosea's: I the cuckolded Hosea to Colette's Gomer? Had she not taken another lover just as the Israelite bride of God had? Me, Hosea: she, Gomer. Surely!

And yet, who cheated on whom in my marriage? Who ran after many other loves, long before Col had her single dalliance? Who deserted his partner and rushed off to Aberystwyth and Israel? Who made love mentally to other loves even while his wife was talking to him? Whose mental adultery drove his wife to another lover?

She, Hosea; Me, Gomer

Is this not the painful truth? Colette suffered her partner using sex for his needs. It was she who was saying, "Come back home, but no sex." Was it not I who had to be taught that sex was not animal lust? Was it not I who had to be shown that the act of sex was supposed to be an outward sign mirroring the inner splendor of two souls intertwined?

"*Me, Gomer!*" The horror of this shocked him. More, it reminded Dave Jackson of an even greater discomfort.

CHAPTER 36

More Than a Cease-Fire

Dave doodled after his last full stop. The temptation to fuzz was intense. Just about anything that now flashed through his mind was immensely more attractive than continuing on to his last point.

He even sketched a tall, bald, theological-college don morphing into a naked self-flagellant, complete with a bloodied back and dangling, dripping whip, its thongs melodramatically pricked with red marker. Did he have to whip himself so thoroughly? Did he have to be so harsh with himself?

"Yes and yes," he shouted loudly across the kitchen table. He stared at the doodle and then realized he was fuzzing more than focusing.

One final problem reared before him. He didn't even have a title for it. Whenever things related to this final point had barged forward, he had quickly ushered them back into his mental pending tray, especially that thoroughly distasteful time when Reverend Caractacus Llewellyn had had the temerity to press him with a silly question.

"Dave!" He winced, remembering the grating Welsh lilt. "If you died tonight, would you be certain of going to heaven and God?"

The resentment still scorched. The cheek of the scoundrel! The absolute effrontery of challenging a fellow dog collar with such religious tripe! Llewelyn might as well have asked, "Are you sure you're a Christian?"

This was definitely not what Dave had wanted to consider after two difficult hours of excruciating self-examination. Had he not already bared enough of his soul to his poor blotter? Surely, five major shifts in husbandship were as much as any reasonable wife could expect. After all, it was merely a difference of religion that lay between them, and what was that between lovers?

"Argh!" His groan, starting as a discreet, self-mocking laughter, climaxed in a fury of exasperation. He had just dismissed the world's number one killer of the human race in a careless mouthful of words. A mere difference of religion! Also, he had overlooked the inconvenient truth that he and Colette had not been lovers for half a year or so, and even then only accidentally, in that midnight misunderstanding.

Deep down, he knew his battle with Colette needed more than a mere cease-fire. It demanded honest reconciliation, and only the complete truth could satisfy. Point number six was the final barrier to peace between them.

There was no escape: their religious differences needed sorting, especially because Colette was still in the thrall of the other man. Llewellyn had not only stolen his wife's body in her vulnerability, but he had also captured her mind and soul, and these last two Llewellyn still seemed to command. Dave's wife still continued to talk as though she were a puppet operated by the long-distance Welsh ventriloquist.

"And while you're mulling things over, Dave," Colette had sharply said, concluding their last telephone conversation, "try sorting out who's going to save you when you go to face God. Are you going to pull yourself up to God by your own shoelaces, or will you let Jesus give you a lift? Which is it, Dave: DIY savior or Divine Savior?"

He had had two sharp reactions to holy language like this ever since his fire hydrant days and his pastor's inviting him to climb aboard Jesus's boat. First, he didn't really "do Jesus" the way Colette and Carac did, and certainly not the American way of his Bronx adopters.

Once again he dwelt on the discomfort of those who forever spouted "Jesus" and "the Holy Spirit" and "Salvation" with an overchummy familiarity. It was intrusive. Bad form! The English did put things so well: "Just not cricket, old boy."

It certainly wasn't the thing that was done in Oxford clergy circles. Fellow dog collars had what they considered to be a far more wholesome and professional approach. Jesus was hardly ever mentioned in private conversation. Talking ecclesiastical nuts and bolts was fine. Poverty and associated economics and the feeding of down-and-outers were all acceptable social issues. Even the Bible in general was permissible, though definitely not quoting selected holy chunks at each other.

His telephone conversation involving Colette and her DIY-savior comment had not ended well. Dave had calmly pointed out his superior standing as an Old Testament expert and published religious author. He had then suggested that her lesser role in an infant reception class did not exactly qualify her to teach him profound theological points.

"Codswallop!" she had promptly dismissed. "You've got your Old Testament in a twist. Oh, Dave, if only you'd let God and his New Testament get a word in edgewise, you'd discover that you're still a theological leprechaun with small ideas of a tiny god—and you're still missing the most amazing truths."

Dave normally relished their mental duels. Most were frivolities, and it did not really matter too much to him who won. It was the taking part, the frisson of romantic jousting. But this God thing was of a different order. This was central. He and Colette needed to be one. Did they really have a hope with such a massive chasm yawning at the heart of their relationship?

He picked up the almost full blotter from his kitchen table of penance. He was moderately content to have almost finished his self-imposed sentence at the scene of the crime, even though the final, unwritten point still nagged.

Such was his concentration as he returned to his study that he caught his toe heavily on the desk leg, which tripped him sideways and sent him falling down heavily onto his stool. The shock jolted his lower back, and pain shot upward, sparking his brain to recall a vague half-truth.

"Yer don't get owt for nowt in this world, me lad!" It was a regular, if monotonous, mantra of the leader of the college's dig, Stan Ramsbottom.

"Pardon," Dave had remembered saying the first time he'd heard the northern phrase.

"Sorry, my dear old foreign Yankee," Stan had said, doing his best to mimic a stilted Oxford accent, "you do not get anything for nothing in this world, my good friend. Does't thee understand that, lad?"

"Aye, I do, Stan," Dave had mimicked back. "I am hearing that none of us gets a free ride, Stan. We all have to pay for the trip, right?"

"S'right, Dave. Spot on. No freebies. Nothing, zilch, a big fat zero, without payment."

"God and religion as well?"

"'Course." Stan had nodded. "Keep yer nose clean, be a good lad, and ye might make it upstairs in t'eaven."

Dave eased his throbbing toe from his suede loafer. *Bruised, not broken,* he concluded. He then bent to recover the blotter that had flown across his desk to lodge cornerwise in his wastepaper basket.

Stan, Dave reckoned, was the average Joe on the street when it came to religion. If you wanted to get to God, you had to deserve him. If you wanted a heavenly suite, the price was divine behavior. You don't get "owt for nowt." Muslims prayed five times a day, gave alms, and made the hajj pilgrimage to Mecca once in a lifetime. Roman Catholics kept sixteen commandments, ten from Moses and six of their own, including a Friday frown on meat. Methodists signed the pledge, wishing Jesus had turned wine into water rather than the other way around. Jehovah's Witnesses knocked on doors, and Episcopalians and Anglicans were good at jumble sales and lotteries to win their way to heaven.

All seemed to be working their way strenuously via charitable works to get into God's good books, except Colette and Carac and the Brooklyn family that had adopted Dave. They claimed they already had a place in eternity, because Jesus had paid for their entrance on the cross of Calvary.

How could they be so presumptuous?

Dave released his "How to Win a Woman" work of art from the blotter's four leather corner triangles and then inserted a fresh sheet. His tender toe, now cooled by fresh air and time, had settled to a steady throb, and his pen hovered, awaiting a full and frank renunciation of his wife's assurance of her heavenly place.

This would form the backbone of his ultimate point. Now that he had thought it through, he took the title his wife had suggested: "DIY Savior versus Divine Savior."

"I need to win her back to my way of thinking and convince her to cut the strings of her Welsh puppet master." Dave struggled with his case. Worse yet, his earlier criticism of Colette and Llewelyn did an about-turn in his mind.

How dare he himself presume he could be good enough to earn a place in heaven! The thought left him numb. Ten minutes later, the blotter and the lonely heading remained untouched.

Tears of frustration pricked as he pressed against his impasse. If he insisted that only he could save himself, then he would lose Colette. If he faked belief for her sake, then he would lose himself. If he failed with this final point, all on blotter sheet number one would be pointless.

The pen was still airborne, yet another ten minutes later it was still waiting for permission to land on a solution that had a long enough runway for landing. At least Dave had not fuzzed or crash-landed for a doodle. His heading looked somehow indecent and lonely.

A further five minutes in a holding pattern brought one glimmer of hope; a tiny irritating controller toward the rear of his mind advised him to crash-land by the seat of his pants and see what unfolded. He could always tidy it up later or even tear up the landing pad. Two ideas propelled him downward.

First, he must set down the opposition's argument to see how to throttle back Colette's overspiritual zest. Second, he needed to do it honestly. Maybe *throttle back* and *love* were somewhat in conflict. He quickly scribbled out the skeleton of his last conversation with his wife on the subject. Surely, this would somehow break through this impossible deadlock.

> Colette: When I give you your baby girl, Dave, are you then going to dump her into this messy life with only an impossible set of commandments to follow?
>
> Dave: 'Course not. She'll be the apple of my eye, and she'll want for nothing. I'll be there every precious step she takes.
>
> C: Do you think God the Father loves his children more or less than you love ours?
>
> D: That's totally different.
>
> C: Are you not the apple of God's eye, Dave?
>
> D: Ah, now be careful you don't take poetic phrases too literally.
>
> C: Okay, Reverend Jackson, allow a mere infant teacher to inquire if you will only love your daughter if she obeys you.
>
> D: Now you're being silly, Col. 'Course not. That's not how love works.

C: The love between you and your God does, Dave. You believe he won't accept you unless you make his grade of perfection.

D: God is the Creator and is therefore different from you and from me.

C: You sure, Dave? Didn't God say that he is love and that those who follow him should love like he loves? And even in your Old Testament, didn't God go on loving his bride Israel even though she cheated on him time and again? In fact, from what I can remember, didn't this Hosea chap act out this unbreakable elastic, never-say-die type of loving? Didn't he even buy back and save his long-lost love even though she didn't deserve it? Isn't this precisely what God's amazing grace is all about?

Dave, in doubt, threw his pen down.

This was getting him nowhere. It still irritated him when somebody lectured him on his own area of expertise. Maybe he was being too fair to his wife's argument. Did he really have to go into such detail? Next thing he'd be writing down were those chunks of Scripture he hated her lobbing in his direction.

Colette had quoted Gospel writer John, saying he'd written "so that people may know they had eternal life," and Jesus telling all and sundry that those who trusted had already passed from death to life. Then there was Paul banging on about being saved by grace and not by good works so that none could boast of how they had gotten themselves into heaven. They were saved only by a Savior paying the price for their sins on the cross. They gained freedom like undeserving Gomer when the price was paid to save her from her hell.

Maybe, after all, setting down the opposing argument in such detail was a waste of a good blotter. Perhaps on this day of bending over backwards to try to win back his Colette, Dave was in danger of twisting and dislocating his long-held beliefs.

After all, he knew life. Had he not learned it in the Brooklyn academy of hard knocks? His mother was his drunken nursery teacher: "Fend for yourself, kiddo. Don't expect handouts in this life." He knew that the only free ride he'd ever get was where she'd left him, on a lower Brooklyn fire hydrant going nowhere.

His secondary education had come at Captain America Church. He'd felt loved, but it always seemed to have strings attached. He'd always believed he'd better keep his nose clean or else he would be back on the hydrant. True, he was amazed by the grace of the pastor and his wife who saved him from jail, and at that time he did toy with the idea that maybe the pastor's God loved him in the same way. But then Dave was no saint, and maybe it was all just too good to be true. At least it had given him a love for the

Old Testament stories. And with his natural gifting, he had a knack for thinking new things about old books and history.

It was this that had begun his college and university education, where he was able to detect that the Bible experts of previous generations had taken some wrong turns. It was his ability to suggest new ways of looking at the old stories that had first brought his name to his seniors and laid the foundation for his present standing.

He was surveying his blotters side by side, now almost certain that he should tear up the latest one, when the telephone rang.

"Hi, Dave Jackson here."

"I can't believe it!" It was Colette.

"What?" Momentarily, he was tempted to duel with her and ask if this last statement meant she was having the odd doubt. Something told him to resist.

"Have you really told my dah you're not bothering with your precious scroll?"

"It makes sense."

"He's absolutely blazing, and he keeps going on about your throwing it all away. Is that right, Dave Jackson?"

"Well, erm, ah ..."

"And you're not going to go swanning off to Israel for months on end?"

"That's right."

"Why?" There was an edge of suspicion in the word. His wife suddenly shouted, "Just what are you doing, Dave? What twisted game are you playing now? Is this your idea of a sick joke?"

"Serious as a judge, Col." Dave suddenly had one of his brain waves. "Look, I'll send something over to you later at Bridie's place."

"Just tell me on the phone."

"We'll end up dueling. This way, you can have time to see where I'm at. Sorry, that sounds pompous. I mean, how I see you and me."

"So this scroll thing and canceling Israel, is that to do with us?"

"Yes."

"You're doing this for me?" Colette's words shot down the phone. When no reply was immediate, Colette quietly asked, "For us?" Dave hesitated with a series of "ers" and "erms."

"You're willing to give it all up, a possible doctorate, the kudos of another book, and all that goes with it, just for us?"

"Well, erm, um ..."

"Yes or no?"

"Yes!"

"That, Reverend David Jackson," she said, her voice level and calm, though it seemed to catch a little on his surname, "is about the nicest ..."

She stopped speaking. Dave dared not offer a word. Silence reigned.

"Okay." Colette's voice was crisp. Gone was the tenderness of moments before. "Whatever you've got, send it. Better be good, Dave Jackson."

Moments after the phone went dead, Dave released the second sheet from the blotter and tore it up. He lifted an often ignored painting off a wall and slipped the first blotter sheet carefully behind framed glass and placed it in his out tray.

He then reached for his precious scroll. He was certainly prepared to lose it, and gladly if it won him back Colette. But he still felt an odd responsibility to Mary the scribe. How could he abandon what she had bequeathed to the mad world below Masada? How could he walk away from Little Sister's tales of love? At the very least, Dave felt that he needed to perfect the fruits he was soon to deliver to colleagues.

CHAPTER 37

On the Threshing Floor

"How will we get to see the king?" I asked Hosea as we walked toward the city walls of royal Samaria, with the dawn mist slowly surrendering to a new sun. "Can anybody just go and knock on his palace door?"

"A nice thought." My brother grinned. "Normally he stays in his palace, but on judgment days he holds court on the threshing floor by the main city gate. Today, the king is supposed to sift through the claims of all parties to get to the seeds of truth in the disputes before him."

"Supposed to?"

"Clever. You continue to learn fast, Sister. Around his throne hover the henchmen of Emperor Tiglath-Pileser. Sometimes judgments are twisted to reflect this truth more than the true facts of individual cases."

"And if those behind the throne give you the thumbs-down ..." I left the thought hanging. I looked up at my brother, who remained tight-lipped, though his Levant tan seemed a shade lighter than normal.

It took two hours to reach the city gates, and another hour to find adequate lodgings. For all but a handful of those minutes, I considered our chances of surviving a royal court that was regularly entertained by assassinations, foreign and domestic coups, and everyday injustice. What chance for an honest prophet and his sister?

When eventually Hosea uttered his first words before King Hoshea, I knew God would have to work overtime if we were to see nightfall.

"You are supposed to judge with justice." Hosea's feet were planted squarely on the threshing floor before the throne upon which the king slouched lethargically. "So judgment will fall on you."

The king yawned. This was yet another tiresome voice in a morning of petitioners, supplicants, and applicants, and he was ready for his lunch. An awful silence gripped the court crowd. They well knew the consequences of royal boredom capriciously snapping into bloodletting.

The only sound was the echo of my brother's voice off Samaria's yellow stone ramparts. Onlookers were wide-eyed at the appearance of this suicidal madman. His words were ones you might whisper to a dear and trusted friend in the middle of a deserted desert, and only then after looking over each shoulder to make sure all horizons were free of inquisitive ears. After a pause for effect, which was substantial, my brother continued.

"You will be like this morning's mist." Such was his confidence; my brother might have addressed royalty every day. "You will be like the early dew that disappears, like chaff swirling from this threshing floor, like smoke escaping through a window—"

"Watch your words, beggar!" a throne henchman growled. My brave Hosi ignored the interrupter and glared at the king with the authority that stopped bears in their tracks.

This king merely shifted a little, carelessly waved away his muscular advisor, and grinned. "We will hear a little more of this lunatic crying in his weird wilderness." Hosea took full advantage.

"When Israel saw how sick she was, she ran to Assyria. You have sown the wind, and now you will reap the whirlwind." The king's grin faltered. This seemed a truth much too close for his comfort.

"You, O Israel, are as useless as a broken pot. You are as stubborn as wild donkeys. The people of Israel go their own way. The Lord says, 'I will send fire that will burn down your palaces and cities. You have sold yourself like prostitutes to the god of Baal and have loved the corn you thought Baal paid you with.'

"Soon, you will not have enough corn and olive oil, and there will be no wine left. The people of Israel will not remain in the Lord's land but will have to go back to Egypt or eat the forbidden food of Assyria. God will break down your altars. You will mourn the loss of Bethel's golden bull, carried off as tribute to Assyria's emperor."

On the edge of the crowd I stood rooted to my spot, nervously grasping and ungrasping the reins of our pack donkey. I was amazed that the crowd listened; that the throne men were rooted to the threshing floor; that King Hoshea still slouched. It was as if they were held by the spell of my brother's cold authority. It was the next words that eventually made the king sit up.

"These people," my brother said, swinging on his heels around the circle of threshing to take in the shocked crowd, "will soon be saying, 'We have no king because we did not fear the Lord.' But what could a king do anyway? They utter empty words and make false promises and useless treaties. The king will be carried off like a chip of wood on water."

Actual Love

A dark and low rumble rose in the crowd as the king lifted himself to sit in his upright throne. It was as if he were about to make a stately judgment, but Hosea lifted his voice directly to him.

"Because you trusted your chariots and the large number of your soldiers instead of the Lord of Israel, war will come to your people and all your fortresses will be destroyed. It will be like the day when King Shalman destroyed the city of Betharbel, and mothers and their children were crushed to death."

A roaring gasp rivaling one of our Galilean hill avalanches rolled out across the crowd. I also recoiled at the mention of the Beth of Arbel. It was an infamous and bloody example of the might of Assyria just a few years before. Many in and around Safed had been deeply thankful that our inland sea and our Galilean hills had stood between us and such a harsh and ferocious force. Like all invading armies set on crushing an enemy, they had killed off the children of the town of Arbel under their barbarous chariot wheels, before eliminating the children's mothers to ensure that the town would have no future.

How could Hosea deliver such a dangerous message? And what about the One who had given it to him? This terrible God carries us through dried-up seas and rivers one day, and then the next he is

311

sending forces to destroy us. What kind of loving monster had given us this Promised Land? Why did it have to be defended with such great cost? I felt that similar questions must echo in other listeners, or were they just too appalled at the madness of this nobody from the north?

At this moment, I was very grateful to be a lone woman with a pack donkey, appearing to have no connection whatsoever with the prophet who had just appalled them. With that thought, guilt flooded in. I felt ashamed at my meekness, and the mess I would have made had God chosen the sister instead of the brother to be his voice for our godless age.

I cringe and yet smile as I look back on this episode. It was to be another of those bittersweet God moments. How was I to know that, within minutes, it would all be totally different? I would want to stand on the donkey's back and shout out at the top of my voice that I was the prophet's sister and he was my very own dear and courageous big brother.

The change came about after the throne men remembered that they were in charge and a puppet king should not be pulling their strings. Nor should they be influenced by a peasant preacher. At their signal, a division of soldiers marched into position around the edges of the threshing floor. We feared we were about to be thrashed and blown away as the chaff.

A scared quietness descended, and once again Hosea took full advantage. His strong voice soon recaptured his audience with his own family saga. It was a brief telling. We knew his marriage saga had flown up and down Israel's trade routes in the handful of days since my brother had first preached it in the souk back at Safed. It was, after all, too great a tale to remain untold, given the thousand evening camps to entertain under the Levant stars.

All those around me seemed to grasp instinctively the shocking implication of his domestic story: Israel, the disobedient and wayward bride, would also one day be cast out of her home.

I watched as dread dawned in their eyes. They had had it so good in the glory days of King Jeroboam II and even in the succeeding killing years, when kings lost their heads before they could wear in their crowns. The trade routes were plied, homes were still sweet and settled, and assassinations were just juicy tales for the evening's entertainment.

But now, just at the moment when the horror hit, my brother introduced hope.

I watched as, one after another, neighbors grasped hold of it as the drowning Egyptians might once have grasped at a rock in the exodus sea. Even after the Israelites' centuries of treachery and idolatry, they knew they did not deserve it—yet Hosea's words were too good to dismiss.

"Israel has a chance to live." An intake of wondering breath greeted this declaration. "But she is too foolish to take it—like a child born who had refused to come out of the womb."

"No." A chorus of cries went up. One voice shouted, "We hear, we hear. We will take the chance."

"Return to the Lord," cried Hosea, "and let this prayer be your offering to him: 'Forgive all our sins and accept this prayer, and we will praise you as we have promised. Assyria can never save us, and warhorses cannot protect us. We will never again say to our idols that they are our god. O Lord, you show mercy to those who have no one else to turn to.'"

"Show us mercy, Lord!" some in the crowd began to call out.

"Yes, we will pray," cried others. After a moment, a roar of approval and cheering broke out as though repentance was no sooner said than done. My brother stared in my direction. I smiled back, nodding encouragement. We had heard it all before. The noise was merely an alloy of sad faces and self-pity, hardly true remorse.

With the lifesaving rope grasped by a fickle crowd, I could imagine Hosea's heart almost breaking. He knew his own domestic saga would irreversibly apply now to God's bride. Israel would not change. A ferocious and cruel foe would storm down from the north and carry Israel away into exile. A bridal nation born to lead a lost world back to God was now to end up lost and homeless.

And yet Hosea was still not finished, and nor was the Source of his words. The never-say-die divine heart still beat, still yearned for his lost bride. In a final twist, and with a prophet's poetic license, he turned Israel from a bride into God's Son.

"'When Israel was a child, I loved him,' says the Lord." Hosea's voice rose majestically over a hushed crowd. "'But the more I called him, the more he turned away from me.

"'Yet I was the one who taught him to walk. I took my people up in my arms. I drew them to me with affection and love. I picked them up and held them to my cheek. I bent down to them and fed them. Yes, war will sweep through their cities. It will destroy my people. Yet, how can I give you up, Israel?'"

"You cannot," was the loud cry that went up from several in the crowd. Hosea smiled at the interruption, and then he continued.

"'Could I ever destroy you as I did Admah or treat you as I did Zeboiim?'"

"No! Never!" Anguished cries went up from several women, no doubt remembering the horrific places more evil than Sodom and Gomorrah.

"The Lord says, 'My heart will not let me do it! My love for you is too strong. I will bring you home. I will not punish you in my anger; I will not destroy Israel again.'"

"Yes! Yes!" went up the cries.

"'My people will follow me when I roar like a lion at their enemies. They will hurry to me from the west. They will come from Egypt as swiftly as birds, from Assyria like doves. I will bring them to their homes again. I, the Lord, have spoken. I will be to the people of Israel like rain in a dry land. You will blossom as flowers, be firmly rooted, and soar tall and strong as the trees of Lebanon.'"

Uncertain smiles were breaking out around me. Murmurs of approval rolled across the threshing area. I was no longer planning paths of escape.

"God is great!" the cry rose up. "Praise our Lord" echoed through the crowd. But Hosea had only just started on his ending.

"There will come a time when Israel will have nothing more to do with idols. God will shelter his people and be their source of blessings. They will be alive with new growth and beautiful like olive trees.

"Israel will be fragrant like the cedars of Lebanon. Once again her children will live under the Lord's protection, flourish like a garden, be fruitful like a vineyard, be as famous as the wine of Lebanon ..."

The rest was lost in a roar of approval. It was then that I wanted to mount the donkey and ride to Hosea's side, shouting, "This is my brother!"

CHAPTER 38

An Old Slave's Tether

We walked out of Samaria at the end of that exhilarating royal day without as much as a scratch.

It is the fondest memory I recall as the party of bearers and I straddle the cemetery path, with my family at last catching up.

My dear Hosi has arrived at this spot entirely through natural causes. No assassin, whether dispatched by king or priest, has brought this about. The God he served simply decided that his faithful servant's job was finished. As a family, we know he has been called home to enjoy a final rest fully deserved.

Many hundreds from Safed and the surrounding hills now shuffle into place as we reach the grave. I look back up to Safed, now probably empty, and I can just make out a few stooped town elders too ancient to risk walking on aged limbs, not even to bury their legend.

"Thank you for being with us today," welcomes Gomer, now slightly stooped but still imposing in her fifty-second summer. Her voice is firm in the late morning air and carries across what has now become a multitude of mourners, despite the family-only request for the burial. My sister-in-law stands by a narrow opening in the sunbaked white rock around the cave-grave opening.

"We are here to commit our beloved Hosea to a God who was so committed to him."

The only other sound is the scuffing of distant sandals on hard clay as the late stragglers slither to catch up. All want to claim they attended the end of this true and brave prophet, true because all that he foretold had come to pass, and brave because rarely did any man dare face up to crooked kings and godless, robbing priests. Rarer still was it that a lone individual should do these things and die of natural causes.

I stand to the left of the path facing Gomer, who is alongside her eldest, Jezreel. My other nephew, Not-Mine, and my niece, Unloved, stand beside him, each having reverted to their birth names once they reached adulthood in their thirteenth summer. Not-My-People had set aside the name David, which I had bestowed on him. Unloved had likewise disowned the name Ahuva.

"We understand why you changed them," my nephew had once explained.

"And we are grateful," my niece had rushed to add, "but you gave us everything we ever needed, together with Mother. You filled our days with deep affection, and we always felt treasured as family and therefore much loved, especially by Daddy Hosea."

"And after all," Not-My-People had said, solemnly taking up the story again in the breaking voice of a boy reaching manhood, "it was not our earthly father who named us. God gave us our names. The Lord ordered Father to make us an example of a wandering Israel that kept getting lost, and we both think it a great honor. Jezreel feels the same and is glad to have kept his original name. We are privileged to have Israel's champion as our father."

I ponder these fond memories as I look at the grave opening beyond Gomer. Mixed tears of joy and nostalgia wet my face. The burial carriers begin to unstrap my Hosi's body from the carrying bier, and I look away to the growing families of my nephews and niece gathered in support of their grandma, so great a number that I often lose count. My heart swells with the love and fullness they have brought to our lives. It no longer matters that I never married or had my own children. Have I not known the joys of adopted motherhood for ten satisfying years? Have I not been amply rewarded as aunt and then great-aunt many times over?

Two of the carriers now take the full weight of my brother's preserved remains, one at the head and one at his feet, and maneuver through the narrow rock opening and beyond to Hosea's final resting place. The elders and family had chosen a site that will later accommodate a small chapel to honor the town's national hero. It will be painted sky-blue, our color symbolizing hope and happiness in God. As the pallbearers reemerge, blinking into strong sunlight, Gomer unties a leather thong from around her waist and holds it high above her veiled head.

"My old slave tether!" she calls out, her face glowing with warmth. "Once I was at the end of this." The mourners nod at each other, some sadly and others with a smile, all knowing the rest of the now famous love story.

"Hosea is my hesed," cries Gomer, "that strong, never-say-die, unbreakable love that he had for me, that he and the Lord also has for Israel." Gomer is still for a minute, and I see her chest rise, the sinews in her neck obviously fighting back rising emotion. She has come so far from the haughty princess of our growing years. Gomer gathers herself. "Only gradually, after many summers, did I really understand what love was actually like.

"I lived by manipulation. I saw what I wanted, and then I schemed to get it. It had worked with Daddy Diblaim, so why not others? Those men who used me at the White Temple did the same. They desired life-giving rain for their dying crops, so they manipulated their god by impregnating sacred prostitutes with new life, hoping Baal would drench the earth with life." Gomer paused, just as her husband would have done after having made a point.

"And then there is my man, my betrothed, who loved me." Her tether hand thumps her breast with that final word. "I was always more important than his own desires. Hosea showed me hesed. He saw what I needed and then, without manipulation, willingly worked to provide it, no matter what the personal cost.

"He ..." she says, her voice catching, "he would have died for me, and yet I mocked. I spurned it and made fun of him. There, right before me, was actual love, and I did not even recognize it. It was a love of a great heart, full of strong emotion, yet guided by a will that could not be broken no matter what I said or did." Gomer almost sobs on the last word. She fights for control.

"It was more than mere human love, a kind that often shows off in selfish robes. I have felt the love of God through this man of Israel. I have felt God's love for Israel herself, and this is why we will never stop being his beloved people." A soft and smiling murmur ripples through an awed crowd, as if savoring a final famous echo of their dead hero.

"The Mighty One who called Hosea to marry me with such hesed is still the lover of Israel." This time the murmur was stronger. "God knew what he was taking on when Israel became his bride, just as did my husband on the day we consummated our marriage. Hesed in Hosea brought me home when I fell, just as one day God will call back his bride." A reverent cheer briefly swells across the cemetery hillside.

Understandable, I think. For twenty summers now, our decimated nation, a mere remnant of the original, has had little to applaud. We have mourned the loss of vast numbers of our people, either killed or forcibly marched off to far-flung reaches of the Assyrian Empire. Hosea's prophecy had indeed happened, as he had so often warned.

At the time of the invasion by Tiglath-Pileser's forces, Hosea had been on one of his preaching tours, this time in another country. He had gone south to Judah, and I had gone with him, wanting to support him in the new prophecy he had received.

He was still God's man, this time to the breakaway twin tribes of Benjamin and Judah that huddled around Jerusalem. They fished and farmed and herded out toward Jericho and the Jordan and down past the Dead Sea and below Masada. They bought and sold and tended goats and orchards down to Beersheba and across to Gaza and back again to their capital.

They also bought and sold their twin nation, selling Israel to the enemy. Just prior to our visit, they had allied themselves with Assyria at a crucial time in Israel's defense. When Israel was at its lowest point and undefended in the south, Judah had, illegally and without pity, advanced her own borders northward.

"This is what the Lord says to you," my brother had said while standing before the temple in Jerusalem to deliver his divine message. "'I am angry because the leaders of Judah have invaded Israel and stolen land from her. So I will pour out punishment on them like a flood. Israel is suffering oppression because she insisted on going for help to those who had none to give. I will bring destruction upon Israel and ruin upon my people Judah.'"

We had heard that, despite this prophecy, Hosea's passing had been mourned as much in the south as up here in the north.

Gomer, now closing her tribute to her husband, reminds all gathered that Hosea and the nation are not forgotten, are still loved. Gomer's arms are wide and high, with the tether in one hand catching a slight breeze.

"I did everything to kill my husband's love, as did Israel with her husband. Yet his love refused to die, as did God's, a determined love even while unreturned and mocked, a love that stood firm even while onlookers taunted and jeered. Had this love faltered for a moment, I would have fallen before stones of hate.

"Such a raw love was too much for me. I found that I could not live with it, nor even understand it. It was a love that would soon be exterminated because the world was hostile to it and to the One who brought it. I lived with the daily fear of being told that my husband had disappeared or been killed. And so I ran to more-manageable lovers whom I could control and who would keep me safe. Soon, in a world short on love, I lost all control and ended up at the end of this terrible tether.

"Be still with me, Hosea!" Gomer pleads as we draw to a close. My heart jumps and I fight to hold back the tears. I echo a silent "amen" as she continues "Let your hesed live in me as it resided in you."

She nods, and four of the carriers step slowly forward to take hold of a rounded slab. With difficulty, they grapple it across the grave entrance.

The sound of silence is perfect. No scuffing or shuffling. We are as statues in memory of our solid rock. It is as though we have stopped living for the briefest of times in recognition of this extraordinary life lived for all of us.

A sob comes. Then another. Our village leader begins his final prayers. He adds readings from Hosea's own scroll and the Psalm of the Shepherd, the latter written by a king who himself had lost family members. There is a blessing, and then a thousand and more feet begin the slow climb back up to their lives in Safed.

They are sent on their way to await the culmination of Hosea's prophecy. All leave with the certain hope that Israel's lover, and theirs, looks down on them and refuses to let them go. Hesed is never-ending.

Next year, maybe, they will return home.

Next year, perhaps, they will be reborn, a united Israel together with Judah in God's Promised Land.

Next year, just possibly, all will come home. Next year, with God's hesed, it will be as a united nation in Jerusalem. Next year, Jerusalem!

CHAPTER 39

"I Wouldn't Have Missed It"

A tale's final full stop should satisfy. But what if that is death? Can such an ending truly gratify?

With time healing much between my brother's passing and the telling of this story, I have come to think so. Mine is a story whose final full stop has yet to come. This is only one ending, but it is not the finish.

We have lost our main character, which for me has been devastating, and yet, as time and reason nurse my emotions, I increasingly glimpse hope. Just like Hosea. He died with the anticipation of putting a face to the voice that had given him his powerful words.

And where is my hope, you might ask? I would not blame you for the question. Have I not played what my Greek customers call "the skeptic"? Have I not recounted some of my most precious God moments but left teller and told still wondering?

For some, my brother's authority before bears and other brutes will be enough. A power more mighty than earthly powers must have protected him. Some will be convinced by one who read the past and present so accurately as to tell the future. Surely he was the voice of one who knew the future. A few will marvel at a lone man taking on kings who assassinated each other as easily as they eliminated lesser opposition.

Still others might choose to believe that my remarkable brother balanced on the brink of death a thousand times yet was an incredible lucky walker of ropes like those in our traveling troupes.

However, it is not like the perfect balance sheets that have ruled my life since I took over Daddy Beer's books. If ever I suspected a figure or column or balance, I would play detective. I would worry the numbers, change them around, and interrogate a customer's bill until eventually I arrived at provable facts.

A scroll of balanced figures is indeed a beautiful picture, almost as stunning as the Galilean hills at sunset. "Now, their beauty is absolute perfection," I once said, challenging my teacher and brother.

"And from where do you think that perfection came?" was the reply. "Would not perfection come from perfection, my little sister? If this beautiful world bubbled out of nothing, how did an unintelligent nothing create such clever rules and laws and financial sheets that can balance perfectly? And where did—"

"Stop!" Even now, years after his passing, he has an answer to everything in my mind's eye. Whenever these scenes filter through my grief, I even catch myself rehearsing the arguments out loud. "Stop!" is a regular shout of mine to drown his quiet and insistent logic.

"I am working on it!" was often how I would end such sessions before storming off to some place my brother was not. In my rare, mischief-filled moods when he was alive, I would even tell him what I thought his supernatural boss needed to do.

"If he is so almighty and great, then why does he not put things beyond doubt?" My chin firmly led in the attack position.

"And just how would he do that, Sister?"

"He would come here."

"Safed?" Hosi smiled.

"To all Israel!"

"And do what, Sister? Precisely how could he win trust?"

"Appear before us. Make everything right. Make the lame walk. Cure the blind. And why not raise the dead?"

"Maybe if he did that, we would end up killing him. If men and women try to kill the messengers, what would they do to the message maker?"

Tears prick my eyes as I now remember this silly challenge. If only God would come now and raise my beloved Hosi out of that narrow grave entrance, then I would believe. Then, I would definitely believe. I think.

And so we have our ending.

And yet the questions go on, and so too does life. Other prophets are already taking my brother's place. God is now piling on the warnings down in Judah with a man called Isaiah.

Here in Safed we are safe. We are the highest town in Israel, so some claim, and the trade travelers assure us that we are certainly one of the coldest. This is probably why Tiglath just sent up a small force and his own local ruler after his invasion. They got rid of a few of our leaders, but it was business as usual before too long.

Now, weeks after the shake-up of my brother's funeral, life has returned to normal. People and travelers and customers come and go, and business bustles on. Some days are so brisk that I forget God and even Hosi. I just live and enjoy the loving remains of Hosea's family and mine.

But in quiet times, I yearn for the lost days as much as I long for my lost brother. They were exciting and filled with adventures and exhilarating danger. We confronted bears and they ran away. Weeks dragged by as I wondered if my preacher-brother would ever come home safely. At times, I would linger by the rose garden's teaching stone, yearning for him to give me another lesson.

Time was truly alive when we knew perverted priests were selecting stones of the right size to dash to death any prophet who threatened their profits. These fearful, frightening, exciting, and exhilarating times I would not have missed for anything.

My own God moments continue to happen. God and I had a fierce exchange when Hosea was taken away. Then I thought that fifty-five years was no miracle and was by no means long enough.

Funny, as time goes by and my upward conversation mellows, I've learned that not only brothers can hear from above. So too can sisters.

CHAPTER 40

The Last Days

Day 120
The madness of the world below has buried my second husband. Tomorrow, it will kill the rest of those I love, all save my children, Magdalen, and the baby within me.

The Roman legions have already breached the outer wall. The cushioning of our inner barricade is greatly frustrating the enemy, but our satisfaction mingles with fear. The barricade has already given us four extra days of life, but Uncle Eleazar tells me that the troops will be through it around midafternoon tomorrow.

There is therefore to be an early morning assembly and a good hearty breakfast for all. Eleazar will then speak for the last time. Lots will then be drawn to decide who will kill whom. The organized deaths will start midmorning, when parents should already have brought their children to peace with the lesser of evils. Many parents are planning to do this as the children sleep tonight. My uncle is a master of planning, yet I fear his end strategy will not fully follow his ideal. How can brains wholly account for the cold killing of loved ones and self when mothers' hearts and the instinct to flee an executioner are all involved?

The last twenty days since my last diary entry have been a mix of emotions from Hades itself: incredibly sad, disturbingly challenging, and, in the last few days since the Romans launched their first attack, really terrifying.

Perhaps the hardest was conquering my pride to apologize to Magdalen for calling her a cannibal. More of this later.

The days and evenings have also been full of scribing, which has brought some relief and even joy. There has been no time to keep up the diary part of my scroll, but at least I have been able to finish the sister's story.

This scroll is now so large when wound around its central rods of wood that I can scarcely carry it without help. For many days now, I have left it out on our work slabs to avoid the strain of constantly moving it. After Magdalen and I were reconciled, she was kind enough to read and check one end while I scribbled away at the other. I am starting this entry early so that all will be finished in time.

We will then carry it, together with its large clay carrying pot, to our cave after dark this evening so that no suspicion will fall on us in the high emotions involved in the lesser of evils.

Why I continue to use this silly phrase, I do not know. I have come to believe that there is nothing more evil than to kill my children and allow myself to be beheaded, thereby losing the baby that dear Isaac gave me.

I must now quickly take you through our last days.

The funerals of Isaac, with the two others killed in the arrow attack, were held within a day. Reactions were strange. Some said Isaac was blessed because he no longer had to await the sword or knife. Others were more generous, sympathizing with the loss of a second husband, and "so soon after your marriage," one kindly added.

"Just a few days' difference, dear," one old crone had cynically cackled as she passed me two days after Isaac was buried. She was typical of a tiny number of old wives and widows who had grown as hard as the calluses on their sandaled feet.

My own feelings are mixed. I did truly admire my husband, and I am sure I loved him, though quite differently from the overwhelming passion I felt for Joseph. I am thankful that Isaac always lit up my days. In normal times, I would have genuinely enjoyed our life together. Certainly, we would not have married so quickly had circumstances been different, but I do believe we would have been together eventually.

I do have to admit my relief at his death. I no longer have to tell Isaac that his new family are not going to obey the death-pact edict. This would have been a difficult discussion to have with Isaac after making my peace with Magdalen.

She and I did not speak until three days after Isaac's funeral, though Magdalen did come to the burial at the far eastern edge of our plateau. She had nodded and waved sympathetically through the crowd of mourners, but this I had pointedly ignored.

She later told me that she had by that time reconciled herself once again to a lone escape. She had concluded that I could no longer bear the company of a cannibal and a follower of a religion responsible for the decimation of Jewish life.

"You were right to scold me," I said once I had eventually stopped Magdalen as she came away from one of our stores.

"This way." She had quickly pointed down an alley and away from the queue still waiting to shop.

"I just wanted—"

"Not here," Magdalen had barked and walked off. I had almost turned away to walk in the opposite direction when I sheepishly realized that she was right again. I had placed her in great danger. Of course we could not talk openly; it had been stupid of me to think so.

I had followed her meekly.

"Sorry," Magdalen had said, abruptly turning to face me as the alley opened out into a deserted square.

"No, no, Magdalen, my fault. I only wanted to admit that I behaved badly when I called you a cannibal. You were right: I had no evidence and believed tales without firsthand facts."

"We eat and drink symbols," Magdalen had explained without emotion. "It is bread and wine. We take them as if taking the body and blood of the One who is the Messiah. We commune with him in our hearts and minds and spirits. Do you understand?"

"No, not really," I had said stiffly. "But because I have come to know and respect you as my friend, I am ready to accept that the stories I heard from my side may not have had all the right facts."

Magdalen's face had wrinkled into a half smile. "And I am truly sorry that so many of your synagogues have been affected, and—"

"Look," I had interrupted. "Right now, Magdalen, the past is gone, and the future of our children—"

"So, you are coming?"

"Yes. The alternative is impossible and horrifies me."

"He will be with us."

"He?"

Magdalen's concern had melted into a beaming smile, knowing that I knew to whom she was referring.

"What, your God?"

Magdalen had grinned. "The one we both believe in. All we disagree about is whether or not he has sent his Messiah. That's our only difference, is it not?"

"Hmm," was all I could reply. In that moment, I had suddenly yearned for a Magdalen-sized faith, or even the Hosea trust that had so completely filled my life for a hundred or so days. All I could muster was the insecurity of being his sister.

Day 121

The alleys were filled with revelers last night. Wineskins seemed to be everywhere as I ventured out into the night. Even the older children were drinking, much to their surprise and delight. One neighbor had confessed that the lesser of evils would begin soon after midnight, when the children were in the deepest of sleeps. The wine would ensure they knew little about the end.

From odd conversations overheard in the night, it seemed that boasting Zealots and Sicarii were trying to outdo each other to prove their courage. God help us when our beliefs have us killing our kin to prove our zeal. This is why I am still able to scribe. There was far too much happening last night for us to safely smuggle the scroll to the cave, and so Magdalen has stayed with us to await our chance in the early hours.

All the rest of our needs await us in the cave thanks to Magdalen's quick trips in the last few days. Even now as I write, just after midnight, I occasionally hear distant screams. I try not to imagine what they mean. They are usually women's cries. I can only assume that the women or their husbands have begun their gruesome task. Occasionally the young twins awaken and start crying, and it is times like these that I pray. I ask that a good God will keep them quiet later in our cavern, until our chance of escape comes.

It is now two hours after midnight. It has been quiet for the last hour. I must finish. Like other parents, I have decided on a late change to our plans. In another few minutes, if all is still quiet, we will wake our children and depart for the cave. God go with us, for I fear we will need much protection in the coming days.

Day 122

Jemima, bless her, smuggled ink and quills in her sack when we left for the cave. It seems she has caught her mother's interest in writing. She has let me use her pot and quill for this last note.

The enemy did not come this afternoon. Uncle Eleazar was obviously given wrong advice. Toward the evening we were able to take our children out for a walk on the safe eastern side of the plateau.

Everything is so quiet. We see few about and hardly any children. It is clear that the lesser of evils has arrived. We stopped at the cave tomb of Isaac and told stories of how he made us laugh, mentioning all the kind things he had done for us. We smiled at the laughter and cried at the memories, and also for what might have been.

We ran back the long way, hoping to tire the children into a good night's sleep. We also wanted to do a final check on our supplies before bedtime. We have several pots of water, thanks to Magdalen half filling kidskins, which she then secreted under her skirts for the trip to the cave and its storage pots. There is enough to last two weeks, but we must save enough to refill two skins for our escape down the Snake Path. Once we reach the bottom, there will be only the undrinkable water of the Dead Sea until we reach the Jordan. We plan to cross the river and settle on the other side in Jordan until times become safer.

Food is plentiful, including well-salted goat. We have picked a good selection of unripe fruit from Masada's orchards.

I may have time to write more if the children will allow and the soldiers do not find us. Later tonight, we plan to dig a hole to the rear of the cavern. At the right moment, or even if the enemy comes too near, we can place this scroll safely in position and swiftly cover it with dry sand. If it is at all possible, I will come back for it—if ever the Romans leave Masada. This is doubtful.

Magdalen has spent much time planning our days, while I have scribed. For the children's sake, she is treating it as an exciting holiday, involving them as much as possible in selecting their favorite games and stories. It is vital that we keep the children occupied. They have yet to listen to the ending of the sister's story.

Our greatest dread is that the twins will catch our fear and start to cry. They have lusty mouths in most activities, but they especially excel when hurt or aggrieved. Make a sound when the soldiers are near and all will be lost.

To keep our sanity, and to keep our minds on creative things, Magdalen and I grab any opportunity to divert each other. Once, while the children were running ahead of us, she took me through our Jewish scriptures and the many prophecies about the expected Messiah. These foretold where he would be born, the gifts he would get as a babe in a manger, the tribe and the house that he would come from, his name, his work in Galilee, how he would be betrayed by a friend, and even how much his friend would be paid. They made clear he would rise from the dead, ascend into heaven, and then send his Spirit to be in his followers. Jesus had apparently fulfilled every one of the hundreds of prophecies about his life.

"This is one great reason I felt able to accept that he was the Promised One," Magdalen had said.

"I just hope one prophecy comes true," I whispered.

"Which one is that, then?" She smiled.

"That your God will go with us as you promised."

The more life and death hang in a fine balance, the more I have prayed as never before. I plead for the safety of all of us. It seems like I am asking for a great many miracles from a God I am struggling to know. I know him as the Lord of our fathers, almighty, with great acts in the past, and quite distant. Magdalen knows him as her Father here and now. That's what I desperately need.

My last prayer is that somebody will find this scroll and then share the ever-giving, sacrificial hesed love of Hosea with a world that only seems to remember how to hate.

Finally, I wish I could scribe my ending as with the sister's story. I would love to be able to describe to you how we all lived on like Gomer and Little Sister. Instead, all I am allowed is this recitation of my fears and hopes.

I fear we may well end like Hosea in the grave or, may God forbid, experience a living fate even worse than that. Of course, hope tries to bury all this. Hope smiles on us and gives us an escape so that we might live on and practice this hesed love that has so filled these last months. Yet hope, it seems to me, depends on a hesed kind of love turning up for us with a few miracles.

It might seem incredulous to some that I should still be so filled with doubt after all that I have written about a loving God turning up for Hosea and Israel many, many times.

Maybe, if we ever get out of this, if he ever turns up for me and especially for my children, well, then I have guaranteed him a convert.

CHAPTER 41

Handed On

"You're not married, are you?" Dave looked intently into Stanley Ramsbottom's eyes.

"Nope." The Lancashire lad grinned cheekily. "Why you asking?"

"Are you thinking about it? You know, engaged or any such thing?"

"Nay, lad; ah can't afford such luxuries."

"So, you're courting then."

"Dave, what're you on about?" Stan's northern bluntness lost patience as they queued in the college canteen.

"I want you to do something for me and you need to be free for it, that's all."

"Well, you sure know how to get a chap's interest up an' running. If you must know, I'm buried up to my eyes in my final master's dissertation, and it's boring me silly. Another thing: college grants don't exactly stretch to flings with fine fillies. So, come on, Dave, spill!"

"It's, erm, the Masada scroll."

"Givin' you trouble? Honestly, what're you dons like! You send us out to godforsaken places like ..."

"Israel, godforsaken? Wash your mouth out, young man," Dave mocked.

"You send us out in t' wilderness to do all that rough digging, sweating in a forty-degree furnace, scrapin', and scratchin'."

"Well." Dave sighed. "If you're not interested ..."

"Did I say that? I'm all ears. Look!" Stan grinned widely, his lips zipped closed by thumb and forefinger.

"Would you consider taking over the work on the scroll?"

"Hmm?" Stan's eyes were wide open.

"You've got first refusal. If you don't want it, then there are a hundred in the queue behind you."

"Lasagna, ta," Stan ordered as they reached the head of the queue.

"Mine's your wonderful old English fish and chips, Mildred," Dave called out.

"Why the free giveaway?" Stan was wary. "I don't understand, Dave. This is your chance to shine, to establish yourself once and for all. It'll make your name, give you fame.

When our latest Dead Sea find hits t' headlines, they'll even know who you are back home in Oswaldtwistle."

"Where? Never mind. Let's just say I've other stuff to do and things I can't afford to lose." They paused to receive their meals and grab drinks and extras before paying.

"Not good enough," Stan muttered as they settled at a table for four to give them ample space for their trays. "If I take this on, I need to know it'll be mine and you won't come scurrying back to claim ownership after I've done all t' hard work."

"My reasons are mine."

"Hey!" Stan looked over a hovering forkful of lasagna. Then he grinned widely. "Of course. It's the marriage thing, isn't it? That's why you were grilling me. You and Col, Dave—are you both okay?"

"Do you want the scroll, guaranteed as Ramsbottom's own find with no interference? Yes or no?"

"What about college?"

"You will do it under their patronage and they share your glory by association with you?"

"And Dean O'Hara? Is he in on it?"

"He's putty in my hands, Stan. He's so disappointed I'm not doing it that he'll jump at the chance of the college backing you."

Stan sat munching on one and then another mouthful of lasagna before stretching a hand across the table. "You've a deal, so long as you bring me up to date and allow me to use your translations and your research so far. You'll get some credit, of course."

"Okay, Stan. We have a deal." Dave got to his feet and formally grasped the offered hand.

"I've got a great ending for the Masada diary part of the scroll," Dave said as he sat back down. "It concerns the two women and five children who escaped. However, if you run with this ending, you'll need to make a strong case, and that might not be easy."

"I'm all ears."

"Well, first things first, Stan." Dave took a folded A4 sheet of notes from the inside pocket of his elbow-patched jacket. "First point: my translation of the scroll is only for guidance. It won't stand up for a moment to the experts. You will need to do your own, paying much closer attention than I have.

"There's also a problem with the Masada diary part. It stretches over more than four months, but some scholars insist Masada survived less than two, whereas others reckon it was more than eight. Some argue for our timescale, but you'll have academic enemies straightaway.

"The paleographic dating on its own is a problem. I think you know that. So, the college will bankroll you for additional carbon 14 dating, and you'll have to persuade the Israeli authorities to part with sample fibers of the scroll for testing. That'll be a full-time job in itself."

"I can cope with them." Stan was grinning and nodding with anticipation.

"And you'll have to have watertight answers to a whole series of queries. For a start, why only now have we found this scroll? The area has been picked clean by professionals and gifted amateurs for well over half a century. How come a thousand digs and searches failed but your small underfinanced team of greenhorn students succeeded? Maybe it's modern and somebody's playing tricks. I'm sure it's not, but you're going to face this and much more skepticism, Stan.

"And how come our scroll is so well preserved? Sure, it's split in one place and its edges are frayed and deteriorating, but it rivals the best of the original Dead Sea finds, and some of those were not just papyrus parchment but were tough animal-skin parchment. Of course, our scroll was not only in a clay pot in dry caves but also buried in dry sand. Has that been enough to make the difference? Lots of questions there, Stan, and you'll have to have convincing answers."

"This'll take years!" Stan said with interest rather than dismay.

"Sure will," drawled Dave as he shoved the A4 sheet across the table. "You can read the rest of the questions, but I reckon the most interesting line of research will be this." Dave eased another two sheets of A4 from another pocket and passed them across.

"Good 'eavens!" Stan said after a few scans.

"Quite a find!" Dave nodded.

"But this is ..." Stan went quiet as he read the remainder. Eventually he looked up, perplexed but smiling. "This is just too good to be true, Dave."

"Yes, siree! There'll be all sorts of accusations flying around with this ending to the Masada scroll."

Stan cleared away their plates onto trays and slid the trays onto a vacant adjoining table.

He then placed the two sheets of paper on which was printed a translation by William Whiston of Hendrickson Publishers of Massachusetts, USA. It was a translation of the siege of Masada by the renowned first-century Jewish historian Josephus Flavius.

"Yet there was an ancient woman," Stan began reading out loud, "and another who was kin to Eleazar, and superior to most women in prudence and learning, with five children, who concealed themselves in caverns underground and had carried water thither for their drink, and were hidden there when the rest were intent upon the slaughter of one another."

CHAPTER 42

"Best Lunch in Years"

"Dynamite, isn't it?" Dave's grin could not be any wider. "I sometimes wonder, Stanley Ramsbottom, why I'm handing you such a treasure. However, needs must—"

"Whatever need is driving you to do this," Stan said, peering at him seriously, "it better be sound, or I'd suggest you need your 'ead examining!"

"Here, listen to this." Dave swiveled one of the pages to read it. "It says that Eleazar urged them to kill their families and that some started to do it even before he had finished. They didn't want to be last to act, in case their courage was challenged by others on Masada.

"It says the husbands tenderly embraced their wives, took their children in their arms, and then gave them the 'longest parting kiss with tears in their eyes.' It then explains they did what they had resolved and that the only thing they had for comfort was the knowledge they would be saved from the enemy."

"And doesn't it say somewhere," interrupted Dave, "that 'it was the lightest of all evils before them'? That's not exactly the same as the scroll, but it is very near it. So, you might get queries on that, too."

"Looks like the twins gave 'em away, do yer think, Dave?"

"Oh yes. The ending, you mean."

"That's right." Dave nodded. "The women came out voluntarily. It seems like the Romans found nothing but a massive fire of clothes and equipment blocking their way when they finally broke through to Masada. Apart from the flames, it says there was 'a perfect silence.' They couldn't find one person, so they went round shouting at the tops of their voices.

"It says they made a noise as loud as a ram hitting a wall. Maybe the twins got scared and started to cry and the women were left with no alternative but to come out of hiding.

"Here it is: 'The women heard the noise and came out of their underground cavern, and informed the Romans what had been done, as it was done, and the second of them clearly described all, both what was said and what was done, and the manner of it.'"

"The second must have been Mary."

Dave pondered over this point. "Yep, that's it. Age would have made the Romans count Magdalen as first. It looks much as though the women were interrogated, but then they left as the soldiers started beating their way through the flames. It states that they found around nine hundred and fifty bodies of men, women, and children, many huddled in family groups. Here again, Stan, it's not exactly what our scroll records, so there might be challenges.

"The soldiers later had no problems talking about the women and children to Josephus and seemed to have nothing to hide. It even seems as though Josephus was later able to find the women and get firsthand information from them.

"Maybe they were allowed to leave or were even escorted down. Probably the latter, for they would have needed them as witnesses for when their superiors quizzed the soldiers as to the success or otherwise of their mission.

"Remember, Roman soldiers who carelessly lost their prisoners in those days usually forfeited their own lives. They had lost nearly a thousand on Masada on that day, and those they found were likely to be well treated so that they could provide good supporting evidence before Governor Flavius Silva."

"So." Stan was hesitant. "What do you make of tying this scroll so closely to Josephus's account?"

"Integrity, Stan. You'll have to handle it with kid gloves and complete honesty. According to William Whiston's translation of Josephus, they are two women who probably belonged to one of the groups, though the second he definitely identifies as being related to Eleazar, leader of the Sicarii. However, the scroll states she belonged to the Zealots. Is that likely? It needs checking to see if other families were split like this."

"And integrity would go farther, Dave?"

"Go on."

"What made these two women go against everybody else? Remember, Dave, we are what we believe. I think I actually got that from one of your first-year lectures." Stan grinned.

"But Mary's beliefs were the same as the others', Stan. Okay, she may have been considering other options with Magdalen, but she was still Jewish. If you're going to take that line, stick to Magdalen. She's a far better example. She must have had strong alternative beliefs to the other nine hundred and fifty or so to stand out against them and risk death. Does this all make sense? Have you got enough to be going on with?"

"It makes plenty sense, but it all needs checking out. I'm sure you've got a whole pile of more stuff for me." A delighted Stan smiled. "Best lunch meeting I've had in years."

"And," said Dave, smiling, "if it stands up to scrutiny, what a great ending for the Masada story."

CHAPTER 43

"I'll Think About It"

Colette Jackson sat in her friend Bridie's flat with a silly grin on her face. She did not do gooey, her least favorite yuk word, but her face had forgotten that at this precise moment.

Before her, lay a framed blotter and two dozen red roses, hand-delivered by a college student.

Her immediate response upon tearing away the brown packaging and string had been surprise at seeing an ornate picture frame that normally graced their lounge wall in the college flat.

"Silly fool!" She had sighed, her practical mind hoping that Dave had been gentle with the original contents.

"*Cheek!*" was her second response as she deciphered the ornate "How to Win a Woman." "If he thinks a posy and a framed doodle are enough to make up for all the rotten ..."

She suddenly stopped. Her throat tightened with a different emotion.

Her hands went to her tummy, now expanding and occasionally rippling around its precious tenant of six months. The emotion she identified was hope, and the last time she had felt that was at that altar rail in the college chapel.

Did the future really have to be as black as she had been viewing it en route to single motherhood? Could it possibly be that a man could change his selfish spots? She had changed hers! She was certain of that. What she now believed had begun to change her behavior and her thinking.

Ah, but can men change? she mused, giggling at her non-PC generalization.

Desperation had driven her to change. She was an addict who had come to the reasonable conclusion that she desperately needed a power greater than herself. That first step had been drummed into her at every Alcoholics Anonymous meeting since she'd started attending them, the day after her pregnancy was confirmed.

Maybe Dave, too, had at last identified his addiction. Hers was a liquid spirit imported from outside and nourished by low self-esteem. His was a selfish survival spirit, born in abandonment on a New York fire hydrant. Maybe desperation was the force now driving them both to change. Dave certainly sounded different, though her inner cynic mocked, *Sure, and what about the actions?!*

Too many thoughts! Too much to cope with! Hope itself seemed too hopeless with a mother and father like hers. Still ...

She took in the subhead below the title, "The Winning of Col: Pros and Cons," and immediately burst out laughing at the word *pillock.*

"*Yes!*" she shouted at the sole item under "Cons." "To be sure, the giant leprechaun himself has got it. Would you praise the Lord now!"

A moment later came a throaty chuckle about her wayward husband's "thinking with a part of his anatomy three feet below sensible."

"Too right, Reverend, sir!" She punched the air. "Now you're thinking with the right part, my lovely boy."

The gooey grin came as Dave's words described how work must make way for her, stating that academia was lightweight "compared to the fullness of being well loved by the one I love."

Her eyes filled upon reading his resolution to start listening to her and cut out his mindless "Sure, babe" con. Col wasn't at all sure what her tears were about. Still, there was the tiny skeptical voice whispering, *Cut the con? Aye, Dave, and Irish pigs might fly over the rainbow!*

A louder voice of hope held sway. She didn't mind the occasional automatic "Yes, dear," so long as when Dave was home, all of him was home, especially the head.

"The *head!*" Colette suddenly exclaimed out loud. "What's the silly fool doing cutting off his wrap-over hair hunk?" A bald husband! *Well, that should be something to see,* she mused.

"Ah, now that's a good one for dueling about." She prodded the scroll where it mentioned "attentive arms" rather than "alms." "Methinks we'll battle that one out a little, to be sure and begorra," she said, pouring on the full brogue.

"Now, why shouldn't a girl hope for both alms and arms now?" she asked herself, but her grin of anticipation was immediately banished from her face as a torrent of old guilt swept up and over her, making it difficult to breathe.

Her eyes had skipped ahead to the mention of Caractacus, and she remembered again, with agony, the kitchen table and the night Dave had burst in on them.

Astonishingly, Dave was now claiming that it was all his own stupid behavior that had caused it. He was the criminal and she the vulnerable victim. Guilt told her at that moment that her husband was taking far more than his fair share of the blame.

She had promised to love Dave "'til death us do part and for better or for worse," whether in a quaint canal maisonette or a pokey flat at his intrusive place of work. And, quite simply, she had not.

Colette knew deep in her heart that she had been flattered by the charming Caractacus. She had loved the idea of this clever Welsh wizard enchanting her humdrum existence in which the only humans who listened to her were infant reception kids.

Sure, Dave had been thick and selfish and inattentive and quite boring at times, "But, hey, what's new?" She mocked herself with head in hands and elbows resting on the blotter. "That's married men, ain't it?"

Colette knew deep down that she had loved the idea of being loved and courted. She chose to ignore the tiny voice that echoed, *Ah, now, isn't the Welshman himself merely make-believe listening so you'll give him what he wants?*

And still she had gone ahead. It was the thrill of it. It was being listened to, appreciated, treated as special, as the only person of note in the world. It was heady, delightful stuff.

Colette made a mental note to discuss the "she, Hosea; me, Gomer" thing. She was not at all sure that was the right way around. And, she underlined in her mind, it would be a discussion. Some things you did not duel or joust with.

The telephone rang in Bridie's house. Colette dried her eyes as she reached for the receiver,

"Hello. Bridie's out at the moment. This is Colette Jackson."

"It's Dave!"

"You've been busy." She smiled.

"On the right things?"

"They made me laugh," she said without laughing.

"Is that all?"

"Erm." There was a long pause. "And fill up."

"Was that in a good way or a bad way?"

"Some good," she said, half-chuckling, though she knew it masked a hint of a sob.

"So, er, where do we go from here, Col?"

"Dinner? A bit of old-fashioned courting?"

"Come home," he said quietly, hopefully.

"This Dead Sea scroll, Dave—are you sure about it? And what about all the Israel work?" Colette felt her guilt resurfacing after the furious meeting with her dad. Was she expecting too much? Would Dave hate her for it later? How could all this relationship stuff work with this sort of pressure?

"It's done, Col." Dave was definite. "Best decision I've made in years."

"What about next week or a year from now? Do you not think you should give this more thought?"

"Too late, Col. It's all signed over to Stan Ramsbottom, who led my discovery team. It's his baby, and if it's not too yucky-Yankee for you, that means I can stay home with my baby."

"Slushy but bearable." She smiled.

Dave's voice deepened. "Col, there really is no competition. I want you. I've missed you. I've missed our double bed, our romantic jousting. I'm missing the half of me that's any good."

"Dave, I'm sorry."

"Pardon?"

"You heard," whispered Colette into the phone. "It's not all your fault, you big lummox."

"I am, too—sorry, I mean … for everything. Come home, Col."

"I'll think about it." Dave heard a chuckle.

"Should I order a new double bed?"

"Don't push it!"

"A cuddle, possibly?"

"Now, that's somewhere between a possibility and a probability." And there was another chuckle. "By the way, Reverend Husband, what about a bit more action from your side of this bargain?"

"And what exactly do you have in mind?"

"How can you be so presumptuous to think you can save yourself?"

"Colette Jackson, don't you ever give up, girl?

"Answer the question, Yank!"

"Is this really the right time and place to tackle this subject?" Dave sounded pained.

"Do you really think you'll get to heaven and boast about doing it on your own? Doesn't your Old Testament Israel prove that we don't deserve anything yet get offered everything time after time after time?"

"Okay." He breathed out in mock exasperation. "Look, I'll think about it."

"Come on, Dave, jump off the fence."

"Don't push it."

"Well, is it something we can talk about?"

"Now, that's a definite probability."

They both laughed easily into the phone.

The dueling was back on. Humor had returned to the agenda, and hope came with it.

$$\Omega$$

Also by Kevin Logan

What Is Love? (Collins-Fount), the inspiration for this novel

Secret Warriors (Paternoster Press), ghostwritten for the original Q of the 007 books, the late Charles Fraser-Smith

To God Be the Glory (Paternoster Press), elucidating the open secret of successful evangelism—churches working together

Paganism and the Occult (Kingsway)

Close Encounters with the New Age (Kingsway)

Satanism and the Occult (Kingsway)

Survival of the Fittest (HarperCollins), a serial-killer thriller in which Britain's Parliament and Buckingham Palace grind to a devastating halt

Responding to the Challenge of Evolution and Creation (David C. Cook, Kingsway, plus a German edition), consisting of easy-to-read arguments on our origins

Joshua—Power to Win (Kingsway)

Note

What Is Love? was updated and republished as an e-book (2015). HarperCollins and Church Pastoral Aid Society kindly allowed me to adapt the first edition of my book, printed in 1976.

The trilogy on paganism, the New Age, and Satanism was condensed and reprinted in one volume, *Paganism and the Occult*, which is available from reachouttrust.org.uk or kevinlogan1@hotmail.co.uk.

The other titles are available at Amazon.com.

Romance

at the

heart of

our universe

This is the e-Book that inspired this novel.

- *A romance to enhance your own*
- *An all-action biblical thriller*
- *A bird's-eye view of the Old Testament*
- *A spiritually satisfying personal read*
- *An 8 to 16 week Bible study group course*
- *A love story that explains the wrath of the Old Testament*
- *A fly-on-the-wall view of killing kings and robber priests*
- *A warming glimpse into the heart of God*
- *A way into that heart for each of us*
- *A vital reminder that God still seeks a bridal people for the final marriage feast in heaven.*

About the Author

Kevin Logan is a former journalist who quit his editorial role to train for the priesthood. His desire to pursue love prompted him to marry Linda, who died of cancer in 2004. He remarried to Ann, who resides with him in Lancashire, Great Britain. This is his tenth book.